# Unseen Companion

### DENISE GOSLINER ORENSTEIN

## KATHERINE TEGEN BOOKS

*AN IMPRINT OF* HARPERCOLLINS*PUBLISHERS*

This book is a work of fiction. References to real people, events, establishments, organizations, or locales are intended only to provide a sense of authenticity, and are used fictitiously. All other characters, and all incidents and dialogue, are drawn from the author's imagination and are not to be construed as real.

Quotes on pages 82, 84, 87, and 95 are excerpted from *Evangeline* by Henry Wadsworth Longfellow (1847).

Unseen Companion

Copyright © 2003 by Denise Gosliner Orenstein

All rights reserved. No part of this book may be used or reproduced in any manner whatsoever without written permission except in the case of brief quotations embodied in critical articles and reviews. Printed in the United States of America. For information address HarperCollins Children's Books, a division of HarperCollins Publishers, 1350 Avenue of the Americas, New York, NY 10019.

Library of Congress Cataloging-in-Publication Data

Orenstein, Denise Gosliner

Unseen companion / by Denise Gosliner Orenstein.— 1st ed.

p. cm.

Summary: In rural Alaska in 1969, the lives of several teenagers come together while they try to find out what happened to a sixteen-year-old boy who is missing.

ISBN 0-06-052056-6 — ISBN 0-06-052057-4 (lib. bdg.) — ISBN 0-06-052058-2 (pbk.)

[1. Orphans—Fiction. 2. Boarding schools—Fiction. 3. Eskimos—Fiction. 4. Alaska—History—1969—Fiction. 5. Schools—Fiction.] I. Title.

PZ7.O6314Un 2003                                              2002152944

[Fic]—dc21                                                              CIP

                                                                              AC

Typography by Andrea Vandergrift

❖

First paperback edition, 2005

www.harpertempest.com

## NO TELLIN' WHAT YOU'RE GONNA SEE.

"Mama? What about those prisoners up at the jail? Do you think they is the murdering types? What about that guy gone all crazy in the head? I'm not so sure that a girl such as myself should be spending any time up there at all. You know I surely don't want folks to start to think of me as prison trash."

Mama shakes her head. "Not everybody spends time in the penitentiary is necessarily trash. And it ain't always clear who's savage and who's not. Once you start looking into people's hearts, no telling what you're gonna see, no matter if they're poor and looking pitiful or cleaned up and dressed real fine. And don't start listening to them folks with badges, or you'll find yourself in a pickle one day soon. Just because a man's wearing a uniform don't mean he walks the straight and narrow his own self. The law's a messy thing—ain't always clear what's right and what ain't. And sometimes those deputy and marshal types know about as much about their prisoners as a two-dollar hooker knows about love."

*To my daughters, Jennifer and Lisa,*
*and to my parents,*
*Julia K. and Bertram J. Gosliner*

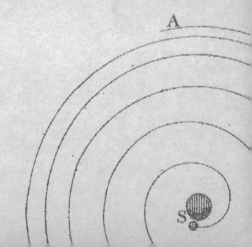

*Our heart always transcends us.*
—Rainer Maria Rilke

# PART
# ONE

*Outer space
is no place
for a person
of breeding.*

—Violet Bonham Carter

# LORRAINE HOBBS

*Bethel, Alaska*
*Spring 1969*

This is the spring we all hear about the wild man locked up in the Bethel town jail. "He ain't got no fingernails," I tell my mama soon as I walk in the front door from buying a strawberry parfait ice-cream pop at the Tundra Shack. "They say that savage, crazy man up at the prison ain't got one single fingernail. Turns out he pulls them all off one by one, smack in front of Marshal Nicholsen."

"And why, pray tell, would anyone do a fool thing like that?"

I can see Mama ain't buying none of it. And ain't it just like her, always wanting to hear more before coming to any judgments at all. Plain dull and boring to always be so calm, if you ask me. She just sits there with a mess of sewing on her lap, not even giving me the courtesy of looking up for a single minute.

"Don't ask me," I answer, sitting down at the kitchen

table next to her, "but it sure don't seem likely that someone's gonna fabricate up something strange as that."

"Oh, no?" Mama chuckles and chews off a knot from a tangled-up piece of yellow thread. "Folks 'round here can stir up a can o' worms quicker than you can say 'land of the midnight sun.' I wouldn't necessarily believe all the chatter goes 'round town."

Mama can be downright aggravating sometimes, never listening to what nobody says about nothing. She's just used to seeing things her own way and probably always will. But I gotta admit it's been hard for her, right from the start, seeing as Mr. Willie Resse Hobbs leaves her after two years of marriage.

"Ain't nothing but a sorrowful man," Mama says whenever his name is mentioned, "but let sleeping dogs lie; never do care to find out whatever happens to that crazy SOB."

So I don't even get to meet him, my daddy, though it sure feels strange calling him that; I never do exactly know how I'm to refer to the man. Goes and leaves my mama with one little baby in Oconee County, South Carolina, and if it isn't for Grandpa Tulley, Mama's own daddy, I just don't know where all of us would be right now. Grandpa Tulley (I don't remember much of him) has a job up Prudhoe Bay, working on that dang pipeline, when he sends for Mama and me, but by the time we make it up north to meet him in Bethel, the old man done up and dies. Just like that.

"When you get to the end of your rope, tie a knot and hang on," Mama says, sitting in this old plywood shack with honeybuckets instead of a proper outhouse. "There's work to be had in this little town, and I'm of the mind to get it."

So we end up just staying right here in Bethel, and my mama, she works herself to the bone, holding two jobs to make ends meet, doing cooking for the jail and the receiving home (the big trailer where the orphan kids live) plus taking in sewing from anyone too lazy or rich to do it themselves.

Poor Mama, she does let herself go, tying back her stick-straight graying hair always in the same bun, always wearing frayed blue-jean overalls or brown corduroy pants and some old plaid flannel shirt, an apron around her waist, needles or straight pins in her mouth. Her face ain't nothing to brag on neither (never a fleck of Max Factor's lipstick or pressed powder, don't you know), kinda square boned about the jaw, her forehead lined deep, her nose wider than it should be, and her lips lopsided as if she's been chewing at a corner of the top, the lower one sticking out more than a smidgen. But when you look into her eyes, and they're hard to resist, you just forget about everything else and get dunked deep into Mama's strange spell. She has a way of staring at you hard so that it's impossible to look away, and then them giant, golden irises start spinning.

There ain't two ways about it—there's just no one in

this here world can pull the wool over my mama's two whirling eyes, and I'm smart enough to just about stop trying.

But I do hate to say it, Mama ain't one to do herself up pretty, and her apron sure has to be let out some every year—seems like she gets wider and wider. And she don't seem to mind a little bit, laughing and smacking her tummy as if she's almost proud. When I mention that it looks like she picks up a little, she just grins and says, "More of me to go around—some lucky man's gonna get a real pile of woman to hold on to. Sometimes I feel uglier than a mud fence after a seven-day rain, but I sure am one hundred percent real woman."

I just laugh right along with her but do wish she wouldn't talk low class like that when anyone else's around. Appearances aren't everything, I know that, for heaven's sake, but it's important for a girl to keep herself up as best as she knows how. I'm also of the mind that it's essential for a person to improve on herself in order to really get anywhere in this world, and no matter what blows life sends you ("Ten Cute Cures for a Clothing Crisis," *Today's Teen*), you just got to make the best of it. And I do fully intend to start by enhancing my natural good looks. The women Mama sews for give her piles of their old beauty and style magazines, and I study them like there's no tomorrow, don't you know. I certainly aim to better myself in every way humanly possible. Here's what I learned from *Modern Style* (Special Anniversary Edition, May 1969):

- *Heat and humidity can destroy your hairdo; use a volumizing shampoo to give hair more of a lift.*
- *Vitamin-rich cucumber and revitalizing ginseng purge impurities and restore natural moisture for soft, beautiful skin.*
- *Pick a brow pencil shade a little lighter than your hair color, and apply it with light, feathery strokes.*
- *Dull-looking hair needs a quick color boost.*
- *Just say no to wishy-washy colors, and take your cues from the glorious hues found in nature.*
- *Instill a note of relaxed, easy grace in your rooms with painted trays set upon stands.*
- *Fulfill your wish for a very romantic bedroom with a luxuriant canopy bed.*
- *A just-for-fun paint job will invest a once-dull room with a new, free-spirited attitude.*

But when I try to convince Mama that we need to start ordering Beautiful Blondes Hair Rinse by Clairol because it takes over two months to be shipped in and the next time we get to Anchorage will be after break-up next June, she just sighs and rolls her eyes.

"You surely don't need a color rinse with your pretty, long hair. That Billy Numbchuk's been studying you ever since. And believe you me, it don't matter to most men what the color of your hair is as long as you got nice lines, if you know what I mean. Up here in the bush that hardly don't matter neither. Ugly enough to make a train take a dirt road and these here Bethel men will still be all over you—those fellas don't have a lot of women to choose from. Even a fat old lady like me has suitors, as is proven by Mr. Samuels, who is more devoted than your daddy ever meant to be."

Mr. Samuels grunts and rubs his knee with the heel of his thick old hands. He's an old coot, probably over sixty, and he just sits around, hardly even saying nothing. Mama says he's from Unalakleet upriver and his people never do have much use for English; they even closed their missionary school last fall. They need the children home for hunting and fish camp, but most everyone in Bethel speaks English real good, so that sometimes you forget they're even Native at all.

Mr. Samuels sits in the same straight-backed chair in our house every evening, his greasy old striped shirt grimy at the neck and sleeves, big old belly hanging over his belt. I can't even stand to think what Mama sees in him, but it don't really matter because he brings her a goodly amount of fish during season and helps with a few chores around the house. Although in my mind that sure isn't exactly enough for full room and board. And it's pretty peculiar if you is to ask me because they hardly ever do anything together and the idea of them in the same bed makes my stomach turn. Sometimes I even think that Mama cares more about that old man than she does about me, always making time to fix him a cup of tea, bake him up a pie, give him his medicines, but seems like always too busy to bother with the likes of Lorraine Hobbs. Sometimes I wonder if my mama has any respect for me at all—seems like she's quick to criticize my ways and never notices how grown up I really am. But she'll surely go on and on chatting with that Mr. Samuels as if he could even understand anything she has to say. Makes me feel kinda lonely sometimes.

Sitting at the kitchen table with Mama, I smell the smoked fish off Mr. Samuels's clothes and move my chair back a few inches.

"Mama," I say again slowly, "you might not be believing all the talk about that wild crazy man from up north holed up in the jail, but I sure wish you'd listen to me when I tell you straight off that we just got to order Beautiful Blondes Hair Rinse along with this powder-blue dotted swiss fabric so I have something to wear to the aurora borealis dance this summer."

I do have to admit sometimes that I am beholden to my mama, who sews just like a professional. I get to design most of my clothing myself and have them made up any way I want. It seems that Lorraine Hobbs is gifted with a special creative vision that allows me to see things (in Technicolor) inside my busy head. I refer to this unique ability as my picture imagination and find it particularly useful for conjuring up original outfits as well as for creating other scenes in my mind's eye: singing "Coat of Many Colors" (written by Miss Dolly Parton) in front of an adoring audience, wearing a tangerine off-the-shoulder chiffon sheath. Sometimes when I picture a particularly extraordinary dress or blouse for Mama to sew up for me, she'll roll her eyes at being asked to trim the sleeves with sequins or create a matching scarf and hat with velvet bows, but most times she just laughs and does what I ask.

Mama takes off her glasses and studies her sewing. "You got more dresses than any girl in this state, Lorraine. I'm not spending more money on fabric until you find yourself a job. We're not as poor as church mice, but some help from your end would surely make a difference. And it sure seems like you might want to develop yourself some new personal interests this summer, child, 'side from always fretting about what clothes to wear."

Mr. Samuels chuckles and reaches across the table to help smooth down a hem. "My days," he mumbles, as if to himself, "them days, I fish all summertime and work in the mines, too. Fifty cents for one hour them old days. I remember digging all day down Bear Creek with Fat Hans." He chuckles again. "Used to see them grizzlies my old days."

"Well, exactly what kind of job do you have in mind?" I ask my mama, trying to ignore the old man, and pretty annoyed that my own mother won't let go of this subject ever since I turn fourteen. "You know perfectly well that I work Northern Commercial until March when Arthur Swanson steals my job right from under me. You gonna say that's my fault?"

Mama absolutely knows that since Arthur Swanson goes on probation for disorderly conduct, he has to stop his drinking ways—that boy spills more liquor than most men drink—and work for his folks again at the store. It's surely no fault of mine. I study my petal-pink fingernails where I've chewed them off on one side.

"I've been thinking about that, Lorraine," Mama says, threading a tiny needle carefully, "and I'm sure I can figure out how you could earn some money this summer, now that school's out come next week. You can wish in one hand and spit in the other to see which one fills up faster, but if you is of a mind to really make some money, you're gonna have to get yourself a real live job."

"Yeah?" I mutter, pretending not to be interested. "What kind of work is that? I'm sure not subbing at the Sleep-Off Center again. Last year Edna Frank puked all over my new red cardigan."

"No, not at the Sleep-Off."

I can see Mama trying to be patient. Mr. Samuels is snoring softly in his chair. It's hard to figure how such a big man can be comfortable in a metal frame straight-backed chair.

"Speaking about that Sleep-Off-Center," she continues,

"reminds me of something that's been on my mind. What if you is to help me with the cooking for the prison and the receiving home?"

"Help with the cooking?"

I'm really aggravated now. Mama knows I can't hardly boil up water without burning it and even hate making my own lunch for school. And what a time to bring up working for that pitiful jail, what with a crazy devil-man sitting right inside.

"Oh, nonsense," Mama says, looking over her bifocals at my most horrified expression. "Even a spotted pig looks black at night. You gonna have to give something a chance before sending it out of your mind. You're just done spoiled living in this house. It don't take much to cook a few meals for the jail. And they pay ten dollars per hour. If them NASA folk gonna walk on the moon this summer, then Lorraine Hobbs sure can get herself a paying job."

I glance over at the *Kuskokwim Kronicle* lying open across the table. The headline is printed in capitals: ASTRONAUTS TRAIN FOR SPACE TRAVEL; and in smaller print below: Scientists Study Starry Expanse While Murky Interior of the Single Atom Still Not Understood. Why anybody in their right mind would actually cram hisself into one of those rubber spacesuits and hurl smack into space is beyond me. What those astronaut folk gonna find out there in the great beyond—if they ever is to actually get there—just gives me the willies, and who knows what savage aliens might be crashing around in space, anyways. It makes me all ashiver to think of all the wild and uncivilized possibilities. I really have no interest in such a thing; I really do not.

"Ten dollars?"

I quickly figure how much I can make over the next few months and ignore any further reference to moon walking, which, I think, in all actuality, is probably a bunch of made-up bunk. I look around this pathetic little town of ours, no flushing toilets 'cept in the rectory house where the minister and his family live (the word is that Mrs. Susanna Weinland, the minister's wife, ran off to Seattle with the town postmaster) and nothing but flat as far as the eye can see. Bethel, Alaska, ain't anything but a mess of old trailers and shanties stuck plumb in the middle of the tundra, like some kinda pitiful arctic slum, for goodness sake. Everyone here may be all atwitter about that moon walk scheduled for some time come July, but I find it hard to believe that some man's gonna march around up there in outer space when it takes the town of Bethel until last winter to get the Norichinka boys to even start a honeybucket service.

"Does the jail pay extra for carrying the meals over and back?" I ask Mama, trying to calculate some pretty impressive figures in my head.

"Imagine so," she replies. "You could do pretty well for yourself if you is of a mind. You gotta run with the big dogs, daughter, else just stay on the porch."

✳

13

So that's how I, Lorraine Hobbs, get the job that changes my life. And don't it figure that I end up having to go to that same jail where that wild man sits locked up behind bars. Not only does that lunatic pull off body parts, but I also hear tell that he eats his food like an ordinary barbarian savage——crouches right down on all fours and laps up his vittles with a wide, purple monkey tongue. At least that's what old Sara Oscar tells me the other day out by Northern Commercial. She gums up a Nabisco vanilla wafer straight from the box with that toothless mouth of hers and gives me the lowdown 'bout what she hears 'round town concerning that prisoner wild man.

But I try to put them nasty thoughts right out of my mind and concentrate on refining my cooking skills. Mama shows me a few tricks, and before I even know it, I'm making three squares a day for everyone in the Bethel jail and for the guards, too. Mama keeps on handling the receiving home part for a spell while I study up on recipes.

I learn to make meat loaf with brown sugar, catsup, and crumbled Post corn flakes (the unfrosted kind) and chicken-fried steak with deer meat that Arnie, second assistant to the Bethel U.S. marshal, says is the best around town. It's definitely not as bad as I expect, all this cooking, and thank goodness for good fortune, I never do have to actually see or talk to any real prisoner, just leave the meals on Arnie's desk in the front office. I might be just a tad curious about those lawless criminal types in the back, but am more than just a little relieved that I never have to come face-to-face with any crazy lunatic man or any other Bethel prisoner for that matter. You can never tell what might could happen when a locked-up man gets a glimpse of a feminine type such as myself.

I may not be the best example of womanly beauty, skinny as a stick where curves oughtta be, and nothing but two little hard grapes for a chest that barely wobble when I jump up and down with natural delight. And my face might be nothing to brag on neither, my droopy-lidded eyes a boring brown with short, pale lashes practically invisible without a dab of thick 'n' rich black mascara. My poor cheeks is so covered with a splatter of freckles that a compact full of peach powder ain't much help at all, and although Mama says my nose is perfect for my long face, I think it sits too flat and wide to be anything close to dainty. My heart-shaped mouth, however, if I do say so myself, is particularly alluring, lips plump and pink as a baby rose—could be that my gums show too much when I smile and my front teeth have an unappealing gap in between, but my blond hair falls to my shoulders real nice and even curls some when I pin it up overnight. Lorraine Hobbs may not look like an actual movie star, but them jail prisoners ain't known to be the most discerning of folk, after all.

When I first start bringing food over to the jail come the end of the month, I write a personal note to all the prisoners:

Dear Boys,

Please excuse this original cooking because I'm just starting to learn. Please, however, do not hesitate to favor me with any questions or comments regarding your nutritious meals.

I will attempt to satisfy all of your wishes as quickly as I can, excepting if you ask for something I don't have or can't make.

Best wishes,
Lorraine Hobbs, Cook

Arnie thinks my writing notes is funny, but I really do it because I have this worry that when the prisoners get out, they might run me down and beat me up or something awful if I'm sending over sorry food with no real explanation at all. I don't tell any of this to Mama, but before every meal, I write a short and sweet note on my best pink-flowered stationery and slip it into the jail's container. Call it insurance.

It's unusual, this metal container the jail folks send over three times a day. It has four layers, all made of steel, and each layer has a lid and slides out from the others, kind of like a pocketknife. So you can prepare four parts to the meal and each section can be kept separate and hot, too. For example, I can make Pillsbury Instant Mashed Potatoes for the first layer, Great Aunt Gertie's Can Casserole for the second, and pour in Del Monte's apricots for dessert. Usually stick in a wad of Wonder Bread or some kinda soda crackers for the last layer. When you slide all the layers back inside, you can carry the whole container by its metal handle while you walk up past the receiving home all the way to the jail. I affectionately refer to this meal container as my Carry-O-Meal and reckon it would make an excellent means to bring along hot and cold meals to outdoor engagements ("Yes! Plan a Party Picnic and Have Fun, Too," *The Elegant Entertainer*).

Saturday and Front Street all empty. I haul the Carry-O-Meal out of Northern Commercial—Arnie gives me some change to buy Kraft's miniature marshmallows so I can garnish my Southwestern Gelatin Fiesta Salad—and I wish I have enough money to buy those new look-like-mother-of-pearl hair barrettes or an extra-large box of Milk Duds. My bubble-gum pink and orange candy cane–striped skirt ("Stir Up Your Wardrobe with Startling Stripes," *Teen Trends*) has two complementary pockets sewn in the shape of flowers. I dig my fingers down deep, looking for more change, but all I find is a small white button and an emery board. I make a mental note to work on my cuticles before the week is over and sigh as I peek at the dirt wedged way down into my pinkie fingernail. Oh, well, it's hopeless, anyway. No matter how hard I do try, my fingernails stay short and stubby, don't matter what, Max Factor's Mostly Mauve polish or not, those doggone nasty nails stay too soft to grow.

I walk slowly toward the jail, thinking on how lonely I am, stuck in this stupid little hick town. I see photographs of Alaska in some of my schoolbooks, or sometimes get a glimpse of them pretty picture postcards in Northern Commercial. And I can tell you what—Bethel don't look much like anything I see anywhere before. No white-capped mountains or green forests. No pretty little cabins perched on a blue lake. Nothing but flat every way you turn, and nothing but bleak up and down every path. The ground is brown with mud in warm months and gray with ice in the cold; even the snow seems dim under that dark, cornerless sky. More like an empty no-man's land, Bethel is. More like a forgotten planet where no human oughtta ever go. I look around me and sigh. Them little crooked plywood Bethel houses don't seem like they belong here either, wobbling on all kinds of old pilings, perched, trembling, and leaning themselves away from the river's sunken mouth. This is a town that's set down on a piece of earth that ain't meant for any kind of folk at all; the tundra yawns and shrugs its wide back, us townsfolk slip-sliding where we never really even belong.

And it's an aggravating place to live, Bethel, with flies

and mosquitoes starting to sprout everywhere late spring and summer. I stop in front of Larsen's Roadhouse to swat some mean little critter, but the buzzing bugger bites anyway. Come June, my legs are so stung that they get all swelled up and it's hard to even get my pumps on real good. But the roadhouse is a fine spot for feeling down in the dumps because there's always so many interesting folk hanging around: brawny bargemen, suited-up government folk, even a few confused-looking tourists from Outside. Guess they ain't expecting the likes of Bethel when they book their spring Alaskan tour!

I look over to the docks, Bethel late afternoons cold and quiet; the dirt blows up from the dried mud, and the Bering Sea spreads its smelly breath of fish and old bone. I shiver, the wind still bitter this time of year. They say the Yup'iks throw whale bone back into the sea once they've made a kill and that the bone stays in the water until it pops up again years later, light as plain old packing foam. Those old Yup'iks believe whale bones need to be given back to the sea so that their spirit will return home, and only after many years underwater will the bone get light enough to float; funny what nonsense people let themselves believe. Mr. Samuels likes to walk on the beach and poke around for bones every once in a while, and carve these flat masks out of the old water-bitten pieces. He uses baleen for eyes and sometimes ivory for the wide, grinning mouth. Those things give me the creeps, they surely do.

I walk slowly past the Bethel Social Services trailer, switching the Carry-O-Meal hand to hand. The lights are off outside and the metal door clangs softly every time the wind hits on by. No one's sitting out at Mr. Petrovitch's general store either, although I see old Sara Oscar hobble up the rickety wooden stairs, probably in search of Skippy creamy peanut butter. That's practically all she eats, day and night, and I hear tell that Mr. Oliver Oscar starts staying out all night last summer, bugging folks in town to cook him a real meal. But then, of course, he kicks the bucket one night coming home from the pool hall with Katie Santini on his arm. Word is that he's just about to slip her a twenty for her services when he goes right down in the Bethel mud. Heart attack. Old Sara tells us that man should never have been out drinking with that floozy Santini woman.

"Old men don't have the heart for that kind of partying no more. Old men sure is silly," she says.

Three boys, looks like eighth graders, ride by on rusty old bikes, and I see stupid Billy Numbchuk throw a water balloon at my feet.

"Hey, Lorraine," he yells at the top of his dumb old lungs, "how would you like to do some messing around tonight? Hate to see you wasting all that pussy while I could be helping you out anytime."

Before I can pick up a rock and throw it right at his

20

head, they're all gone. Bumping away down the dock past leftover piles of dirty snow, leaving a trail of bottle caps and Milky Way wrappers behind. The wrappers are suddenly picked up by the wind and wave in midair, but then drop into the water, more trash to join the ring of garbage on the river's floor.

"You're a jerk, Billy Numbchuk," I yell, although I do prefer not to use those kinds of words. "You can go to hell."

And for no reason at all, I feel like just sitting down and bawling. But I keep walking anyways. You're not never going to catch Lorraine Hobbs sobbing on some Bethel street. Not for the likes of stupid Billy Numbchuk or any other fool boy.

My hands are hurting from the Carry-O-Meal I lug all the way from the store, and I set it down on the dried mud street. Straight in front of me, I can see the teenagers hanging out in front of the Tundra Shack, the only ice cream place in town, and it's only open come late spring. The kids are all talking together, sharing their ice creams and leaning on their bicycles. Half of them are twisted around each other, stuck in some long kiss or just staring into each other's eyes. Not exactly my idea of romance. I'd prefer a moment of privacy with my man and a chance to get him to tell me all about his love feelings ("Love Talk— Get Him to Gush," *Beauty and Charm*).

I see Wilbur Kwagley and Sammy Agaiak just smoking and watching all the action. They're both wearing short jean jackets like they're real tough, and I hear Wilbur gets a tattoo on his right shoulder that says "Eat My Dust." A lot of the teenagers around here think it's cool to not care about anything but smoking and booze, which I think absolutely immature. You won't catch Lorraine Hobbs messing around with that kind of stuff, and it's not hard to notice the brown bag near Sammy's feet; every once in a while, someone will take a swig and pass it around.

Suddenly who do I see but old Mr. Samuels, walking what we call the tundra step, pulling each foot way high up before setting it down again. It's the usual tundra walk you see from the bush Natives. Yup'ik folk from the little villages up- and downriver aren't used to anything but plain, soft tundra. And when they try to walk on a wooden boardwalk, like the ones we have here in Bethel to cover the mud and permafrost, they do this funny tundra step, cross between a skip and a hop. I guess the stiffness of the boardwalk slats feels pretty different from the springy, spongy tundra under your feet. Mr. Samuels walks slowly past the Shack, and I can see some of the kids pointing and laughing. I don't know exactly why, but the sight of that old coot hobbling past a mess of stupid kids makes me feel kinda sad and lonely. As if he's some sort of visitor from an entirely different universe, as if he's stepping bravely, all by his lonesome self, onto the surface of a distant, foreign world. But I know better than to get myself started on sorrowful feelings of any kind as I'm late for my one P.M.

22

delivery. Slowly I pick up my lunchtime fixings and head straight across the road to the jail.

The old door creaks as I kick it open with my size-six-and-one-half (extra-narrow) patent leather party shoe.

"Why, if it isn't Miss Lorraine." Arnie stands up behind the desk as I walk in and clears a place for my Carry-O-Meal. "What do you cook up for us today, little lady? I'm sure standing in need of some nourishments, hungry as I am."

I feel myself blush and set down my freshly made lunch. I'm absolutely glad that my hair's just washed and fluffed with Prell's specially patented, enriched formula—leave it in for ten minutes for maximum effect—and I've already selected a wardrobe change (green plaid knit jumper with coordinated red scarf and beret) for my suppertime delivery.

Arnie's from Texas, like a lot of Bethel folk come north to begin work on that old oil pipeline up Prudhoe Bay. But like many of the others, he gets sidetracked by good money along the way, finds himself the second assistant to the Bethel U.S. marshal position when Ivan Kotenovich, the last second assistant, runs away some five years ago with Marshal Nicholsen's hippie wife. She was some kinda woman, the marshal's wife, a pretty young, big-bosomed item gallivanting around town with looks like no decent brassiere support, if you know what I mean, and tossing about her long, wild (naturally curly?) hair every which way. They say she marries the marshal just so as she don't have to go to jail for smoking up those marijuana cigarettes and going on them psychedelic LSD acid trips. Anyhow, no two ways about it, sure costs a pretty penny to live up here in the north, but the wages is high and I hear much better than Outside. Many folks like Arnie, most of them from Texas too, just find the cash too tempting on the way to the pipeline, and never even make it up Prudhoe Bay.

"We got fish sticks with real tartar sauce," I finally reply smugly. "Libby's green beans stirred up in cream of mushroom soup ("Get Him Greedy for Greens," *Decorating and Dining*), and scalloped potatoes enriched with evaporated milk. Also bake up a Grape Punch Pie with special fluted edgings. And all of it piping hot and in peak condition." Arnie's face lights right up, and he pats his stomach slowly.

"You sure is going to make a man lose his boyish figure." He grins. "I get better eating up here at the jail than back at home with my woman."

Arnie's married to Bertha Sam, a Native girl from upriver. They say he meets her on a hunting trip and carries her right back to Bethel to get married, but I'm certainly not quite sure what he sees in her. Arnie's not a bad specimen of a man, if you is to ask me, and he does cut quite a figure in his khaki uniform, all pressed up and creased real nice. If he ain't spoken for and married, I'd might likely be swimmy-headed for him myself, and don't mind admitting that my eyes do wander just a bit whenever he's around.

Arnie leans over to my Carry-O-Meal and slides open a compartment full of steaming potatoes. He spreads a shiny smirk over his face and then sticks his thumb right up into my Betty Crocker scalloped potatoes sprinkled with imitation Parmesan cheese. I watch him nibble those potatoes right off his thick thumb and then lick his lips loudly.

"Mighty good." He smiles.

"Hey," I say, "that ain't exactly no proper manners. Hey, your hands might be full of some multiplying bacteria and all. What if some of them prisoners gets your bacteria germs and turn poorly because of you?"

He licks his thumb again and laughs.

"What if? What if that were to happen, Miss Lorraine? Who's to know?" He sits down in his chair and leans back. I can't help but to notice a few curly blond hairs popping right through the opening of his shirt, and a muscle or two stretching up across his wide shoulders. "And believe me," he continues slowly, "them boys in the back, it wouldn't hurt me none to see any one of them get sick. Hey, Lorraine"— he leans forward again and closes his pale eyes almost shut—"you don't know the half of it. You don't even want to know what them animals in the back is like. Don't you even know that there's a wild lunatic hunkered down there in the smallest cell."

He lowers his voice to a whisper. "You don't even want to know what could happen if he was to be all alone with a young girl like you. Why, that crazy retard don't even know how to talk, just stares at you with these mean, bugged-out eyes. And that's just one small part of it. He's nothing more than a savage, mixed-breed boy from Stony River who surely attacked one of the fine, upstanding white teachers down at Japonski Island. Way down by Sitka at that Indian boarding school. They get him down at the Juneau Detention Center for a few months, but are carting him back north to some place in Fairbanks. Say he goes plumb crazy one day in class and goes after his own teacher like the low-down savage that he truly is. And for no goodly reason at all. Our state of Alaska income taxes taken out of each and every one of our pockets and sent up to them black Indian schools. Good civilized folk trying like hell to educate and tame them useless barbarians. And what do we get back? The colored bastard beats up his own lily white teacher to an inch of his life. Ain't the kind that a young lady like yourself wants to bother with, I can tell you that. I can tell you that right now."

I don't say nothing then but carefully tighten the Reynolds tin foil wrap around the corners of my cherry-lime Instant Jell-O Soufflé (add bits of Dole's canned pineapple for a special touch). Suddenly its heavy, sweet odor makes me sick to my stomach.

✦

"Mama," I say that evening as we're clearing the dinner table, "what exact laws do you expect them prisoners up at the jail to break? I know they stick Frank Paul up there to sober him up when the Sleep-Off's full, but what about the others? I hear tell this one guy, this crazy madman I speak to you about the other day, he tries to kill his school-teacher with his own hands."

Mama rubs her neck and sighs. As usual, Mr. Samuels is sitting in his favorite chair and don't say nothing.

"Are you sure about all of your information, Lorraine? Can't always believe what you hear. A lot of people in this town gossip just to hear themselves talk. Don't call any man a cowboy, honey, unless you see him ride."

"But what about it?" I continue. "Could all of Arnie's chatter be true?"

She sighs again and sits down at the table. "Whew, it's stuffy." Mama fans herself with the kitchen towel. "Warm enough for the chickens to pluck themselves tonight in this little house of ours."

"Mama?"

"What, child?"

"What about those prisoners up at the jail? Do you think they is the murdering types? What about that guy gone all crazy in the head? I'm not so sure that a girl such as myself should be spending any time up there at all. It might not be all that good for a girl's personal reputation around town, polite company and all. You know I surely don't want folks to start to think of me as prison trash."

Mama shakes her head. "I'll tell you something, daughter, I really will. Not everybody spends time in the penitentiary is necessarily trash. And it ain't always clear who's savage and who's not. Once you start looking into peoples' hearts, no telling what you're gonna see, no matter if they're poor and looking pitiful or cleaned up and dressed real fine. You just take a minute and look around this little town of yours—you'd be surprised at what you see. Sometimes them folks living on the highest hill with their noses in the air, sometimes them folks got nothing in their hearts but ice . . . you just never know. And don't start listening to them folks with badges, or you'll find yourself in a pickle one day soon. Just because a man's wearing a uniform don't mean he walks the straight and narrow his own self. The law's a messy thing—ain't always clear what's right and what ain't. And sometimes those deputy and marshal types know about as much about their prisoners as a two-dollar hooker knows about love."

"Mama!"

She laughs and wipes the back of her neck with a kitchen towel, then reaches over to flick a stray hair off my face. "Don't know how a daughter of mine is turned so darn finicky. You know it ain't the words that is bad, daughter, it's the people. No word never hurt nobody."

She sits back in her chair and suddenly looks tired.

"Seems like I'm all done in, honey. Sure is a lot of hours in a twenty-four-hour day."

I start rinsing the plates with water boiled up in the kettle.

"Mama," I say slowly, "sometimes I just don't know what's gonna become of me. There don't seem any one exact place where I belong. I finally find some work that I'm good at—I actually begin to enjoy myself cooking up all them deluxe gourmet meals for the prison—and then I have to go and find out that I'm working for a bunch of murdering criminals. I mean, I'm not dumb or nothing, I surely know that they're prisoners and all, but I just never stop to think about the serious nature of their crimes. Fixing my mind on all that like to make my stomach turn. Oh, Mama, I just don't rightly know. Sometimes I just get the feeling that I'll never find me a proper profession. Sometimes I just don't even know where I belong or where I'm ever gonna end up."

I turn around to hand Mama a plastic daisy chain patterned plate for drying, but her head is dropped right over to one shoulder. She's snoring softly and her mouth is opened wide.

"Sometimes the jail is somewhere else," Mr. Samuels suddenly murmurs, slowly lifting his chin from his chest. "Sometimes that key gotta be found." He taps the torn shirt pocket over his heart and, as usual, I ignore him. What does an old man know about anything? He don't make any sense with his silly chatter, anyways.

"Mama," I whisper, turning myself right around, "Mama, you'd better move yourself to bed now."

But she just sighs and swings her head to the other side. "Why, if that don't figure," I mutter angrily to myself. "Why, if that don't top everything at all. You'd surely think that Mama would be a little interested in her own daughter's deepest and darkest of feelings. But no, look here. I open myself up to this mama of mine, and what do I get but a barrelful of snoring. Why, she falls clear asleep without hearing a dang word." I shake my head and turn off the kitchen light. I make a mental note not to ever tell Mama anything ever again.

And I figure that she can find her own doggone way to bed.

But I do end up bringing breakfast treats to the jail the next morning, just like always (scrambled eggs made up from real dried egg powder, griddle cakes with a canned corn fritter variation, and fried deer steak sliced into minibites). I must admit that frying up meat first thing in the morning gives a body a moment's pause, but then again, I figure those prisoners, insane murderers or not, probably need something to stick to their bones.

When I set my Carry-O-Meal on Arnie's desk, seems like no one is around.

"Arnie?" I call, peering down the hall, "Arnie, anyone here at all?"

No answer.

I look down the prison hall again. The lights are cut off and it's real dark. My buttercup yellow scoopneck sweater and matching A-line skirt trimmed with faux white fur along the hem ("Fun, Festive, Faux Fashion," *Miss Mode*) and paired with navy tights and navy shirt makes a crinkling noise as I start to walk. I don't mind saying that I'm just a bit nervous and jittery seeing as I'm all alone, me, Lorraine Hobbs, in a jail prison with no second assistant to the Bethel U.S. marshal, or even first assistant nearby. No Bethel U.S. marshal neither.

"Anybody here?" I call again, but still no reply. The hall walls are covered with black-and-white photographs of wanted criminals. They give me the creeps, but I do start reading one down the hall a piece because I happen to be naturally inquisitive and might be just the very one to notice a stray criminal here or there around town. As I lean closer to examine the photographs, I suddenly hear something behind me. I hold my breath and freeze. Something rustles.

"Anyone there?" I call out again, not moving one single inch. "Arnie? Anyone there?"

Slowly, holding my breath, I turn around. To my horror and surprise, I am face-to-face with nothing less

31

than a real live prisoner. He is standing right behind the iron bars, his cell exactly across from me. I can hardly believe that I don't see him before.

He don't say nothing.

I don't say nothing.

I take one step back. And then another again.

"Well, hello," I finally stammer, figuring it would be best to get on his good side right away. "I'm so sorry to intrude, but don't realize there is actual live prisoners right here in this one particular hall."

He still don't speak.

"Well," I continue slowly, "I suppose I should introduce myself. My name is Lorraine Hobbs, and I have the unique pleasure of cooking your meals."

I gotta say, I'm feeling pretty proud right then about not fainting dead away from old-fashioned fear. My poor mouth feels all dry and my tongue lumpy; it's a wonder that I don't break out in a cold sweat. The prisoner still don't say nothing but moves over to one corner of his cell. My eyes start to get used to the darkness, and I notice that he's real, real tall, and I also notice that he's pretty young. His eyes flash and then shine up fuzzy like he's getting ready to bawl, but I know that can't be. No prisoner I ever hear about is the type to actually set his self down for a good cry.

"Hey," I say all cheerful like ("Keeping Up Your Chin When Adversity Strikes," *Modern Style*), "my name is

Lorraine Hobbs, and I'm certainly happy to meet you."

The man takes another step backward and is suddenly hit by a square of light from the small window above. All at once his face is lit up with dusty sunshine and I can really see him clearly. The sun shines right in his eyes and he blinks.

This prisoner looks like no one I've ever seen before; it's as if he's rubbed all over with a soft, yellow light and his whole face practically glistens. He's real tall but all filled out so he don't look skinny, just strong, wide shoulders and long, thick arms. His hair is shiny and black, worn long over the ears, his skin almost golden, the prettiest color golden, and I'm wondering where he's from. Don't look Yup'ik, don't look Athapascan, maybe not Native at all.

And his features especially sure don't look usual, with the long, narrow nose and wide, surprised-looking eyes, his cheekbones high as if pushed right out from the inside, and his mouth soft, his lips full, half open. When he shifts in place, I notice that one side of his face is puffed up red and blue and one eye is swollen shut. A long, mean mark winds its way from his chin to his right cheek; I look closer and see that he's cut; I see that he's hurt bad, the blood dried up into tiny, dark beads covering the right side of his jaw. I try not to let my mouth drop open wide.

He stands real still, his head flung back, as if about to

33

speak, and looks at me for a minute and then looks away again. I think I see him move his lips. I think I hear him speak. And just like that, with no warning at all, just like that, I feel my face flush up hot ("Physical Attraction, Fact or Fiction?" *The Contemporary Woman*).

Someone taps me on my shoulder and I jump.

"Jeez, Lorraine," Arnie says, "what are you doing back here? Don't you know that it's against the Bethel jail regulations to have visitors in the back, no exceptions but on holidays, birthdays, and break-up, of course. You could get yourself in a heap of trouble, girl, if anyone is to know. Come on, let's you and me head on back to the front office. What in the Lord's name are you doin' back in here with them prisoners?"

I shrug and follow him out of the hall, but not before I take one more good look at the man behind bars.

"What you looking at, girl?" Arnie pulls on my arm and sounds downright aggravated. "Ain't you seen a real certified criminal before?"

"Guess not," I answer, determined not to let my hot-blooded feelings be known. "Guess I've never really come face-to-face with a prisoner before. And this one's hurt real bad—looks like someone's been beating all over his face. Don't you have any medicine or ointments or the like to help heal him up some? It ain't right to leave a man's face all split open and tender, no matter what crime he's done. What's he in for, anyway? Where's he from?"

"Well you certainly have a mess of questions, don't you, Miss Lorraine?" Arnie stuffs a wad of chewing tobacco in his mouth and opens the hallway door for me. "You're pretty nosy for such a little slip of a young thing. But I suppose there's no harm in lettin' you know the facts of life, the way things are 'n' all. Even a girl such as yourself shouldn't be walking around without knowing that nasty things could happen before you can count up your numbers from one to ten. Nope. I suppose it's no secret and won't hurt you any to know. But I wouldn't go back in the cells no more, if I was you, or something pretty ugly might like to happen."

"So," I ask again, trying not to look as though I care, "what's that man's name, anyway?"

Arnie stops and laughs. "Don't know if I'd even call him a man, being he's only sixteen. Why, that's the crazy fool from Stony River I'm telling you about the other day, honey. Don't you be worrying about him being hurt any. That's Dove Alexie, the crazy, savage half-breed who practically kills some white teacher down by Sitka. Dove Alexie from Stony River."

# ANNETTE WEINLAND

*Bethel, Alaska*
*Spring 1969*

I was seventeen when my mother left, exactly one year ago. The twins were only several months old, DeWitt seven, and Garrett just five.

"Why did she go?" Garrett still asks me every night as I give him his bath. "Where did she go, and when's she coming home?" I hold my breath each time and look away.

"You know, Garrett," I say, trying not to get annoyed at the same question day after day. "You know why Mommy left."

"Tell me again, Nettie, tell me again so I'll really, really know."

I sigh and sculpt his fine blond hair into a peak of streaked shampoo.

"Because," I whisper, looking away, "because she wanted to live Outside with her new friend."

"Mr. Simon?" he asks, bobbing his skinny white body up and down in the water.

"Stop, Garrett, stop. You're getting me all wet."

"Tell me, tell me, tell me again!"

I reach for the towel and take another deep breath. My shirt is damp, and I'm irritated that I will have to change before I put the chicken on to boil.

"Okay, okay. Mommy left to live with Mr. Simon Outside. She needed to get away for a while, and maybe one day she will come back."

"But Daddy won't let her," he murmurs into my neck as I wrap the frayed gray towel around him twice. "Daddy would rather see her burn in hell." His body, held against mine, feels hot, his head on my shoulder suddenly very heavy.

"We'll see. We'll just have to see." I catch a glimpse of myself in the cracked mirror as I turn to close the door, a heavy-set, dark-haired girl, arms filled with the slippery flesh and splintery bones of my shivering little brother.

When we first moved up to Bethel six years ago, I would write letters back home to friends in Cincinnati and tell them how I would return soon. We were living in the trailer then, the missionary house not yet complete, and I can see my pale hand lying flat on the lavender perfumed stationery sent as a gift from Outside. I'd help my mother check the oven to see if the sugar cookies were ready for the potluck at the church or the dinner up at the school, and touch their soft centers gingerly. My mother's face would be flushed from the oven's heat, and she would look up from rolling out the dough and smile. I remember that one of her front teeth was chipped, and her mouth would be twisted, as if she couldn't quite decide whether to laugh or remain grim. Her black hair was long and curly then, held at the nape of her neck by a wooden clothespin. Why a clothespin? I never knew, but secretly wished to buy her a silver comb, one like those pictured in a fairy-tale book. One like the comb worn by the queen or the fair maiden or the girl whisked off on the bravest knight's fastest horse.

I would hear the wind blow outside the window; I would feel the floor shudder ever so slightly, and smile as I sat down at the new Formica kitchen table bought at J. C. Penney during our vacation in Anchorage. The pen in my hand was blue, the one with the matching tassel that hung from the top, and the green oval rug would have just been vacuumed, the pillows set on the couch just so, the small kitchen cozy with the smell of cookies baking, and the sheets on my bed smooth and soft; nothing wrinkled there.

I might hear the wind outside; I might even feel a quick chill, but still I would be smiling, still I would be safe in the little white trailer house with dark-green shutters. All of us were together, and one day soon we would return home to our friends and relatives in Cincinnati.

Before my mother left, we would check the calendar every month and mark the days until our return home. The problem was that we never had a definite date, and weeks became months; months turned into years.

On Saturdays I would help my mother prepare lunch for the other missionary wives: deviled ham spread on small, soft dinner rolls; pink cookies with single chocolate drops; sweet tea mixed with evaporated milk. The wives would trade patterns for dresses, finger each other's newly crocheted pastel scarves, plan their next visits Outside. We knew the missionary families and nobody else, only in Alaska temporarily in service to our church. We never walked through a muddy Bethel street and always stepped carefully onto the boardwalks in our short, transparent boots. The children were taught at home by the women, and we never saw anything we didn't understand; we were really never living here at all.

My father brings me one of the twins now and sits him on my lap. A stained diaper hangs over my left shoulder and the smell of sour milk is on my hands, my chest. The baby tugs at my shirt and I feel his wet mouth slide over my bare arm. My mother always said that each baby was bigger than the last, and the twins the largest by far. Their feet are fat, their dimpled hands strong, and each time I hold them, I can feel the broadness of their backs.

My father watches me, his hair thinner than before, and behind his silent mouth, I can see the grimace of another little boy.

There is a playpen in our living room, a crib in the kitchen, and two in the corner bedroom now. At night when I get up to check on the twins, the others rustle, their mouths moving silently for something more. I roll the smallest baby over as soon as I hear him whimper, and the rest of the house is hushed. If I close my eyes, I can pretend no one at all is even breathing.

On Sundays before church, my father sits on the front-room couch with the eldest, DeWitt, and reads him the Bible.

"Son," I hear him whisper in my brother's ear, "it's my job to teach you the way. I'm bound and determined to teach you what others may never learn."

I am in the kitchen, watching Garrett sing the spider song to the babies, but I turn to see my father's arm tight over DeWitt's shoulder.

DeWitt and his father are sitting on the front-room couch together, holding the Bible like a rudder.

My father's fingers are short and white. He taps them on the table as he eats his lunch.

"'Hot Cross Buns'?" I hear Garrett ask, his face hopeful.

Father shakes his head, angrily.

"'Row, Row, Row'?"

Father shakes his head and taps again.

"'America the Beautiful'?"

Father takes Garrett's small face in his hands. I hear him sigh with disappointment. His eyes are small and blue, and the spots on his nose from his glasses are soft, dark pink.

"Listen this time," he says to his son. "You aren't listening for the rhythm or the tune. There's only one particular way to hear this song."

Garrett bows down his head, and I sit at the kitchen table watching them both slide back in their chairs so that they are sitting farther and farther apart.

We are silent at the dinner table when Father asks for the boiled potatoes.

"Not tonight," I finally say, tucking the edges of my napkin between my legs. "I thought I'd try something different tonight."

He looks up slowly, and in the evening light I can see the soft yellow hairs of his pink cheeks, delicate peach down. The sun flickers in his eyes, and he brushes it away as if there were insects, summer mosquitoes or flies.

The cracks in our table rise up like a field of winter ice, and I hold on tightly so nothing will move. I feel a rumble at the bottom of my water glass. He points to the plate of potatoes.

"This is what you made?" he asks.

"Twice-baked potatoes," I answer softly. "Stella Petrovitch gave me the recipe. What you do is take the potatoes and bake them in the oven for a while until they're soft, then scoop them out and mix the pulp with powdered milk and butter. Then you bake them again. Look how fluffy. I tasted them, Father, I tasted them before and I know they are something you might like. Please. Just try one bite."

He looks away. A button is missing from his shirt, and he fingers the spot absentmindedly.

"When are you going to mend my clothes?" he whispers, still looking away, as if he's not talking to anyone at all. "You always say, 'Yes, Father, I'll get to it soon, Father,' and then suddenly in the middle of my day, when I'm at my desk or speaking with someone from the Naknek church, suddenly I'll look down and notice that there is a rip or a button missing. How do you think that makes me feel, Annette, how do you think I feel?"

I pass the potatoes and feel my feet sink into the floor.

"Please just try one," I urge, "just to see if you like it. Just try."

He stands up and folds the napkin neatly on the table. His hands are white and the knuckles glisten as if polished stone.

"Father?"

He stares at me then with rock-hard eyes and picks up the platter of sliced meat. It drips onto the tablecloth, brown and bright red.

"Next time," he murmurs, still holding the plate, "fix me an edible meal. I can see blood. This meat is underdone." And then, with his surprising grace, he carefully sets down the meat and wipes his hands with a single, careful motion.

I see his back, neat and straight, as he walks slowly into another, darker room.

I walk across the road in front of the receiving home and then down to the jail, a baby on each hip. My dress, the same one I wear day after day, is ripped at the hem and thankfully covered by my mother's old black knee-length parka. I wonder how this dress still fits after all this time, since my mother first made it for my sixteenth birthday. Over the past year, my body, once slim and agile, has bloated up curveless, seamless, like a buoy out at sea. It's as if someone sneaks into my room at night and pumps me up while I sleep. I can't remember eating enough to grow so big. My cotton dress, ruffled with a narrow white eyelet trim at the neck, wrists, and hem, now faded but once bright blue with a rim of yellow roses, still fits, although I can't imagine how. The elastic where the sash once was is stretched flat.

I can feel it scratch against my skin through the thin, almost transparent fabric.

The babies suck on my arms, the warmth of their mouths always surprising me. "Shhh, shhh," I whisper to the bigger one, who starts to cry, "we're almost there now." He raises his heavy head, a strand of wet hair plastered to his shiny cheek, and looks across my chest to his brother, fallen asleep on my shoulder. "Ahh, baby," I say softly, "shhh." But their weight is suddenly too much, and I must shift them to regain a steady grasp. The bigger one grabs onto my hair and pulls.

I stand silently at the jail door, feeling each tug shoot down my neck to my shoulders, down to my separated heart.

"Anybody there?" I call. No answer. "Anybody there? It's Annette Weinland, the minister's daughter." The screen door flaps and a circle of flies buzzes toward the babies' heads. "Go away. . . ." I nod toward them, and the bigger baby laughs at the motion. The little one stays asleep. My arm feels numb.

It's exactly the same every week, Tuesday, the same day, the same exact time. Father has volunteered for me to help with the jail paperwork, now that I am finished with my schooling, and I sit at the same desk each week, filling out forms and typing letters and reports. I can leave the older boys with our neighbor but need to bring the twins with me each time. There's a small holding cell in the jail's front office, and I lock both babies inside with their blankets, their bottles, and their toys. They usually play quietly for a while, but it isn't long before they pull themselves up on the iron bars and start to cry. I see their damp, round faces and listen to them call but keep typing steadily, never missing a word.

And then it starts again, always exactly the same. I never plan, I never think about it at all. But after I file the papers away, carefully lining up each document so that nothing is out of order, after I cover the typewriter and put each pencil back in the drawer, I stand up slowly and reach for the key.

It's always in the same exact place, under the edge of

44

the coffee-stained blotter, and I feel the same flutter as I finger its short, rough edge. It feels warm, not like metal at all, and the surface is smooth, stamped with only a few tiny words: *It Is Unlawful to Duplicate This Key.*

Almost like sleepwalking, I turn around in a pleasant haze.

And even though the babies are wailing by now, even though I know he will be back soon, I fit the warm key into the bottom file cabinet lock and pull open the metal drawer. Always exactly the same, the money in the same cigar box marked Petty Cash, usually ten or twelve dollar bills, sometimes a twenty or a five. And always a boxful of shining coins, copper and silver, too many to count at one time.

I cup the coins in my hands and blow.

I make a deep and beautiful sound.

The coins slide back into the box, one by one, but I slip a fistful into my pocket. Sometimes it's several half dollars, sometimes a dozen quarters, sometimes ten dimes. Then, quickly, everything is put back in order, the box closed, the drawer locked, the key hidden. Everything back to the same again as if nothing had been even touched at all.

I sit back down in my chair, smooth the wrinkles from my skirt, and look at the babies lying asleep on the jail floor. They have finished crying for a while by now, their little cotton blankets twisted up in wet, slippery knots, their bottles rolling slightly back and forth on the uneven cement floor.

And then the door flies open and Arnie, all red and blustery, stomps his way in. He is carrying a brown paper bag, usually damp at the sides, a wet stain seeping larger and larger right before my eyes, a widening circle of blood from meat or oil from chicken fried up thick in white lard. He drops the bag carelessly on the desk and I push my chair back against the wall. He smiles at me. The babies whimper in their sleep. And slowly, exactly the same each time, he walks up to me until he can't walk up any closer.

"Remember, love," he whispers into my cold ear, "remember, one day soon, I'm gonna have my way. What do you think old minister Daddy would do if he knew what I know about his little girl? I'm gonna set a time and a place, just you and me, and then we'll see who's really in charge in this stinking little town."

And then the stench of what we know together seeps up through our clothes like a poison gas filling a small windowless room. Just as I am about to pull back, pull myself away, he laughs and pushes me roughly. He sits on the corner of the desk, one leg left steady on the floor.

"Don't forget your pretty babies." He grins, cracking open a chicken wing or slicing a fat slab of cold meat. "How much did you get this time, anyways, little Miss Minister's Girl? Do you have enough for a new dress this time? You sure as shooting could use a fancy little dress."

But by now I'm not even listening, gathering up the twins into my arms.

"Thanks for your help, darling," he calls as I turn to walk away. "See you next week, same place and same time."

And the babies cry in their sleep, burrowing themselves into my shoulders, trying to dig a path back into somebody else's womb.

Father is home early for dinner. He stands behind me in the kitchen as I fry halibut in an old iron skillet. The pan is ridged across the bottom, and small pieces of fish begin to flake off and burn.

"Here, this way," he says as we watch our dinner disintegrate. "If you would just listen and flip it over this way, the fish won't fall apart."

"I want to see the moon walk on television," I say suddenly, hearing my own voice echo in this small room. "Do you think we might be able to go to Anchorage at the end of July? The twentieth, I think."

He frowns, concentrating on the scorched food.

"Why would you ask such a question, child? You know that I have much too much work. And the expense is prohibitive. It's not important that we see the event on television, anyway; everybody in town seems to be talking about going to the city to watch the TV, but I find that a ridiculous indulgence. We can read about it in the paper the next day."

"I don't know," I reply, handing him the black, bent spatula and turning my attention to a pot of steaming water just about ready to boil. The potatoes are green and hard, but I know we are lucky to get them at all any time of year. "They say that outer space is the final frontier. I think it would be exciting to see the walk as it happens. Anyway, I'm eighteen now. I have some money saved, should be able to go places on my own. I could go to Anchorage by myself."

No one speaks for a moment, and I can hear my father inhale sharply.

"Forget it, Annette," he says, scraping the spatula on the skillet's bottom. "You certainly will not go alone."

I watch as he flips the fish one more time until each and every edge is burned through and through.

The next afternoon Garrett crawls up on my lap before dinner. His brown hair, recently shaved close like a soldier's, brushes my chin, and I inhale his still-sweet little-boy breath.

"Nettie," he says, pinching my cheek with plump fingers, "DeWitt says I'm never gonna get bigger. DeWitt says bad boys don't get bigger, but I am, right, Nettie, I'm gonna get bigger and bigger."

I hug him tightly.

"Of course you're going to get bigger, baby," I whisper into his warm ear. "Bigger and bigger and bigger."

"Bigger than Daddy?"

"Maybe."

"Even if I'm a bad boy, I'm still gonna get bigger than my daddy?"

I stroke the top of his head, feeling rows of bristle

flatten and spring back up straight under my palm.

"You're not a bad boy, Gary. Why do you think you're bad?"

"I am bad." He wiggles his head as if a dog shaking off water and smiles. "I'm a bad boy. DeWitt says so. DeWitt says bad boys don't even grow big like Daddy and DeWitt says it's bad to suck your thumb and make messes. I can dip my toast in milk and then it's all mushy and funny in my mouth. I'm a bad boy, but maybe I'll still get big and eat whatever I want even for breakfast—I'll pick up all the crumbs with my fingers. I'll get big fingers, Nettie, won't I? I'm hungry, Nettie, hungry to eat right now."

"You're hungry? But you just had your afternoon snack."

"No, I don't eat any snack. Can I have it now 'cause I don't eat any snack before?"

"Gary." I tickle him gently under the chin and laugh. "If you didn't eat your snack, where did all those crackers and jam go?"

"I dunno." He slides off my lap and runs into the kitchen. "DeWitt," he calls, "Nettie says I'm gonna grow as tall as you someday. Even bigger than you. Bigger!"

I stand up and realize that it's time to start dinner but dread the same routine of defrosting meat and opening a can of beans or corn. Father is eating with the school board at the church tonight, and I'm tempted to just fry up some cheese sandwiches for the boys. I hear them fighting in the kitchen and sigh. It seems as though DeWitt is

49

giving Garrett a pretty hard time these days.

"Boys," I call weakly, "what's the problem, what's all this yelling about?" I feel myself grow more and more irritable. It's as if I never have any air of my own to breathe. Garrett runs from the kitchen with his hand on his wrist.

"DeWitt bit me!" he finally manages to sob. "DeWitt bit me with his bad, bad teeth." He throws his arms around my legs, rubbing his face into my skirt until I pick him up.

"Let Nettie see." His face quivers against my chest and I feel the warmth of his tears on my neck. His wrist is held up, little and white with four small red marks.

"Gary tells DeWitt that he's gonna be bigger and he says no. DeWitt bites little Gary on the hand. See?"

I try not to smile at how he speaks of himself in the third person when needing sympathy and cuddling.

"DeWitt," I say, trying to imitate my father's deep voice, "did you bite your brother on the wrist?"

He shrugs. "Garrett's not going to be bigger than me and Daddy. You shouldn't tell him that."

"DeWitt." I feel my face flush with anger. "Did you bite Garrett on the wrist? Did you or didn't you?"

"He said things that aren't true. Garrett lied to me, Annette. You should teach him not to lie."

I sigh, trying to keep my temper and bend to stand Garrett up on the floor. He hangs on to my arms and I have to push him away, surprised at my own impatience with his clinginess.

50

"DeWitt, this is the last time I'm going to ask you. . . ."

"Well, I'm not going to tell. You're not my mommy, anyway; you're just a stupid old girl."

DeWitt turns his back to me and stands there perfectly still. "I'm not going to eat or breathe anymore because you like Garrett better than me. See, I'm not breathing. You'll be sorry when I'm dead, and my daddy will be mad and mean 'cause I'm not breathing at all."

Garrett runs to his brother and pulls at his pants.

"Don't die, DeWitt, don't die. I won't do bad things if you just don't die."

DeWitt turns around and looks down at Garrett's worried face.

"We're all going to die, Garrett. Don't you know that by now? We're all going to die and go to heaven. Unless we do bad things like Mommy, unless we're really bad. And then I bet you don't even know what happens then, do you, do you even know what happens then?"

"Yes, I do too. Listen, listen. I do too." Garrett raises both arms and jumps up and down happily. "You go and burn in hell," he yells, his face lit up with pure joy. "When you're really bad bad bad, you burn right in hell."

My brothers smile at each other and for a moment I think they are going to hug. They both look at me suddenly, and their laughter echoes through this small, shuttered house.

✳

Tuesday morning again and I wait for Arnie to come. Delicate dimes fill my pockets and I listen to them jingle: silver Christmas bells. The babies' breathing is steady, and I look over to where they lie. Both wear hand-me-downs, torn blue corduroy pants, rolled up at the hem, and miniature hooded sweatshirts, one black and one white. They lie on their backs, side to side, with their little knees curling up and down as they sigh in their sleep.

I lean over the arm of my chair so I can see their faces, but Arnie's green raincoat is hung on a black hook, blocking my view. It swings slowly in a breeze from an open window, arms outstretched, back stiff and straight, a body of its own. I rub my arms and bow my head. The pile of papers on the desk lifts and settles, softly whistling its secrets, and the wind slaps the prison's front wall, making the windows rattle. I can see through to the iron bars covering a thin quavering of glass.

I look down at my hands and suddenly notice how the flesh is changing. Once smooth, the knuckles pucker mercilessly from washing dishes, cleaning house, caring for babies. The vast landscape of skin, from my fingertips to my wrists, divides into tiny graphs, like minuscule crossings for tic-tac-toe. Only eighteen years old, I suddenly see myself aging.

This is what loneliness looks like, discolored and pocked, full of seams and indelible markings.

The door swings open and he storms in, his face red

and angry, his forehead bright with sweat. Suddenly I see there is someone else behind him, a tall young man he is dragging in by handcuffed wrists. The boy's face is down, but he looks up suddenly, and for a minute I see his black eyes roll with fear. His face is unusual, distinctive: clear-cut, elegant features unlike any I have ever seen before. It's almost as if the boy is foreign, from some far-off country, but I can't put my finger on where. His long hair is dark and thick, his skin is golden, the color of honey, and for a minute it almost looks liquid in the moving afternoon light. My eyes quickly move to a gash on his lower lip that leaves a bright crimson trail across one cheek and along the jaw, all the way down to his neck. The boy stumbles, and Arnie pulls him up by his shirt and then shoves him forward.

It all happens so fast that I am not sure of what I am seeing.

"Don't mess with me, you good-for-nothing half-breed."

Arnie's flushed face, his knotted mouth, are right up to the young man's ear. He spits out each word, slowly, one by one.

"I told you when they turned you over at the airport, and I'm telling you now. Why, I don't even want to dirty my white hands on the likes of you, a filthy black Indian with no home of your own. A good-for-nothing mixed-breed mongrel who has the nerve to raise a fist to a white man. Just look at me the wrong way, and I'll give you more of the same. You think I messed you up outside, well, you ain't seen nothing yet. Where I come from, I could slice your black throat right open and no God-fearing white man gonna give no never mind. Where I come from, any dark-skinned coon raises his fist to a white man, well, that's grounds for the electric chair."

I stand, but Arnie ignores me; he strides on by as if I'm not even here, and I inhale so that my breathing won't make a sound. Then there's the bang of a cell closing, that particular sound of iron hitting iron, of locks clicked neatly into place. An echo trembles across the walls, and I reach to steady myself on the desk's sharp metal edge. Everything is still.

He appears suddenly, wiping his face with a soiled handkerchief. "What are you staring at?" he asks me as I step back against the wall. "What the hell are you still doing here, anyway? You should be gone now; get the hell out of my sight."

As I scramble to gather the babies, I trip on my own feet and fall down. A stream of silver drains from my pockets onto the floor and I hear him laugh.

"I still get a kick out of you, Miss Minister's Daughter. And if I had a minute, I'd show you exactly how much. But you better get that pretty little bottom of yours outa here right quick now. I got some business in the back with a black bastard who don't even know his own name. But don't be worrying, honey. I'll surely get to you come next week."

And then he throws a rusty ring of keys to me and watches it fall, still spinning, at my feet.

"Put these on my desk, lover," he calls. "I can't be bothered myself right now."

That night I have trouble eating, and think about the boy imprisoned by Arnie, a victim of his guard's hatred and of his fist. Whatever the crime, is it fair to be treated with such violence, with such disdain? And exactly what does skin color have to do with anything at all? I watch my father chewing his meat and yearn to turn to him in my distress. But I am frightened to bring up anything at all having to do with the jail. What if he confronted Arnie and my secret was revealed? Nothing would give Arnie more pleasure than humiliating the minister and the minister's daughter with the unthinkable truth.

I live in terror that my father will find out.

His own daughter is a criminal, a common thief.

Why is it that I can't control myself, why do I have to unlock what should remain contained?

Why can't I be like the other churchwomen, proper, placid, obedient, unashamed?

Every single minute of the day, I think about what my father might do if he ever found out who I truly am.

He would be furious.

His fury would be monstrous, terrible to see.

He would be hurt.

He would be riddled with shame and pain.

He would say I am just like my mother.

I must keep going over everything in my mind.

Everyone must be kept content.

If I make sure that Father and Arnie remain happy, then there would be no reason for anyone to find out anything.

Soon, I will stop the stealing.

Soon, I will behave appropriately, the minister's daughter.

It won't be long before I can control myself, simply do my work at the jail, and then go home again.

I will not want anything more.

I will not open that small drawer, turn that tiny key. Everything will remain shut up tight.

Arnie will forget it ever happened and leave me alone.

I will tell Father that I don't choose to work at the prison anymore and maybe he will understand.

Until then, I will do my work perfectly.

I will cook hearty and healthy meals for the family at home.

The house will be clean, the children quiet and content, the air around us still and fresh. The windows will be opened in the warm months, and the oven sputtering heat in the coldest of winter.

It will all be over soon if I can just hold on.

No one else has to know.

I live in terror that he will find out.

# THELMA COOKE

*Mt. Edgecumbe High School, Japonski Island, Alaska*
*Fall 1968*

Sometimes I can't even remember how I get here and sometimes I wake up mornings and can't even remember where I am. I lie in bed, my eyes half closed, the room in front of me zigzagging with morning. Seems too bright to me, the whole world dizzy, different, as if I've been stolen away from home and left on some brightly lit, newly exploded planet where everything stands on its prickly edge. Seems I don't know anyone here. Even the folks from home look strange.

And I miss Rosie. Don't seem fair that she's taken somewhere else. Don't seem fair that those folks keep my littlest sister up at the receiving home and send me away. Rosie don't go nowhere by herself before—never even leaves Sleetmute until that day we go up to the Bethel receiving home together after Grandpa dies and Auntie's gone 'cause her husband John gets a job at a cannery down Bristol Bay. He's her second husband, that big gussak who never likes us kids much, and I can tell it makes Auntie feel real bad that we can't stay with her no more. After Grandpa dies last year, Auntie lets us live there, but all that's before Gussak John gets a job and there ain't nothing left for them in Sleetmute no more.

So last summer, Rosie and me, we get to go to Bethel and stay in the receiving home with them other kids and it's not so bad after all; we all get to be kinda friends, and Rosie sleeps right next to me then. I can smell her sweet breath nights when she blows powdery dream air with her small mouth. Sometimes I see her tiny dreams in my own sleep—she dreams of silly times, Grandpa teaching us to dance drum stories and us kids chasing each other out on the tundra ice. I'm glad I see Rosie's dreams, 'cause that means she and I are always close together. No matter where she is. No matter how far she's gone.

But come fall they send me here to Mt. Edgecumbe boarding school, since I'm fourteen and it's time to go to high school. There ain't no real high schools up north in the bush, and all the kids get sent away. And it's not fair how much I miss Rosie, who has to stay back at the home. I miss her, different from before, different from missing our parents when they get killed in that hunting accident out there on the winter ice. I'm only nine years old then, Rosie just a little baby, and I can't remember much about that day, just sometimes the wind will pick up all thick and salty and I will think about how Grandpa holds me in his arms.

*"You have your mother's name, Thelma,"* he says to me, *"your momma gonna always live in your heart."*

The day my parents both get killed and never come back.

But missing Rosie is different. I lie here in my little school bed, the brightness of day making my head hurt, and I'm trying to remember the part of that poem I've got to memorize for English class. Somehow just can't remember any of it—nothing stays in my mind and none of the words I read make any sense.

My roommate's dabbing herself with perfume and pulling an ice-blue sweater over her head. She's an Aleut from King Salmon and she don't talk except to the other Aleut kids. She don't even say hi when I first get here, and so I put all my little things in this one drawer. Lotsa drawers in the chest still empty, but I'm scared to put more things away, scared someone'll get mad, so I keep everything else under the bed. Most of my things are piled there, folded carefully, the edges of my clothes turning cold from the hard floor. And no one here to hold on my lap or to laugh with or even to touch. I miss touching. I miss Rosie like I don't even know I can miss somebody. I know I'll see her come summer, but it's like a part of my body is missing, some arm or leg or shoulder or my whole entire face just gone. I hear that when Sammy Paul gets his leg shut in a trap hunting down Admiralty Island, and when he loses his leg, he still feels it staying there.

Same thing with me and Rosie. She ain't even here no more, and still I can feel the same hurt as when they pull her out of my arms away. That lady takes her right from me and says, "Thelma, you know it's best for everyone. Thelma, let's show Rosie that everything's going to be all right." But everything ain't all right no more, everything ain't all right at all. Rosie cries and calls for me and I gotta just stand there saying nothing. In the morning when I can't open my eyes, in the brightness under my lids, I can see her small face and hear my name called again just like it was back in the receiving home with no one there to do anything and no one there who could even help.

Get a note in my mailbox. It's written in red print and says "Thelma Cooke: 9:00 A.M. Appointment with school counselor (Alex Davidson)." I stick the paper in my pocket and look at the big hall clock. Eight fifty-five. Only got five minutes and don't know where the school counselor's office is. Don't even know what a school counselor really does. I think I'm in trouble. Maybe I filled out all the school papers wrong. Maybe they're mad I still haven't signed up to recite that poem for English class. I know I'm not smart enough for Edgecumbe.

But I manage to find his office after all. Some old lady with a black notebook points the way, and it turns out to be right downstairs at the end of the hall. I knock on the door and walk in. He's sitting at a big metal desk, talking on the phone. He looks up at me and smiles.

His skin is pale, even for a gussak, and he has a narrow, pretty nose, his face almost delicate like a girl's; his hair, dark brown, is straight and shiny, the bangs cut right across so it looks like he's wearing a hat. He has a dark beard, trimmed up neat, and it looks real soft, and his white, white skin looks glistening slick, clammy, as though he's been sweating. At first I can't see his eyes real good because of the glasses, but when he takes them off to rub the bridge of his nose, I notice them eyes are shaped long and narrow, the pupils black. What about him makes me feel as if I've seen or met him somewhere else before? Sure don't look like anybody from Sleetmute or Bethel. He hangs up the phone and smiles again.

"Thelma Cooke?"

I nod.

"Come on right in. Have a seat."

I sit down across the desk from him. I feel scared. I watch as he leans back in his chair and crosses his legs. He's wearing a dark-blue suit and a reddish tie. I notice he's not too tall and is real slim. His hands are square, the knuckles kinda chapped, the nails look bitten, and he keeps them moving from his face to his arm to his neck to the papers on his desk. He takes off his glasses and looks at me now. He grins and winks. His lips look bruised, swollen. Feel like turning my head away, but I don't. Can't.

"So, Thelma," he says, "it shouldn't be hard for a pretty girl like you to find her way at Edgecumbe. Your grades from home are excellent—looks like we have a smart one on our hands."

I look down. I feel ashamed. I don't exactly know why.

"Are you settled in your room? Everything going well with your roommate?"

I nod.

"Good. And I want you to feel free to come down to talk to me anytime. Anytime at all." He taps the desk with his pencil and stares at me for a moment. Suddenly he looks young, real young, maybe even twenty-one or twenty-two. I wonder how a young guy like him gets a big job as counselor at a big school like Mt. Edgecumbe. I wonder how he even ends up here.

"You know," he says, as if he can hear what I'm thinking, "I'm not from this neck of the woods myself, Thelma. I'm pretty far away from home myself."

I look at my hands.

He laughs.

"Guess where I'm from," he asks.

I shrug.

"Hey, Thelma." He smiles. "You're sure a shy one, aren't you?"

I look up. He is leaning over the desk, looking right into my face. I hold my breath. Something in my stomach flutters.

"Well, now." He sighs. "Won't do to be so quiet, you know. This is the first time away from your village?"

I nod.

"I know it's a big change. But that's why I'm here. To help you with any adjustment problems. Now, I don't want you to worry. Just come see me if you run into any problems at all."

We both stand up. Nobody says nothing, and I don't know if I should just leave or what.

"That'll be all, Thelma," he finally says. "That'll be all."

At night I wait until the last minute before brushing my teeth and peeing. Don't want to go into the bathroom with all them other girls, even the Yup'ik ones I know like Mary Beans and Sophia Pastinak from Hooper Bay. All of them laughing and curling up each other's hair. They wear long, see-through nightgowns with little ribbons up top, and some of them have dark, pointed fingernails. It seems like everyone stops talking when I come in. Seems like everyone stops talking and looks at me. So I wait until just before the last bell and run down the hall with a sweater over my long underwear 'cause I don't even got one little nightgown at all. I'm holding a tin cup in one hand and my blue toothbrush and toothpaste in the other. First I brush my teeth real fast, watching out of the corner of my eye, then quickly slip into a stall. Sometimes there's all kinds of pads and Tampax and things right on the floor next to the toilet and I have to step carefully. It's pretty nice having a toilet that flushes every time, but I can't get used to the noise and the smell of the disinfectant and wet mop.

The worst is when I have to take a shower, because you got to wait in line and some girls just stand around in their bras and panties, flicking back their hair and twisting in front of the sink mirrors. I can shower before the first bell if I'm real quiet and I try to keep it to once a week. Somehow taking off all of my clothes in a strange place feels wrong. I wish for the hot bathwater back home with me and Rosie soaping each other in front of the smoky woodstove.

One night my Aleut roommate, whose name is Zena, don't get back to the room until after the last bell. The dormitory resident, who's also the school nurse, opens the door and looks confused. I'm already in bed, lying down completely still. I don't want anyone to say anything to me about nothing. But she does.

"Hey," she says, "where's number 301 at? Zena Petrinkovich."

"Don't know," I answer real soft.

"Hey," she says again, "don't get smart with me. You know where she is. Don't give me any of that crap."

I slip deeper into the bed.

"You know," she continues, walking into the room, "you could get yourself into big trouble if you don't let on. You could get study hall for two straight weeks."

I think of the long cafeteria room and all those kids having to sit right next to each other all evening. Don't want to be one of those kids.

"She's in the bathroom," I finally say. "She'll be right back."

"Well, why didn't you say so in the first place?" The nurse frowns. "I got a date tonight and have to get ready. Don't have any time for this nonsense. You sure she's in the john?"

I nod.

"Well, tell her to stay the hell in the room after last bell. I find her missing one more time and there'll be trouble. You understand?"

I nod again.

"Good," she says quickly. "Good," she says, slamming the door.

Zena don't get back until the middle of the night. I'm all asleep when I hear some big crash. I sit up, terrified.

"Shhh," she says. I can see her body's outline in the dark.

I hold my breath.

Another crash and I see her trip on something and fall down.

"Shit," she says out loud, "shit."

"You better keep quiet," I finally whisper. "You're suppose to be here a long time ago."

She laughs and sits down at the foot of my bed.

"Is that so?" she leans over and whispers right into my face. "That so?"

Her breath is sharp. Smells like beer and I recognize the familiar slur in her speech. "You gotta stop worrying so much, little black Eskimo girl." She laughs. "You won't live to be a hundred if you keep worrying so."

"Shhh," I say again. "If they catch you now, we're both in big trouble."

"Yeah?" She lays down on her back, my toes under her shoulders. "Big trouble, huh? What'll that turn out to be?"

I shrug. I realize I really don't know. Study hall ain't exactly big trouble, but still trouble.

"You think they'll send us to jail?" she asks, suddenly sitting up straight. "'Cause this place is worse than any old jail."

I don't say nothing. I'm thinking hard.

"Think they'll send us home?"

"I dunno." I look at my hands.

Zena slides up the bed until she is sitting right up close to my face. "'Cause sending us home is just what I

want. Hell." She waves her arms above her head as if dancing to music. "The fact is, my little Eskimo friend, the
fact is it don't matter what the hell we do, 'cause they can't
do anything back worse than what's already been done. It's
just like we're all in the middle of this big nightmare, the
worst nightmare we ever have, and it's all come true. So we
might as well forget trying to be ourselves anymore, forget
trying to be good or what they want. We already go right
to hell here in this so-called school, and there ain't any
place worse than that."

She bends over me and brushes the hair off my face.
The smell of liquor washes over me and I turn. She rests
her head on my shoulder for a moment and I hold my
breath. The moon drifts in through the window, and I see
one of Rosie's dreams clear as day. Grandpa and me are
feeding the dogs, all staked out one by one in our little
summer garden. The wind picks up and Rosie floats by.
She's wearing a pink *kuspuk* and her black hair is long and
curly. "Take care," she calls as the wind pushes her on by.
"Take care, Thelma." And me and Grandpa just stand there
looking up, our mouths wide open. Rosie's high over our
heads, turning smaller and smaller, like some kind of pink
balloon. And then we can't even see her no more. We can't
even see nothing.

Zena shifts, and I can feel her pick up her feet and slip
over my side. Her arms drape around my chest and her
knees curl up behind mine. The moon sucks itself back

into the black sky and two girls suddenly sigh. They are falling asleep together in a little dormitory cot, the air around them choked up sudden with somebody else's small dream just sliding on by.

This boy named Dove Alexie sits by himself in the cafeteria. He stares down at his lunch on the tray and then begins eating slowly, just looking out into space. I know his name from Zena, who thinks he's good-looking, and I gotta agree. This boy has a face that looks like it is dug out from stone, all chipped away so that its edges are sharp and clean. His chin, his jaw, his cheekbones are finished off definite, nothing blended there. If you look closely, you can see exactly where each section of his face begins and ends. The jaw, the cheeks, the nose, the forehead, all separate, yet fit just right. Kinda like a statue, kinda like a soapstone chiseled up all edgy and fine.

"That Dove boy's really put together right," Zena whispers to me at lunch.

We're both holding our forks midair, and a fleck of macaroni drifts down to my plate.

"Just look at him." She laughs. "I wouldn't mind getting my hands on that piece of work."

"Zena!" Suddenly I'm embarrassed and feel my face flush up hot.

"What's the matter, Thelma? Ain't you ever wishing for something else in your bed? And that boy's got everything you might be needing. Too bad he's from Stony River or I'd march up to his table all by myself."

She sighs and stops chewing for a moment.

"What's wrong with Stony River?" I ask, raising my head again.

The boy across the room tosses back his long black hair and stands up. The air around him shakes up sudden and ripples over his shoulders, a fluorescent glow. I'm surprised by his height and the bulk of his chest in contrast to his slim hips. He's very tall for a Native kid, tall and muscular, his black T-shirt tucked carelessly into his worn jeans. Nobody sits at the table with him, but somehow the room seems to quiet as he stands up straight.

"Don't you know nothing?" Zena pats me on the arm reassuringly. "Oh well, guess it's my place in life to educate this poor girl from up north. Stony River, well, it's a village deep in the interior, you know, where there's this thick forest, pine trees 'n' all. Never see a forest myself, but hear talk they're all around Sitka, way across the bridge. Never go that far myself. Anyway, Stony River people, they're not Yup'ik or Athapascan, Aleut or Haida or Tsimshian or anything else. They're full of mixed-bloods, crazy in the heads from all the bloods running through their bodies, and them's a murdering lot. They say them Stony River people got cold river water in their veins. Their hearts are made of stone, and each and every one of them will stick a knife in your heart without even saying boo.

And there's nothing worse than getting hooked up with anyone from those mixed-blood parts. They'll look at you with their hungry eyes and curse you with old Indian shaman breath."

I shiver.

"You watch," Zena continues, "ain't nobody 'round here gonna mess with the likes of Dove Alexie. He may look good, but there's nothing but trouble inside his bones. You watch, ain't nobody gonna be speaking to that boy and he ain't gonna last long here. He'll be back in that Stony River place before you can ever turn around."

I study Dove Alexie as he walks slowly out of the cafeteria, his back straight, and a draft from the window softly lifts his heavy hair. Everyone shifts in their seats as he walks on by.

"Thelma."

I hear my name in the main hall as I try to make my way to breakfast. Turn around, but no one's there.

"Thelma Cooke."

He's suddenly standing right there next to me, so close to my face that I can feel his warm words on my skin.

"Everything going all right? I haven't heard from you at all. Remember, anytime you need anything, I'll be in my office. That's what a counselor is for, you know, to help with any problems you may be having, help with anything at all."

I see a red tongue darting inside of his full mouth. He smiles and takes my elbow in his hand.

"Goddamn, Thelma, you look scared to death."

He laughs, and I get a sudden urge to reach out and touch his soft beard. I take a step back.

"Gotta go to class," I say.

He moves toward me again and pats my shoulder. I can feel the heat from his hand through my clothes.

Zena's got black underwear with lace.

She ordered it from the Montgomery Ward catalogue. She laughs. "Whew, my mother says them catalogues sure do change over the years. In her day all they got were white cotton briefs. Come on, Thelma. Don't just stand there with your mouth wide open. Come on over here and I'll show you what I mean. You can borrow one of these bras if you want."

I walk over to the dresser. Zena's things fall out of the drawers, all except one, the one stuffed with my stupid wool socks and long underwear.

"Come on. Nothing to be scared of, for heaven's sake."

I take one of the bras in my hand. The straps are black satin, slick to the touch, and the top of the cups is scratchy black lace. It looks uncomfortable. It has wires sewn underneath and the cups are stiff.

I giggle.

"What's so funny? Ain't you ever seen a black bra before? When's the last time you get out of that village of yours, Sleetetown, whatever."

"Sleetmute," I say.

"Sleetmute. Try it on. We're about the same size, although I can't see much of anything under all them clothes you got on. Don't you get hot with all them clothes on?"

I nod.

"Well, what you waiting for? Try it on. Jesus Christ, I never see anyone as slow moving as you before."

I look at the bra in my hands. Somehow, it don't look like an ordinary piece of clothing. Looks like something breathing, something alive, some new kind of discovered animal. The Black Satin Seal, newly discovered under Mt. Edgecumbe dormitory ice.

I giggle again.

"Thelma!"

She's shaking her head, hands on hips.

I walk back over to my bed and slowly undress, somehow feeling shy in front of Zena, although she often parades around the room without anything on at all. The air is cold against my bare skin.

"Jesus, Thelma. Look at you. You got a real nice pair on you. Why the hell do you keep them hidden behind all those flannel shirts?"

I shrug. I can feel my whole body blushing. The black bra feels tight at first, but when I adjust the hooks, it falls over my body like it was made only for me. I look in the mirror. The tops of my breasts protrude a little and everything is lifted out and up. I don't look like myself. I look like somebody else, somebody I don't even see before.

Zena whistles through her teeth.

"Jeez," she says softly, "Jeez, Thelma, you are something else. Jeez, you better look out."

So I end up sitting with the Aleut girls at lunch since Zena starts saving me a place at meals. At first they aren't real friendly and look at me with little eyes, but soon they forget I'm even there and start messing around like always. But when I see them in class or run into any of them in the hall, they turn their delicate faces and pretend they don't even know who I am.

Aleut girls are beautiful. They look different from the other Natives; they have different faces and different expressions. And even their skin color is different, too, less yellow than Yup'ik, more coppery, the color of new autumn tundra grass. Sometimes when Zena looks at me, I can see a whole lot of colors flashing through her skin so that it's almost as if her entire face moves. She'll smile or laugh, and the colors all race to her cheeks and circle quickly under the elegant lift of narrow cheekbones. Her eyes, a color I can't even name, but somehow both yellowish and gold, can look mean and hard—they gleam up so sharp for so long that it's impossible to look at them straight on.

Her nose is slim and chiseled, her mouth wide, and her hair, cut straight at the shoulders, hangs thick and shiny from a gleaming middle part so that every time she turns her head, the air around her just burns up smoky like firecrackers. Of course, not all the Aleut girls look like Zena, but they all seem to have her shined-up colors, her narrow face, her lean, wiry frame. Standing next to her when we speak in the hallways or lean against the dormitory window sharing a smoke, I feel short and wide, my round face sallow, my rocky bones bulky thick.

To my surprise, today one of Zena's friends, Nadia Cherkov, waves a graceful hand when she sees me in class and motions for me to sit down next to her. I feel the Yup'ik girls' eyes on my back as I slowly walk across the room and hear Mary Beans hiss, "Black Russian Thelma, Black Russian Thelma." I slide into my seat quietly, head down, and Nadia looks at me and laughs.

"What ya doing, Thelma Cooke?" she sneers. "This chair ain't saved for any stupid Eskimo girl."

I feel my eyes burn as I try to slip into the back of the room where the Yup'ik girls wait for me, anger decaying their pink mouths black.

He's in his office, just like before, and barely looks up when I come in.

"Mr. Davidson," I say quietly. "Mr. Davidson, you busy?"

He keeps writing but says, "Have a seat. Be with you in a minute."

I sit across from him as he writes with a red pen. Once more I notice the fingernails are bitten, the skin around them raw.

"Well," he finally says, setting the pen down with a smack, "what can I do for you? Don't you have a meeting scheduled? Should be something already scheduled if you're a freshman."

"Another one?" I ask.

"Another what?"

"Another meeting? I met with you already last week."

"Oh," he says, looking surprised. "Oh, of course, last week, Thelma Cooke. I'm sorry, love, having the responsibility overseeing so many students, I'm not always able to remember each one. But Thelma Cooke. Of course, last week. Everything going all right with your roommate?"

I nod.

"Any problems at all?"

I shake my head.

I leave the room without saying anything at all.


Dove Alexie comes in late to science, and the only chair left is in the back, right across from mine. Mr. Huddleston clears his throat and looks at Dove angrily, but he continues his lecture without a break. Dove rummages through his papers, finally settling on one, and starts to write quickly. I wonder if he's taking notes. Nobody I know ever bothers to take notes. A small slip of paper falls from his desk, landing at my feet. I reach for it but miss. His head juts up suddenly and I can see half of his face bathed in light, the other half turned away, dark. Slowly, I pick up the paper and offer it, my hand shaking as if cold.

He doesn't move for a minute and then softly pulls it from my fingers. He nods.

I peer at him through my downcast eyes and watch as he continues to write, his motions small and quick. I notice his hands are dark and square. I notice his skin looks thick and tough, puckered and scarred, the skin of a walrus or a seal. The skin of something wild.

The next time I see Dove Alexie, he's standing alone outside the main building, smoking. He doesn't look up as I walk past him slowly. The skin on the back of my neck knots and prickles.

"Zena," I say softly into the black air as we lay in our beds that night, "what do you think would happen if we ran away?"

"What do you mean, ran away?" She yawns loudly and I hear her turn over in bed.

"You know, back home."

"Oh. But you know, there really ain't much left for us

back home, not anymore. Nothing to do, just the same old people all of the time."

"But don't you miss your family? Don't you want to get out of here and go back?"

"I don't know." She rustles around in her sheets and I see her sit up, a long, shadowy figure. "I sure as hell want to get out of here, that's no joke. But I don't really want to go back home, don't want that either. I don't know, I just want something exciting to happen, wanna go somewhere, but somewhere far away. What about you?"

"I want to go home. I want to get Rosie and go back home. I want things to be the way they were. I want people around me not to be so angry and mean all the time. That's what I want. I want people to be happy again and not so mad anymore."

"Oh." Zena sighs. "Yeah," she says softly, "I know what you mean."

The next day I get to science after the bell and sit way in the back, making sure the seat next to me is empty. And right on cue, about five minutes late, Dove Alexie walks in, sits right down across from me, and begins to write. He doesn't even look up as Mr. Huddleston sighs and clears his throat.

That evening after dinner, I sit on the cafeteria's steps, looking out at the harbor and the mountains above. The boats rock slowly in the water, a few people working on their decks, painting, cleaning, some just sitting and talking. The sky behind the mountains is all gray, no other colors tonight, and the rain disappears right into the thick, billowing air. Sometimes I can hardly even believe that Japonski Island is part of the same world as back home. Sleetmute and Bethel feel so far away, their flat tundra back home almost difficult to remember in this rocky, jagged place. It seems like Japonski Island is nothing but a mess of different-sized rocks, even the earth underneath tiny rock pebbles, and the mountains and volcano a single endless, enormous, black boulder. The tundra back home in Sleetmute stretches itself out flat, but Mt. Edgecumbe spits up endless gravel and pebbles like the breathing of underwater fish. Every time you take a step, blown formations of rock and stone are shot out hard and fast. The ground under your feet is so solid, so thick and deep, that footprints left behind are just rock chalk quickly blown away. No mark is made. Nothing ever sinks in.

I notice a bright-yellow station wagon pulling up to the curb and recognize Mr. Davidson inside. He waves to me and opens the door. I tighten my arms around the books on my lap.

"Get in," he calls softly. "Hurry and get in."

So, before I can even think about what to do, I find myself next to him in the front seat of his car. He starts the engine again without saying a word, a cigarette dangling from one corner of his mouth. The air outside darkens and then pours inside the open windows. He looks at me out of the corner of his eye and nods. One arm is on the wheel, the other draped over the back of my seat.

"Thought you might like going for a ride," he says softly. "That okay?"

I nod and he steps harder on the gas, giving the car a sudden jolt. I notice a bottle of beer held between his knees. The car smells sweet, cologne and warm beer. I inhale slowly.

"Ever been over the Sitka bridge?" he asks, leaning back in his seat as if relaxing in a chair. "It sure is one hell of a view."

I shake my head, somehow scared to speak, but he doesn't seem to notice.

"Cigarette?" he asks.

I shake my head again and we drive in silence down the rocky island road. Soon I don't recognize where we are anymore until the bridge looms up silver and sudden. The cars in front of us seem to be flying, their red brake lights burning quickly into the night air, and I hold on tight to the edge of my seat. I see water below and the town of Sitka glowing ahead. I somehow know I will never cross a bridge exactly this way ever again.

"So, Thelma Cooke," he finally says, inhaling without taking the cigarette from his mouth. "Let's not even talk about school. This is my night off, and if it's all right with you, I'd prefer to forget everything about that goddamn place."

I shrink back in my seat. Suddenly I feel very far away and long to be back in my empty, odorless dormitory room.

"Tell me about yourself," he continues. "Tell me what the real Thelma Cooke is like. Any boyfriends back home?"

I shrug and shake my head. "Not really," I finally say.

"What? A pretty girl like you? That's hard to believe. What about the guys down here? Been out on any hot dates?"

I shake my head again. "Don't really know anyone here," I say. "Don't know too many people at all."

"You don't?" He sounds surprised. "Hmmm. Must be pretty lonely for a girl like you. So far away from home. We'll have to make an effort to set you up with somebody real soon. Maybe you should join one of the clubs or try out for cheerleading, always a good way to meet people. You've got the body for it. Hey Thelma"—he laughs and slaps his knee—"look at me, talking about school after all. Doesn't that figure? Work so hard that I just can't seem to get my job outa mind. Just goes to show you, doesn't it, just goes to show you that it doesn't pay off to always work so goddamned hard. Never thought that I'd end up in such a godforsaken place when I started graduate school, never thought that after paying all that tuition money and wasting my time in classes, I'd end up a stupid counselor at a hick high school dormitory in godforsaken Alaska, for God's sake, but it's the only job I got offered. Who would have thought? And with all my degrees, I'm spending most of my day filling up dormitory soda machines and sitting at my desk writing out forms. I tell you, I can hardly believe it myself."

He looks up suddenly, as if remembering that I am sitting next to him, smiles, and takes a swig from the bottle. "I'd offer you some, Thelma Cooke, but you know it's against the law, I could get in big trouble giving a drink to a minor. How old are you, anyway? Fifteen or sixteen?"

"Fourteen."

"Ahh." He takes another sip and is quiet for a moment.

I begin to wonder exactly where we are going and if I'm going to be late for the last bell. Wonder what Zena's doing.

"Well, love, look to your left. That's Sheldon Jackson College, where you'll probably end up if you graduate from Edgecumbe. That is, unless you want to go to a real college." He laughs.

I press myself to the window, not able to see much in the dark. I can only make out a few houses on top of a steep hill.

"And this," he finally says, slowing down the car, "this is Totem Park. Ever heard anything about Totem Park?"

I shake my head.

"You'll find it a real educational experience." He laughs

again, sucking on the bottle between breaths. "The Tlingit Indians carved totems out here and left them to rot all through the forest. But shhh, we can't make much noise. No cars are supposed to be driving through." His voice drops to a whisper. "See, we'll go real slow so no one catches on."

I roll down my window and feel a night breeze travel across my chest. The slow rocking of the car on soft, piney earth makes me sleepy and I lean my head back against the seat and somehow the dumb poem I have to memorize for English class suddenly drifts through my head: "This is the forest primeval. The murmuring pines and the hemlocks . . ." I close my eyes and think of Rosie. Think of her tiny sweet face. I think of Dove and wonder if I'll ever see him again.

"Thelma?" The car stops and his hand gently brushes my cheek. It's scratchy and warm. He slides his index finger down my jaw to my chin. "Do you know how pretty you are," he whispers softly into my ear. "Such a pretty, pretty girl."

I keep my eyes closed. "Bearded with moss, and in garments green, indistinct in the twilight . . ." He pulls me to his chest and I lie there, my arms at my sides, his loosely circling my back. His chest is firm. I hear his heart beating and his stomach making small sounds.

*"Listen, Thelma," my father would say, pressing my head to his chest. "Listen carefully and tell me what you hear. Do you hear the old-time songs I am singing from*

*way inside my heart? Can you tell me what they are?"*

*"Don't hear any songs, Papa," I would whisper back,*
*just happy to be held in his large, warm lap.*

*But then all of a sudden, I would know. I'd hear a kind*
*of trilling like a winter bird. I'd hear my papa's enormous*
*heart humming all the songs I ever knew in one long*
*lilting tune.*

*I'd smile and press my eyes tighter. I'd wish not to be*
*ever moved.*


"Thelma, you awake?"

I stir suddenly to his voice and feel his arms tighten
as I start to lift up.

"Shhh, don't move, love, don't move at all. Don't you
know how good it feels just to hold you like this? Just for
a moment. Shhh."

I relax and feel his hand softly stroke my hair. His
breath is warm, smells salty as he whispers more and more.

"You're such a pretty girl, Thelma. You know you're
not a child anymore. First time all alone, far away from
your family, from your home. Must be hard for you. And
I'm lonely too." He speaks slowly, softly, carefully. "Don't
know too many people myself, no friends to speak of, it's
lonely for me too. . . . Who would have thought, in some
nowhere place with nothing to do, not even a goddamn
movie theater in town for God's sake, not even a decent place
to buy a meal."

His words circle over my head but I hardly hear them, sleepy and lulled by the warmth of his body and his steady breathing. His lips brush my forehead, my eyes, my cheeks, softly, so softly that from the inside of my eyelids I see another one of Rosie's dreams, this one all colors, no people, no places, just different dark colors swirling around a deep center. "This is the forest primeval; but where are the hearts that beneath . . ."

He slowly slides me around so that I am lying below him and his soft beard rubs against my neck, my shirt seems to open by itself, each button slipping wide, his words whispery and warm, his lips on my lips, he takes my face in both of his hands and gently pulls my mouth with his teeth.

"Thelma."

His hand is light on my breasts, my shirt pushed up to my shoulders, my eyes pressed tightly closed, and I see still another dream, Rosie's dream, her little body floating on the Arctic ice, she's only wearing a summer *kuspuck*, and I call her, "No, Rosie, no, you'll be too cold, you're too little to be out there all on your own." And she lifts up her tiny, heavy head, her mouth opens calling, but I can't hear the words. . . .

"Thelma."

His hands slide down my legs and back up to my jeans' zipper.

"No," I say, suddenly pulling away, "no," I say, but it's

as if he's humming his own song by then, softly moaning and calling my name.

"Thelma."

I feel his warm hand on my stomach and I try to roll away, but he pins himself down over me so that now I can't feel anything, my pants down around my ankles, my underwear at my knees, and then he is inside me, but it doesn't hurt at all, it's as if I'm not even there, I know he's close in me and that something should hurt, something should hurt and startle, but nothing, I feel nothing. That part of me down below so wide and deep that even with him way inside I feel nothing but the flattening of flesh, nothing I can do about it anymore, all of me swallowing whatever comes my way, the folds of my skin, the gathering of my hips, I feel nothing at all but the spread of ponds, rivers, and lakes, crossing wide and deep.

Zena wags her finger at me as we get dressed the next morning.

"You bad girl, you . . ." She laughs. "So you're not Goody Two-Shoes from Sleetmute after all. Well, I gotta say, you sure surprise me, Thelma girl."

I turn around to button my sweater and keep my head down.

"Where were you last night, anyway? I had to make up some story to keep you out of trouble. Where were you?"

I shrug. "Nowhere, really."

"Nowhere?" She laughs again. "Come on, I can't believe you're keeping something from old Zena. Bet you sneak into that party up in the senior dorms."

"Yeah, that's it," I answer. "Yeah, but it wasn't much of anything. Wasn't much of anything at all."

His office is empty the next few times I stop by. I know he lives in the staff dormitory wing and start waiting outside by that front door. He never goes in or out. I don't see him in the hallways either. Not exactly sure what I'm feeling but know that now I have someone of my own, like Rosie, now I have someone of my own who I can touch whenever I want. Don't matter who it is, just someone. I like thinking about that. It's nice to remember holding someone's hand or having a warm arm around your shoulder when no one else is around. I stand outside by the staff wing and try to remember what his smell is like, how his beard feels against skin, I remember feeling close and I remember the gentle touching. . . . It's hard to think about my schoolwork, somehow I still can't even finish learning that poem, somehow I can't finish anything at all, and Zena watches, asking me questions, but I know enough to never tell.

And finally one afternoon I run into him in the hallway and reach to touch his arm. He's wearing a dark-blue jacket and a blue-and-red striped tie. I notice how neatly he's always dressed, his clothes perfectly pressed, his shoes shined up real bright. He slowly takes my hand from his arm and nods.

"Mr. Davidson," I say, and he nods again. He looks at his watch, slips into the crowd of students, and is gone. I'm standing in the long hallway, my arms glued to my sides, without anybody to even touch at all.

I wonder what I did to make him mad. I lay in my bed at night, wondering why he don't like me anymore, wondering how I changed since the other night. Somehow he's all I think about, even more than Rosie, I even start missing him more than I'm missing her. I hear them soft words in my ears, I hear him telling me how I make him feel, I breathe his mixed-up sweet salty smell. His skin rough against mine. His skin warm. "The forest primeval. Indistinct in the twilight." I close my eyes and try to see one of Rosie's dreams, but they hide themselves, saving their flickering for someone else's restless night.

I stop going to English class. Nobody notices and I can't memorize any part of that poem anyway. And the thought of reciting in front of the entire class makes my stomach hurt. During English period, I wait by his office and watch who goes in and out of his door. I don't say a thing. Nobody even notices I'm there. Every once in a while, he'll leave or come back, always nodding and sometimes saying my name. But he never stops to talk or invites me in. Still, once a day during English, I stay by that door, feeling the cold wall against my back, wondering if I'll ever get to touch him at all.

Finally one afternoon he grabs my elbow and walks me inside. Neither of us sits down.

"Now, Thelma," he says, looking over my shoulder as if I'm not even there. "You've got to stop standing outside my office making a spectacle. Somebody'll notice, somebody'll say something, and I know you don't want that."

"I don't care," I say. "I don't care about that."

"What?" He steps back as if pushed.

"I don't care."

"Thelma, listen." He sits on the edge of his desk and squeezes a pack of cigarettes in his hand. "Listen, you know that was just a mistake, you know that can't ever happen again. Listen, you could get sent away."

"Why?" I ask. "Why can't I just be with you? It doesn't have to be like that night. I just want to be near you. Why can't I be near you anymore?"

He sighs and throws a cigarette pack on his desk, sits down, stands again, then paces back and forth.

"You're kidding," he finally says. "You must be kidding."

I don't say nothing. We stay there, looking at each other quiet.

"You're just a kid," he finally says, and sighs. "Look, you just need a boyfriend your own age and you'll be perfectly fine. And I'm getting notices from your English teacher that you haven't even been to class. Listen, Thelma, this all has just got to stop. Right now. I don't want to hear anything else about it."

"I can't stay with you? Now? Anytime at all?"

He shakes his head. "Not now. Not anytime at all. It was all a mistake. Surely you know. I wasn't myself. Had a particularly hard day. These things just happen. A mistake. Just a damn stupid mistake."

I look down at my shoes. The room starts to spin around and around.

"Thelma?"

I open my mouth and then close it. He is standing in front of me, not even looking at who I am. Things just happen. I'm just a kid. Just a damn stupid mistake.

He holds the door open.

I lean toward him as I walk out, as if to inhale what I have already lost.

I don't go to any of my classes anymore. Zena gets up each morning and sits on the edge of my bed, but I won't move. She takes my hand. Her skin is soft with lemony lotion. "Thelma," she says every morning, "you gotta get out of bed. You're gonna get in big trouble real soon."

I don't say a word. I press my head to the pillow. I don't see anything but black. Never see none of Rosie's dreams no more. Just nothing.

"Thelma," Zena says, "you sick? Want me to get the nurse?"

But I just shake my head and start to cry. "Don't want no nurse," I sob into my pillow. "Don't want nobody."

So she leaves me every morning, carrying her books in her arms, her bracelets rattling like bones. I fall back to sleep, not even moving an inch, and only wake when the room sinks from white to gray and I hear the doorknob turn and her quick steps come back to me again.

Zena brings me a note from my mailbox. I turn my head to the wall.

"Thelma," she says, "this is serious. You've got to do something or they'll send you somewhere else. Look," she continues, "you know that you won't get to go home. Sometimes they send you down south to this reform school in Oregon. I know. I have friends who go there. Thelma, look, if it's the poem, don't worry. I'll help you memorize it—you just gotta do a few lines. Don't let it get to you; you can't let any of it get to you."

I roll over on my back and look at the ceiling. It has cracks in the shape of enormous Arctic hares.

"Listen," she continues, "this note is a warning notice. You can't just ignore what they tell you; you can't pretend that they're not in charge."

"Leave me alone," I finally whisper. "I'm tired and just

want to sleep. Leave me alone." I peek out from under the blankets and see her cover her face with both hands.

And she doesn't leave me alone but comes back later that afternoon with Nadia Cherkov. They both stand by my bed not saying nothing.

"Thelma," Zena finally whispers. "Thelma, Nadia's come to help us with the poem. She already recites her lines in class today and she does it just right. You should hear her; she don't miss a single word. She shows them, she really does."

I pull the pillow over my head.

"Thelma," she continues, "your name's on the list for next week. Nadia and me, we'll help you learn it—we'll help you out until you get it just right. Come on, you can't give up without trying, you can't give in, not before you've already tried."

So for the next three days they both come at the same time, standing by my bed and reading that same stupid poem again and again. On the fourth day, Zena comes in alone. She's panting, as if out of breath, and she sits down on the edge of the bed next to me.

"You'll never guess," she says quickly, as if in a rush to get out her words, "you'll never guess what just happened."

I turn over on my back.

"That Dove Alexie boy, you know that sharp-looking Stony River kid from way up inside the interior, he socks old Huddleston right in the mouth. In the middle of science class, you should have seen, oh, Thelma, I still can't believe it. No one can. Old Huddleston's just standing there, just like usual, droning on and on about volcanoes and extinction and stuff, when he notices Dove writing something on his desk. Huddleston walks to the back of the room, whips the papers right outa Dove's hands, and rips them straight across and says 'You ignorant boy, don't you know better than to write when I'm speaking.' Or something like that. Well, Dove ain't taking any of that—he shoots up to his feet and lays one on the old man, just like that. And then he walks right out of the room like nothing happens. Huddleston's flat against the blackboard, holding his bloody nose with one hand and yelling, 'Somebody get that boy! Somebody get that black Indian boy right now!' But we just sit there, hardly even believing our own eyes. We just sit there, our mouths wide open, until Huddleston gets it together and stands himself back up. 'Class dismissed,' he mumbles, and then kinda stumbles out of the room. And we're still sitting there in our chairs, crammed tight into those little desks that never really fit, and I see John Moran, that quiet Yup'ik guy from Hooper Bay, start to clap his hands hard. And then soon, before you know it, we're all clapping and shouting so loud that Mr. Davidson, the counselor, comes running in and sends us all back to our rooms."

"What happens to Dove Alexie?" I ask, sitting up

suddenly. "Do you know what happens to Dove?"

Zena shrugs and looks down. "Nobody really knows," she says quietly, "but I hear they lock him up and gonna send him away somewhere far. Maybe to Chimawa or maybe to jail." She hugs herself as if cold and then smiles. "But you know what, Thelma, you know what? That boy may be from Stony River and all, but you gotta admire him a little for what he does. Imagine, right in front of everybody and in the middle of class. He stands himself up and smacks old Huddleston right in the jaw. Imagine that."

I sigh and slide back down into the bed. The afternoon light from the window drifts inside, making dusty circles in the air. It looks like a clear day outside and I strain to see if the Mt. Edgecumbe volcano is hidden or visible.

The next afternoon, when Zena and Nadia come in, I'm sitting on the cot's edge, dressed in my usual flannel shirt and jeans. Neither of them say nothing, as if they don't notice anything different, but keep reading the poem aloud. By the next day I'm standing by the window, my hair washed, and I'm looking out all the way to the volcano and the Sitka bridge. You can only see that far when the air's perfectly clear. Again, they don't say nothing but keep reading and reading the part of the poem that's been assigned to me. Finally, after six days, I'm sitting at the desk when they come, the book already opened. Still, I can't get all the words straight; they feel uncomfortable on my tongue, as if I'm saying something in another language, something I don't even understand. But both Zena and Nadia don't say a word, never making fun or laughing at my mistakes. They just sit there quietly, day after day, listening to me try to get all the words right.

"Again," Zena urges, "say it again, this time without stumbling over any of the lines."

"Again," Nadia insists, "do it again, but this time try to slow down and speak up louder."

So over and over, I repeat the lines, not really listening to what I'm saying, but letting the words roll off my tongue without even thinking, the stanzas coming up from some place deep inside that I never even know is there. It's as if the poem finally becomes part of me, it almost recites itself, just borrowing my mouth the way music borrows an instrument, the way songs borrow someone's voice. Over and over, I recite the poem for both of them, again and again, until at last all three of us are satisfied with what I have finally learned.

Zena and I are wearing matching black bras under our sweaters. As usual, she sits with the Aleut girls and as usual, I'm sitting with the Yup'ik ones, but this time, we're all in the same row. The teacher takes out her attendance book and calls my name. I walk up to the front of the room, as if dreaming, as if walking in my sleep. I turn around slowly.

"'Still stands the forest primeval,'" I recite, "'but under the shade of its branches / Dwells another race, with other customs and language. . . .'"

Zena sits up straight in her seat and smiles, and in a small Bethel house, my sister Rosie opens her eyes wide to see one of my own dreams flicker and edge itself ahead.

# EDGAR KWAGLEY

*Mt. Edgecumbe High School, Japonski Island, Alaska*
*Fall 1968*

When I live in Hooper Bay, John Moran is the one who does most of the pranks. That's a long time ago when we are just little kids but it was pretty funny back then, John always doing the jokes. He gets the smoke bombs and likes to make all the girls scream. I hide behind Nick's store and watch him tease the girls with Ethan Kitchok. Them girls, Ella Koonuk and Sophia Pastinak and the rest, just laugh and shake their fat fists, but John keeps at it, keeps after them. I see John Moran running after them, laughing and calling. That was a long time ago when we are just little kids. Things sure is different now that we're at Edgecumbe.

I remember our village of Hooper Bay when everyone plays pranks on each other. Them days it's a happy place. Some of the kids get squirt guns, lotsa fun, and we all have the chew and even some of us some booze. Them days we go to fish camp all summer. Happy times. All the little childrens, they run around naked those summertimes. We have little bushes for trees at fish camp, those trees all gone now, and we go climbing, lots of grass, the beach stretches on and on and you can walk all the way to Numapitchuk. We live in tents at fish camp. All of that's changed. Still, when I hear the sound of an old outboard motor, when the sun gets hot and the grasses come up yellow, I can close my eyes and almost see them old days. The aunties cutting up muktuk by the beach and all us kids playing story knife, doing the dances with the old mens, just living at fish camp.

But soon we get older and things change. We start wanting something more, new things to see, jobs so that we can work and earn some cash. The only real work around Hooper Bay is in the village office, filing the mail with Lucy Tajuracov or standing around waiting for phone calls and trying to get the Tribal Council to meet. Sometimes you can also find jobs at the Northern Commercial, hauling cartons sometimes in Nick's store. Nick's store the only place I ever get good work, but the old mens, they sit around by the woodstove drinking Russian tea and talking Yup'ik all day. Pretty boring. That place, it always smell the same, all type of fish, real strong smell but still kinda nice. Nick's got dried pike, whitefish, dried seal, king salmon, chubs. He also sells all kinds of groceries, canned things, clothing, socks, jeans, jackets, medicines, even Ski-Doos and outboard motors. Some days, a hunter'll get a wolf and he'll tack it right up on Nick's wall behind the cash register, waiting for a good price.

Before we know it, the village elders, the Tribal Council, they say us kids need to get some education and go to the new Mt. Edgecumbe High School way south. No high school in Hooper Bay and Japonski Island's all the way past Naknek, east of Bristol Bay. Way far from this village. We hear there's hardly any snow. We hear there's even no ice. But they say down Edgecumbe there's this big volcano mountain that can still explode. I kinda want to see that.

My older sisters go to Edgecumbe before me, the first ones ever to go to school away from home, but they don't know nothing else but Hooper Bay when they go off. They're real scared, seem like they never want to leave home. But when they come back from Edgecumbe for the summer, they get real mean. They come back meaner than the rest of us, we can't say "Salt" at the dinner table anymore, we gotta say "Please pass the salt." My oldest sister, Lara, she's strong with manners after Mt. Edgecumbe. I don't remember getting scolded before that, before she went to school. But I sure get plenty of looks for punishment, seems like when my grandma gives me the silent treatment I'm scared to look at her. The worst punishment you can get is the silent treatment, your grandma giving it to you bad. Those old eyes are smiling at the other grandsons all the day and all the night.

So I worry about when I got to go to Edgecumbe. I sure don't want to get meaner. Not like my sisters do. But it happens just that way. I'm scared to leave home at first but still I gotta get out, not much happening at home. I'm supposed to go to school and come back during the summer to help with the fishing. The council back home is always telling us kids to get an education but then to come back to the village and work. Don't leave for good or anything like that. But sometimes us kids don't want to go home after. Seems like there's not much left there anymore, some of the aunties dead now, no more fish camp, not the way it was, the little trees, the beach gone, everyone just sitting around waiting for the village corporation checks to come in so they can blow all the money drinking or getting to Fairbanks to hit the bars out by the Native Hospital.

Why not stay away and party? They only got one TV station at home, anyway, and you get used to more, get used to something else. Funny, when I go to Anchorage at Fur Rendezvous, there they all are, hanging out by McDonald's near First Street. Or on Northern Lights Boulevard. Some of my cousins, they learn to live on them streets, smoking butts from the sidewalk, asking folks for change. They drink, they party, they stay with different relatives. They don't want to go home. They don't know how to anymore. Things sure do change.

Now everything's different for me, too. Being here at Mt. Edgecumbe, it's like something happened to my village heart. Don't want no village job no more. Too boring. And anyway, after Edgecumbe, seems like Hooper Bay's just some stupid bush town. Don't want to stay home. I want to get to Anchorage or even Outside. Some of my friends go to technical school in Seward, want to fix machinery, Ski-Doos, motors, and stuff. Pretty good money. I hear that Wiggins John from Akiachak goes to Seward and gets a job making a lot of money. I wouldn't mind that. Look at my dad. Used to be a mechanic long time ago. But he left few years ago to join the army. They say he's overseas now. Left town, just like all the rest.

But it don't really matter if we want to leave home; we gotta go to Edgecumbe, like it or not. And we learn never to show it if we're unhappy. At home we're taught never to show anger; don't show anger. Don't matter who's talking to you or who says what, you just turn away and don't show no feelings. You learn to keep the anger from spilling out all over.

This year it's just John Moran and me old enough to leave home for school and it's a long trip, Wein Air Alaska to Anchorage and then a jet all the way south. And when we get there it seems like a whole different world. Edgecumbe isn't like any place I see before, so many kids, such big buildings. Being from the coast, I'm used to the tundra—clear, open, flat spaces where you can keep seeing and seeing as far as you want. Japonski's different, an island surrounded by mountains and this old volcano, too—you can only see what's right in front of you, no farther than that. Some evenings the clouds cover the white volcano crater at the top and you can forget it's even there.

When I first arrive, I don't know anything about the volcano 'cause we get socked in with fog whiteout. Can't see no mountains, no sky, no volcano, nothing. And suddenly, one day I look around, the fog lifts and what do I see but blue sky and a circle of mountains, never see anything like it before. And smack in the middle, this volcano, kind of glimmering up in the sun. The Mt. Edgecumbe volcano, hitting off the water with its reflection, shining all over the place, just sitting there like nothing even unusual. I can tell you that thing makes me nervous sometimes. I'm always wondering if it will still explode.

The school bell rings and I don't even know what it is at first, just see all these kids pushing and shoving in the halls. Sure ain't used to so many people all in one place at one time. Soon John Moran and I meet up with some kids from villages near home, some from Napaskiak and Aniak and one from Unalakleet, a few of them even our cousins. That makes us feel better, and it's not long before we realize nobody much knows we're around anyway. Seems like the teachers never even see us. We start to sneak smokes into the classrooms, all of us, and light up, right there in front of them teachers 'cause they never know our names.

Like we're not even there.

This one, this real young blond teacher, she's so scared of everyone, she doesn't even look up from what she's reading. Just keeps on talking, eyes down, reading some old dumb book. She's pretty sexy, I guess, that one, yellow hair and short skirts. I stare at her knees all during class. Sometimes we follow her after school, but she lives in downtown Sitka and drives right off in her blue car.

"Like to get some of that," Floyd Kookesh says, and we all slap each other on the back, watching her little car speed off Japonski Island over that silver Sitka bridge. That's one bridge for sure that we'll never get a chance to cross—it's pretty long, longer and higher than any bridge we ever see. Seems like we'd get pretty scared crossing all the way over to the other side.

"One of the more explosive volcanic eruptions," Mr. Huddleston, the science teacher, whispers to the class, "is the vulcanian. In this phase, the lava accumulates between consecutive explosions."

Mr. Huddleston's one of the smallest men I ever see, not only real short but real thin too. His skin's white as halibut, he's hardly got any hair, and when he speaks it's never louder than a low whisper. He stands hunched in front of the class, reading from this real thick book, wearing a brown suit and brown tie. Seems like the same suit and same tie always.

"When the explosive gases have reached a critical point

within the volcano," Mr. Huddleston continues, "masses of solid and liquid rock erupt into the air and clouds of vapor form over the crater. But the peléean phase is the most violent of volcanic actions, spreading fine ash; hot, gas-charged fragments of lava; and a steam cloud that travels downhill at great speed. In 1902 such an explosion occurred from Mount Pelée on Martinique."

He puts down his book and smiles for just a moment, then licks his tiny lips as if tasting something sweet.

"That particular series of explosions," he continues, "formed a cloud that annihilated all life in its path; finally the mountain itself was blown apart."

Nobody says nothing then, but I'm wondering what a mountain looks like after that, if a whole mountain can just disappear. I'm wondering if anything at all is even left behind.

Some days I miss the closeness. Seems like when we get out from home, for me sometimes seems like nothing's right. There's certain things in a village that you don't do here, like go visit friends all hours of a day and they won't mind. Here it's different. Everybody at home sees when you want what, like when someone needs water and wood, others just get it for him. Everybody takes care of everybody else, no matter how little or big, how young or how old. That's a good thing, but at school, I learn to just watch out for myself. I'm always checking over my shoulder, and just looking out for me takes up all my time and

103

my thinking now. Seems like I can't ever remember any of my village heart, it's been lost so far for so long.

Nights, we get Andy Agimuk from Kwethluk to buy a couple of six-packs or a bottle down over at the base store. Being that Andy's nineteen, we never have any trouble buying and he gets a couple of extra swigs for the trouble. Sometimes we talk fat Mary Beans from Napaskiak into coming along and give Mr. Edwards, the junior assistant coach, a couple of beers so that he'll let us borrow his truck. Everybody gets in with Mary stuck right between Sammy Cooke and Ethan Akiak and we drive to the end of the island by Sheldon Jackson College, where they make the kids go to Christian services all day. I once hear that a long time ago, students at SJC get beaten up if they ever even speak Yup'ik to each other, even at all. We're taught three years of Yup'ik at home but it's mostly the old people who talk them words. Long time ago them missionaries back home hit the children if they ever speak. You get hit even if you pray in Yup'ik long time ago. We all learn never to pray in our own language. I never pray at all if you want to know the truth, even though I'm a Christian. We all are.

So we drive past Sheldon Jackson College real fast and leave the car out by Totem Park, where no one is ever going to see us. And in the middle of the park, this old Indian rain forest that's supposed to be real spiritual or something, we all get loaded and feel up Mary Beans, one right after another. By then she pretty much passes out from the booze and doesn't even know what's happening. They say that her auntie from McGrath is the same way, anything for a swig from the bottle.

All these creepy old Indian totems are staring down at us. Lucky for me I don't believe those crazy legends, don't even believe any of the Yup'ik ones neither, but it still gets kind of weird in the middle of the night, not a star out, not a sound, just old Mary Beans breathing hard. That creepy old raven is carved into most of the totems. Lotta people say that the raven makes the world, digs the world out of sand with his claws, but I get sick of seeing his ugly black face, black eyes just staring out everywhere. That raven, he sure don't say nothing when we're feeling up Mary Beans.

And so, before I even know it, we start getting into trouble all the time. Some of the Indian and Aleut kids wait for us behind the gym and usually kick the shit out of us, but sometimes we get them real good. And some Yup'ik kid from Nunivak Island starts selling us this real good weed and we get to cutting class, walk way out by the Sitka Airport and lie on the end of the runway, just smoking and waiting for planes to zap right over us. Most times it's raining, not hard, just that everyday kinda rain, kinda Sitka mist. And even the ground's all wet, even with the rain, I'm always feeling too warm, too hot. We all take off our coats, sometimes our shirts, too, sweaty after walking all this way out to the airport from school. Us kids from up north are always hot. Feels like summer all the winter long here way south.

Sometimes I want to just run outside, breaking the glass on all the windows up at the school, gotta get more air. Seems like you just can't breathe. Sometimes I just get sick of the Sitka mountains everywhere you look, not like home, the tundra where you can see as far as you want. These Sitka mountains, and the Mt. Edgecumbe volcano, too, feels like we're just surrounded by mountains everywhere, feels like we're surrounded. Still, it's cool on the runway, the planes, even those big jets going Outside, they zap right over us, making our whole bodies shake, even the ground shakes. It feels for sure that's we'll all just up and die. Andy, John, Sammy, Russell, all of us. We feel dead for sure.


"There are three kinds of volcanoes," Mr. Huddleston says. He is standing at the blackboard squeezing a small piece of chalk. "Active, dormant, and extinct. Who can tell me how each kind is different?"

Nobody says nothing. He puts down the chalk and wipes his hands on his pants, leaving white prints, just like from light animal in heavy snow. "Is anybody listening or am talking to myself?"

I look at Floyd, whose head is down on his desk—but I know he's hearing.

"Active," Mr. Huddleston continues, "means that the

volcano is actually erupting. Dormant means that it's quiet for a time, but still might erupt during an active phase. Just like our Mt. Edgecumbe volcano right here. There hasn't been any activity for quite a number of years, and yet you really never know what kind of pressure is building up below. And extinct"—he smiles with his mean mouth, lips pressed tight—"extinct means that anything active, any possibility of eruption at all, is completely gone. Extinct. Nothing alive there anymore."

No one says anything then, but all of us, all of us Yup'ik boys, we know to look right down at the floor. The rest of the Native kids shift in their seats way up in the front of the room; their thick shoulders twitch together into a single rope, a long mountain ridge of white muscle and bone, shaking, waiting to explode.


This mixed-blood boy thinks he's hot shit. Got some stupid bird name and walks around like he's real tough. Dove Alexie. Dove Alexie from Stony River. We all know about that place. We all know about the mixed-blood kids. Losers, all of them, though he's the first I really meet, and those of us from Hooper Bay know how to stay away. But this Dove creep all the sudden shows up in science class and kind of keeps on irking us 'cause he asks Huddleston all these dumb questions. Don't know how to leave well enough alone and thinks he's smarter then the rest of us, thinks he knows more. Don't even know to keep his damn mouth closed. Nobody else speaks in science, but this Alexie kid don't know when to shut up. Even the old fart Huddleston don't like his smart mouth. Always asking why and what about. . . . He's got nerve, that Alexie kid, and we stay real far away.

But there's this one day in class that's almost funny, then ends up somehow not being funny at all. Alexie keeps on raising his hand and getting Mr. Huddleston to answer some crazy question. Something about volcanoes and extinction and who really gives a shit. Mr. Huddleston is standing there, breathing real quiet like, just as if he's run a mile. His face gets pinker and pinker each time Alexie's hand shoots up. But even I got to admit that mixed-blood kid has a brain in his ugly head, 'cause he says words we don't even understand.

"Yes?" Mr. Huddleston sighs and nods toward Alexie's waving arm. "What can I do for you now?" I notice the old man's forehead is shiny with sweat.

"Ain't there any volcanoes leave something worthwhile behind?" Alexie is sitting on the edge of his seat, looks like about ready to jump to his feet. "Not all them eruptions destroy everything that's there before. And some even do good, make a change in the world for the good. I read in our textbook that in 1883 a volcano near Java erupted, sending ash into the sky that drifts all the way around the globe. Darkens the whole world for a while, but ends up creating these real bright skies at sunset for years."

"Well," Mr. Huddleston says quickly, "it is true that the ejection of incandescent volcanic vapors can form luminous clouds. But what you don't understand is that it is a temporary condition. . . . When lava steam and ash are expelled through a vent in the earth's crust, total destruction is imminent. That which cannot stand up to the volcano's power is immediately eliminated. Many native cultures, not unlike your own, young man, have been completely and permanently obliterated."

Dove Alexie stands himself up in front of his chair. "Maybe there's ways to see things different that you don't understand. And maybe there's reasons for explosions no one really knows. This here world don't necessarily spin 'round according to what's in them science books."

"And pray what might that be?"

Alexie shrugs and looks away. "You don't know everything," he mutters under his breath. "Them elders believe that the aurora borealis is the souls of dead children playing in the sky. Science don't explain it all, don't explain everything there is to know."

"Souls of dead children?" Mr. Huddleston looks angry, then confused.

Alexie stares straight at the teacher and shakes his head. He begins to laugh. I can see Mr. Huddleston getting madder and madder; his lip is quivering.

"Well, boy," the old man says, teeth all clenched up tight, "what do you find particularly funny? I'm sure that the class would like to share in your mirth."

But Alexie just laughs and laughs until he's gasping for air. For a minute his eyes widen and almost roll in his head; for a minute his face gets so pale, it's like he's choking and I think maybe he can't even breathe. But of course, he's fine in the end, wiping off his cheeks as if he's been crying, his eyes puffed up suddenly red. He takes a deep breath and sighs.

"Ain't nobody speaks for us," he whispers into the air. "Ain't nobody speaks for us at all."

"What's he say?" Floyd Kookesh says loudly into my face. "What does that Indian bastard say after all?"

But I just shake my head and look down, Floyd's heavy breathing curdling up inside my ear.

They're showing this movie on VD, some kind of sex disease, in the cafeteria after dinner. The kids from way up north are sitting at the same table in the back. Even the girls sit with them. Everything smells sour, like that stuff they clean with, and the long white tables are sticky. We keep our hands in our pockets. The Indian kids are all up front—they stand every once in a while and wave their reflections onto the gray, blinking screen. All the gussaks, boys and girls, sit over to one side of the room with some of them girls sitting on their boyfriends' laps. I look around for Dove Alexie, but he ain't even here. We Yup'iks just get a small space at the other corner table, but the school nurse and Mr. Huddleston start setting up the projector right next to us. The lights get turned on and off and everyone's just quiet. The school nurse—we never learn her name—stands up and claps her hands. She looks pretty young, red hair and a raw, fleshy face, and is thick and tall. She's not wearing her usual white dress but has put on dark pants and a tan sweater.

"Like to get some of that," Floyd whispers.

"May I have your attention?" the nurse calls. I'm surprised at the sharpness of her voice. "I'd like all of you to pay close attention to this film. It's on a very important topic, the spread of epidemic disease."

The girls at the gussak table start to giggle.

And then the movie starts and we begin to understand what it's about. There's this Yup'ik guy who ends up in a big city and gets a real pretty girlfriend. But after a while he feels so sick that he goes to the doctor, who tells him it's too late and he's gonna die.

"Why's he gonna die?" Floyd whispers in my ear. I shrug. I don't know yet. So this army guy is lying in the army hospital and gets a letter from the pretty girl that says she's sick because they had sex together and she has this syphilis disease and he'd better be careful or he'll get it too, but it's all too late and the army guy dies right there in the hospital with no one who even cares. The last part shows his parents at home crying, and then you see these pictures of what you'll look like if you get the disease, pretty bad, but

III

we all know it's just a movie and probably not even true. The gussaks are laughing and I see some of them making out. But the movie's over pretty quick and we have to go back to our rooms.

"Still don't get it," Floyd says as we're walking out. "This stuff don't make any sense. They gotta have medicine for things like that." We all shrug and nod, but I think that we all see pictures in our heads. We see pictures of our villages, of our own grandmas and grandpas. We see our grandmas and grandpas crying for us, too.

Mr. Nikolai, one of the assistant coaches, is an Aleut from Unalaska, but sometimes he talks to us anyway because his great-grandfather is Yup'ik. So he tells us about the Mt. Edgecumbe volcano and he even makes us laugh. Thinking about that volcano still gives me the creeps and still gets me wondering. Seems like some years past one of the Sitka gussaks decides to make a joke. He flies this car tire, just some old pickup truck tire, all the way up to the volcano in his Cessna plane. Drops the tire smack in the volcano's crater. Somehow—I never understand this part—he covers the tire with gasoline and lights it up on fire. Just like that. Well, that old volcano starts smoking like crazy and the folks down in Sitka see it and go nuts thinking it's starting to explode. They're thinking they better hightail it out of town, and some of them even start to leave, start packing up their boats and planes. But word gets spread pretty quick that it's just a joke and everyone says, "Oh, sure, we knew that." But I would have got a kick out of seeing all those rich gussak Sitka folk running around, scared out of their minds and having to leave the only place they've ever lived, the only home they know.

Sometimes I wonder why all that gasoline and fire don't really get the volcano going and I try to imagine what a real eruption would look like. Sometimes I think I see the Mt. Edgecumbe volcano still smoking; I wonder what it'll be like when it explodes. Seems like it could wipe out any trace of us. Wipe us all off the face of the earth. Sometimes it feels like that's happened anyway. Wiped clear away.


This Indian kid's name is Ernie Dominicks. I've seen him around the auto mechanics room. They say he can fix anything with a motor and he's from Kake, some Tlingit village in the southeast.

He's waiting for me outside the cafeteria. I see his shadow first. Nighttime—it's already dark.

"So Eskimo boy," he says, puffing on a smoke, "where do you think you're going, anyway?" I shrug. I keep walking.

"Hey," he's starting to yell, "hey, where do you think you're going?" He walks up behind me, then suddenly gives me a shove. I trip but don't look around. I don't stop walking at all.

"Stupid ass," I hear him mutter as I walk away. "Stupid little ass."

But I never do tell anyone about this. No one at all. And sometimes I get to feeling like just what Ernie Dominicks says—I'm just a stupid little ass. Don't even know how to stand up to an Indian for myself or for my friends. Just a chicken stupid ass.

"Alaska's own volcanic mountain chain," Mr. Huddleston begins, "the Aleutian Range, is part of the volcanic belt that rings the Pacific Ocean, and as you may know, it has been active in recent years, particularly at Katmai. And one of the greatest eruptions in history was that of Novarupta in 1912."

I shift in my seat nervously. "All plant and animal life in the area was destroyed by the ash and lava. The Valley of Ten Thousand Smokes in this dying volcanic region has countless holes and cracks through which hot gasses have passed to the surface; all but a few are now extinct. The entire region is inaccessible except to specially equipped expeditions."

I see Dove Alexie's hand shoot up and close my eyes for a moment, imagining the Mt. Edgecumbe volcano covered with holes and cracks. I wonder if it's worse to be in a dying volcanic region or an active one, a mountain still exploding with burning lava and catching everything in its path with white-hot ash.

John Moran's in my room looking sick. His face's all yellow and his eyes shiny. "What's the matter?" I ask him.

I lie on my bed thinking about nothing. He doesn't say anything then but sits down by the desk. "Wanna smoke?" He shakes his head and starts to spin his chair by holding out one leg. I notice all the laces on his sneakers are broken.

"Going home," he says quietly. I can hardly hear him at all. No one says anything then. He reaches for my cigarette and takes a long puff. His shaggy hair is greasy and hangs over his face like a hood. I can't see his eyes then.

"Why you saying that? You can't just decide to go home. Why you saying that, anyway?"

"Whadda you think?" He looks away. "Got enough cash. Only books I buy are for science and art. And them teachers never even notice. They don't notice me at all, and when I leave nobody'll even notice that. I'm going to make myself disappear, like I was never even here before. Just like them herds and herds of caribou up home. You can stay put if you want, Edgar Kwagley, but I'm thinking about my little sisters and cousins back home. You know old Grandma can't take care alone and needs someone to help. But mostly I miss my little sisters. How can you stay here and leave yourself behind?"

"You're crazy." I'm watching him pretty careful. "You just can't disappear like that."

He shrugs again.

"Don't care what you say. Don't care what anyone says. I'm thinking about my little sisters and brothers. I'm thinking about what they're doing and I know I shouldn't be

115

here. I'm thinking about freeze-up and going hunting. I'm old enough now. They need me at home. Never no place for me here. I can't find no place."

Well, I don't know what to say right then but look up at the cracks in the ceiling and start feeling scared. For John and for the rest of us. If he leaves, then there's less of us here. If he leaves, there'll be more of them.

"You're just crazy," I say. "You're not leaving at all."

And the next morning, John Moran's right there at breakfast, but when I put down my tray next to his, he moves away. Same thing at lunch, at dinner. John Moran's not sitting with nobody anymore. In science I get there early and save him a seat, way in the back, just like always, but when he shuffles in, head tucked, coat held across his chest, he don't even say nothing. He moves way over to the other side and sits down there. At night, he stops coming to my room—he shakes his head when we sneak off downtown and steps aside each time we pass him in the hall.

"Explosive eruptions"—Mr. Huddleston is patting his little face with a torn handkerchief—"build up steep-sided cones, while the nonexplosive ones usually form broad, low lava cones. Eruptions also occur under the sea. The soil resulting from decomposition of volcanic materials is extremely fertile, and the ash itself is a good polishing and cleansing agent. A notable eruption is that of the peak of Tristan da Queen, whose eruption in 1961 caused an entire settlement to be evacuated. Think about it, if you will, an entire settlement. These people and their culture have disappeared off the face of the earth. One has to admire the scope and the force of such an eruption."

Floyd Kookesh leans over to my desk and rolls his eyes. "The peak of what?" he whispers in my ear. "What's he talking about, anyway?"

I shrug and look away. I see Dove Alexie's hand already up in the air and notice John Moran turns his whole face to the wall.

And so it goes on for a few weeks, John acting strange, and soon I don't even think about it at all. I almost forget about John Moran, forget that he's even here at Edgecumbe with me at all. Get real busy with my other friends, cutting class and getting drunk nights. So when one Friday afternoon, when John is nowhere, not in class, not at dinner, not nowhere at all, I'm not even surprised. I'm not surprised when nobody notices and I'm not surprised nobody even cares. But when I go up to my room and find three books on my bed, something in my stomach begins to hurt. The books are spread neatly on the pillow, looks like in order of size, with the big, flat one on top and the narrow, thin one at the bottom. I recognize the science book from class and trace the cover drawing of a volcano with my thumb. Suddenly I see his name written on the edge in red ink: John Moran, Hooper Bay, Alaska.

"Edgar?" Mr. Nikolai opens my door and stands just outside in the hall, as if ready to make a quick getaway. One hand is on the doorknob, the other at his throat, shaking. "Edgar?" he asks again, stepping back farther into the hall.

A crowd of kids starts to gather behind him. I see Mary Beans crying and Floyd Kookesh opening and closing his fists. Sammy Cooke and Ethan Akiak move closer to Mr. Nikolai as if getting ready for a fight. Nobody says nothing then, but I carefully pick up the books and hold them close to my chest.

"Edgar, there's been an accident," Mr. Nikolai finally says. "We don't know how it could have happened, but there's been a terrible accident." He coughs and rubs his arms. "Somehow," he continues quietly, "John Moran has had an accident. He fell and drowned trying to cross to Sitka over the bridge, the Sitka bridge. Listen, I know this is difficult. Listen, I really don't know what to say. Edgar, are you all right, do you understand?"

I don't say a word but my mouth opens and closes as if I'm gasping for air.

"Listen, I'll be in my office tonight, as late as I can, in case anyone, just in case anyone needs me at all. I'll make sure to check up on you then. Right now, I need to finish answering some questions from, you know, the police, and meet with some of the administration. Edgar"—he stops for a minute and shakes his head—"I just don't know how something like this could have happened."

I don't say anything then. I don't even say a word. The books in my arms slide to the floor and spread themselves out just like our story knife games on thick winter ice.

That night no one says nothing at all. We can't eat any dinner and we can't look at one another's faces. When we pull back the covers for bed, the same shadow falls over our pressed dormitory sheets. The night flaps its wings and we can see its black beak and we can hear its claws scratching. We all go to sleep lying flat on our backs with our eyes wide open. We dream of dancing with the grandfathers and the grandmothers, with the aunties, with the uncles, we dream of dancing with the cousins, with the little brothers and the little sisters, we dream of white ash pouring down over our long tundra night.

So things continue as usual. We keep to ourselves, most often cut class, dream of going home. I hear Dove Alexie beats up old Huddleston one day in class, one day I'm at the airport stoned and lying flat on the ground. Sorry I missed it, sure hate to miss that. Hear old Alexie gets kicked out, finally gets sent back where he belongs, to some jail up north, guess he never makes it all the way back to his goddamn black interior. But nobody really knows much for sure. Who cares, anyway. I'm glad to see the bastard go, him always causing trouble, never letting things just be the way they are. It's kind of a relief, to tell the truth, not having to listen to him question old Huddleston and pretend that there's something more to learn, something that might change. Easier to just close your eyes and sit back. Easier to let things alone.

We Yup'ik kids still keep to ourselves and just slide around over the wide, smooth school hall floor as if at home on the winter ice, but here our shoulders are hunched, our heads tucked down, eyes lowered, hands jammed in pockets of thin cloth. Sweating, always real hot, jackets unzipped but we won't take them off, poking each other in the ribs with our skinny elbows, we're just slipping around a faraway earth where words are spoken so fast, so loud, that we can't even hear.

Sometimes Ethan Akiak takes out a pack of Juicy Fruit and we all chew some real slow like and then spit it all out on the floor and watch them girls walk straight ahead. We line up against the cold school walls, me, Ethan, Sammy, Andy Numbchuk, Floyd Kookesh, and look down at our feet like we don't know nothing about nothing. They come walking fast, those smart, quick ones with their long, light hair, wearing tight Levi's and the softest, whitest sweaters, their small, pointed feet clicking against the floor like paws on ice. They're talking real fast and giggling, looking straight ahead, not even seeing five stupid Yup'ik boys from the bush flat against the wall. And then we hear them squeal; we even hear them curse. "Goddamn it, what's this, disgusting!" And we don't say nothing, just press our backs to the wall and feel ourselves gone. Not a trace left anywhere. Sometimes it's good to be invisible.

We look at each other and wink.

We disappear.

# PART
# TWO

*Over the soundless depths of space for a hundred million miles*
*Speeds the soul of me, silent thunder, struck from a harp of fire.*
*Before my eyes the planets wheel and a universe defiles,*
*I but a luminant speck of dust upborne in a vast desire.*

—Edgar Lee Masters,
*Spoon River Anthology*

# LORRAINE HOBBS

*Bethel, Alaska*
*Spring 1969*

"Don't fret that the horse is blind, daughter, just load the wagon," Mama says to me as I stir up a new recipe for No-Bake Cream Puff Pie ("Rowan and Martin's Prime-Time Pies," *Elegant Entertaining*), and complain that Crisco shortening just ain't the same as the real dairy butter called for in the directions.

"I do believe you're trying to tell me something," I say in my most sarcastic know-it-all voice. "And I do hate to say it, but I can tell you that I have plenty of your back-road redneck sayings, Mama, I really do."

Mama puts a chocolate-coated spoon right down on the table and don't say nothing. I hold my breath. I know I'm in a heap of trouble now.

"Don't you dare be ugly to me, young lady," she says carefully. "Your mama has enough worry these days. Now, you mind, I may purely love you but that don't mean I got all the patience in the world and can't wash out your mouth with soap if I'm of a mind to. It appears that a body don't get a moment's pause around here without hearing something nasty out of your mouth, and I can tell you I'm surely not going to let you get by with it, daughter or no daughter."

My heart drops down a ways.

"Oh, Mama, I'm sorry, don't mean to be common rude." I take a deep breath in and let it out slowly ("One-Minute Stress Stoppers," *Teen Trends*). "It's just that I have something on my mind worrying me, something bothering me for a while."

"Well, now." She picks up her spoon again and continues mixing the batter. "Sorry don't feed the bulldog, girl, but if something's eating away at you then that's a different situation altogether. But it's best that you shoot straight from the hip, Lorraine. Never does a body much good keeping all that feeling shut up inside."

"I know, Mama, but some things is hard to talk about right out loud."

"Try me. It takes more to plow the field than just turning it over in your mind, child. Just maybe your old mama can help you figure things out."

I wipe my hands with a paper towel and sit down.

"Mama," I say slowly, "have you ever met someone that you got a feeling about right off? I mean, just the very first time you is to set your eyes on him?"

"Him?" My mama's voice is suddenly quiet. "Don't

tell me that my baby girl is studying some young man around town. Who is he, honey? Maybe he could come to supper one Sunday night."

"No, Mama, no." I'm wishing that I never even open my big mouth. "You don't understand. It's more than that. You don't understand at all."

"Well, help me understand then, Lorraine. Am I wrong in thinking that you've gone soft over someone? Maybe someone new just come to Bethel? Listen, I'm happy to hear it, child. Now that you're fourteen, you might be needing a little romance in your life. But you mind, don't let any young fella do wrong by you. You be sure to be treated the way you deserve. Don't you take nothing from nobody."

"I know, Mama."

"So, ain't you even gonna tell me who this lucky boy might be. Anyone I meet?"

I shake my head. "Actually, it's somebody you don't even know. Just somebody I have a few words with a few weeks ago, somebody I see just for a minute."

"Just for a minute? Don't seem enough time to make up your mind about anything, daughter. What about this fella turns your head around so?"

"I don't know. Mama . . ."

"Yes, honey?"

"It's someone up at the jail. One of the prisoners, in fact. Don't worry"—I see her eyes widen, like to fall out of her head—"not a real hardened criminal type or nothing like that. They say he's crazy insane, you know, that wild man folks talking about, but to me he just looks like some young boy, some young boy who is sent away from home. You should see him, Mama, all beat up. His face all different colors with bruising. Never see anyone hurt that bad up close before."

"It's no fun to see anyone hurtin' bad." Mama touches my hand lightly. "Guess he must get himself into some kind of big trouble."

"Yes. No. I don't exactly remember. But the thing is, he's just a boy, no more than sixteen years old, and it don't seem right to me that they're keeping him locked up back there in the prison cells like any regular adult criminal. His one eye all swollen up so it's almost closed up tight shut. Even though it's been a few weeks, I just can't get that out of my mind, him being so young and all. Wonder where his family could be."

"Hmm." Mama doesn't say nothing for a minute and just sits there, studying her hands. "How do you know he's sixteen, Lorraine? Could be he just looks young for his age. They wouldn't keep a youngster up at the Bethel jail—they got special places for young'uns under eighteen. You never really know about how many years a person gets under his belt from just looking."

"Listen, Mama. Arnie tells me this his own self. I ask him right off and he tells me, he says, 'Lorraine, that boy ain't more than sixteen years old.' I just don't know what to say. Maybe I should do something back then, but I can tell you, I keep thinking and thinking on it until I can't think anymore. . . ."

I stop talking then. It feels like I might could cry. Something about that boy, something about his beat-up face, the idea of him all alone, holed up there with all those others. It just makes me want to cry.

"Well," Mama says, "I reckon we got us a situation here. I can tell you, I don't like the sound of this at all. I'm guessing this boy ain't no white man. Am I right?"

I nod.

"But that's not the point. He's not locked up in there because of his color. That's not the point here, Mama. You just don't understand anything at all."

"I understand more than you know, child."

I can tell my mama's getting annoyed.

"Well, maybe you do and maybe you don't," I say under my breath ("Confronting Authority: How to Stay Cool and in Control," *The Contemporary Woman*). My azure-blue and white flowered pedal pushers ride up my calves, leaving pale, freckled skin exposed, and I sigh heavily, wishing I could get me a nice summer tan for once in my pitiful life. I look over at Mama, who leaves her spoon and mixing bowl right there on the table, with batter spread all over the counter, for heaven's sake. She wipes her hands right on her overalls—a grown woman in overalls looks mighty peculiar, if you have a mind to ask me—and clears

129

her throat. Her face is all pink and I can see her brown eyes heating up something fierce behind those dime-store glasses.

Sometimes I just sit back and look at my mama and think about how I might could give her some fancy beauty makeover one day, but she would never go for that, her main goal in life being comfortable. "Why should I bother changing how I look?" she'd probably say. "Nothing really makes a woman look snazzy anyways excepting for five or six cocktails in a man."

"What about it, Lorraine?" I look up suddenly and realize Mama's been asking me something.

"What about what?"

"How 'bout you and me taking a walk up to the jail and talking to that second assistant fellow. Never do like the looks of him," she mutters, "always struttin' around like a doggone kitty cat gone and swallowed a fish. That boy may look pretty, but I can tell you something right about now. I can tell you that no matter how hard you are trying, no matter what in the heck you do, there ain't no earthly way to perfume a pig. No earthly way at all."

So the next thing I know, me and Mama ends up walking over to the jail together. She's still wearing those same jean overalls with some faded red, plaid flannel shirt, and I sigh as I notice chocolate stains right over her chest.

"What's the matter, Lorraine?" she asks, not missing

a beat. "You got something to say or is your indigestion just acting up again?"

"Mama." I stop in front of the jail steps and sigh again. "I really would appreciate it if you don't embarrass me in front of Arnie or anyone. You might find it difficult to understand, but these jail folks up here have some kind of respect for me. They treat me just like a grown woman, not like some little child or nothing."

"Well, is that so?" She laughs and pats my cheek. "I guess I can resist for a few minutes or so. But it sure might be rightly fun teasing this little huffy daughter of mine."

"Mama, please."

"Oh, all right. But I can tell you that it really irks me to see some yellow-bellied lawman pushing a child around. Don't matter your age, if you're a different color, speak a different language, wear different clothes, or believe in a different god. Always someone ready to push you around. It gets my dander up, it surely does. But enough of my chatter, here we is at the jail anyways. Why don't you go ahead and lead the way, seeing as you is such an expert on jailhouse doings. I'll keep quiet as long as I can, but I really is of the mind to give that Arnie fellow a talking to. Or Marshal Nicholsen, for that matter."

But when we actually do get ourselves seated across from Arnie in the jail office, Mama stays pretty quiet. In fact, she leaves most of the talking to me.

"What can I do for you, ladies?" Arnie smiles and rubs

his cheek as if deep in thought. "I can tell you right off, Mrs. Hobbs, that it is a pleasure to see you here today looking as pretty as your young daughter here. I certainly can see where Miss Lorraine gets her good looks." I feel myself blush and lower my freshly mascaraed lashes. "And I sure gotta compliment you on teaching your little daughter how to cook up a storm. Why, her Red-Eye Gravy and Onion Pie is better than my own mama makes. You lovely ladies got any plans to see the moon walk come July? Why, me and the missus is planning a trip to Anchorage just to see the whole darn thing on the TV."

"Arnie," I finally say softly, "me and my mama ain't currently planning to see the moon walk, but we is somewhat concerned about that beat-up boy locked up in here when he's no more than sixteen years of age. We're wondering if maybe some mistake is made. Just don't seem right to keep a boy locked up in a prison cell."

"Why, Miss Lorraine"—Arnie looks surprised— "what young boy is you referring to? I tell you what, I suspect you get your information confused or something. Ain't no boy locked up here in the Bethel jail as far as I can tell."

I hear Mama like to speak. She clears her throat and shifts in her chair. I know she's just dying to get a word in edgewise.

"Well"—I'm feeling mighty fidgety myself—"maybe I don't understand you right. But hardly more than two weeks ago, you tell me that a sixteen-year-old boy is sitting right here in this here Bethel jail. We is standing over there in the hallway and you tell me about the prisoner from Stony River." I feel my voice getting louder and take a deep breath in. "Are you saying today, Arnie, are you saying that I hear you wrong and there ain't such a fellow? 'Cause if you is to tell me that, I'm liable to object. I see this prisoner with my own eyes, you know I do. How can you stand there today and tell me something different?"

I look out the corner of my eye at Mama. She's leaning forward, holding tight to the arms of her chair. I can see that she's just itching to speak.

"Now Miss Lorraine"—Arnie's voice is real quiet—"don't get yourself in a hissy fit, girl. I'm fixing to explain everything, so just don't worry your pretty little head about nothing. You is bound to grow old before your time if you get yourself all excited over nothing at all. Ain't that right, Mrs. Hobbs? And I'm not exactly certain that it's fitting for a girl such as yourself to question a law officer of the state."

I'm not exactly sure what to say then. I'm having trouble believing what I hear. I look over at Mama, who raises her eyebrows, as if to ask permission to speak. I nod and she stands up and leans over toward Arnie, her big hands right on his desk.

"I've heard enough tomfoolery, young man. Now you mind, unless you tell my daughter what happens to that young boy, I'll be writing a formal letter of complaint directly to Marshal Nicholsen with a copy to the full Bethel Town Council. I'm guessing that this whole matter can be cleared up in a few minutes."

Arnie looks right at Mama for a minute, blinks those baby blues real quick, then clears his throat.

"Now Mrs. Hobbs," he says slowly, "there ain't no reason to get so upset. Why, you two ladies is like to get yourselves all riled up. All I is saying to Miss Lorraine here is that no young man of sixteen years is in our jail right now. Never do say anything about some week past."

Mama smacks the desk with the heel of her hand and sits back down. "That's better." She turns toward me and smiles. "Why don't you continue with your questions, Lorraine? Seems like our second assistant here is likely to speak up a bit more now that he's had a chance to remember."

"Well," I begin again, "as I just mention, we is wondering why a young man of sixteen years is all beat up and locked here in an adult prison. Now mark my words," I continue carefully, "I do understand that this boy may not be here right this minute, but I think you know that's not what's troubling me. I want to know what he's doing in jail at all."

"I'm not at liberty to discuss the particulars of them prisoners, Miss Lorraine." I see Arnie sneak a quick look at Mama and then continue. "But seeing as you and your mama take the time to come all the way up here, I do believe that I can share some of the facts. It seems that the young man in question is a certifiably insane murdering criminal of the worst kind. As I mention to you before, Miss Lorraine, he's arrested for attacking a respectable white teacher. Seems like this boy hates us church-goin', God-fearin' white folk and he don't know right from wrong. Why, this boy don't even speak a single word at all since he's been locked up here in Bethel—seems like he's born that way, just the same as any ordinary animal, looks just the same as one of us human beings, walks like one of us, but don't have nothing inside his head but air and nothing in his heart but evil. Same as any plain old wild creature, any wild beast. Don't know nothing about human decency and this here civilized world. I know it's hard for you lovely ladies to imagine such an individual, but when you work in law enforcement as long as I do, you learn to face them facts of life head on."

I don't say nothing. Arnie leans back and looks at his fingernails carefully.

"Miss Lorraine, if you is of a mind to try to be of any assistance to that sorry figure of a man, I'd think twice. I'd think twice, I really would. Now, under ordinary circumstances, we don't jail up anyone under the age of eighteen, and I surely do understand your confusion on the subject. But seeing as this particular individual is so dangerous and all, the authorities don't find any other secure place. And the boy ain't here no longer than a few minutes or so. Why, you can check in the back yourselves if you're so inclined. Surely got nothing to hide from two such fine Bethel women."

"What about the receiving home?" Mama asks irritably. "I thought the receiving home's the place for children who don't have anywhere else to go."

"Now Mrs. Hobbs." Arnie speaks slowly as if Mama is deaf. "Do you really think that a dangerous individual such as Dove Alexie should be placed in a home full of innocent children?"

"If he really is so dangerous," I interrupt, "how do you know that he's really all that bad, anyways? You can't fault a man without first giving him a hearing and all, especially a young boy. It ain't fair, it just ain't fair." ("Winning Without Whining: Assertiveness Secrets of the Stars," *Modern Style.*)

"And seeing this boy's only sixteen," Mama continues, "seems like you'd give him extra considerations. We're pretty curious, Lorraine and me, just where this young man is right now. Where does he get sent, this child being barely sixteen and in need of medical attention?"

"I'm not at liberty to release that information, Mrs. Hobbs," Arnie answers, smiling. "I'm afraid you gonna have to wait for an official report and that'll take a formal requisition from the state. And seeing as Marshal Nicholsen's out of town for the next two months, traveling to attend a series of meetings of a confidential nature, well, it seems that you're going to have to wait for that particular piece of information. But I can tell you this right now: You two ladies has no need to worry at all. I can assure both of you that the prisoner's been taken care of in accordance with the state of Alaska's rules and regulations, probably to a group home for problem juveniles. Don't you be worrying anymore about some kind of murdering retard. That boy's nothing more than a crazy, savage retard."

"Don't call any man a cowboy," Mama and I say suddenly at the exact same time, "until you see him ride."

All in all, Mama and I feel pretty satisfied with our prison talk and figure we do as much as anyone can. It's clear that the boy, Dove Alexie, is sent somewhere else, and it appears like we ain't gonna see or hear of him again.

"That's just the way it goes," Mama says to me as we walk out the jail's front door. "At least we do our darndest not to let that Arnie fellow think he can get away with anything he wants, the marshal being out of town and everything. Why, I bet Marshal Nicholsen don't know nothing about that child being locked up in the penitentiary and all. I surely do think that if that Arnie individual was a horse, they most certainly would shoot him by now. I can't rightly stand that slick-talking SOB."

I don't say nothing to Mama then. I'm feeling rightly proud about standing up to Arnie and speaking my mind, even though it's mighty hard to get that Dove Alexie out of my thoughts. I just can't help thinking about his face and how it looks like he's just about to speak. Like he believes that I can help—somehow I just know he needs me to help, like something bad is gonna happen to him real soon if I don't do something right off. Ain't too many times in my short little life that someone's needing any of my help, and it pains me that I can't do nothing, nothing at all. But I also think that not just anyone would march herself up to the jail and question an official of the prison like Mama and I do.

Maybe I should talk to that Steven Roberts fellow, that young hippie guy from back east who moves up to Bethel to work on the *Kuskokwim Kronicle*. He's always nosing around and writing penetrating articles about one thing or another, like the time Mayor Plumb spent town funds for a personal, deluxe waterbed shipped all the way up from Outside. Maybe Mr. Roberts would like to have a sit-down with me and jot down my thoughts on the goings-on at our Bethel jail.

And I do thank my lucky stars for the article on the waterbed scandal, because once them funds were recovered, the town council could afford a real, certified honeybucket service. If it wasn't for Bethel Honeybuckets, Inc., we'd all still be dumping our buckets out by Honeybucket Lake, where the piles often end up being high as a trailer. Eventually Herbert Elser, who is living up there by the lake, leaves two buckets filled to the brim right on the counter up at town hall. Anyways, it's these two buckets along with the returned waterbed cash that finally convinces Bethel Public Works to start a bucket service. We all got to change our buckets from metal to plastic so that the honeybucket workers (Ernest and Jake Norichinka) just have to nudge the side of the pail once with their boots in order to get everything emptied out.

"I surely do admire those Norichinkas," Mama says that first freezing day we don't have to march up by Honeybucket Lake. "It's cold enough to freeze the balls off a billiard table and our buckets is as clean as a whistle without either of us even lifting a finger."

I'm remembering all of this and thinking of sitting down, incognito, with Mr. Roberts—could be a red nylon wig and dark glasses would suit me real good—not paying attention to where I'm going, when I trip on a step walking down the jail stairs and end up flat on my back. When I stand up and brush off my pedal pushers (thank goodness I'm not wearing a skirt), I find myself face-to-face with two very dirty children, a small boy and a taller girl. They both stare at me like they never see anyone trip on a step before.

"Do you skin your legs?" Mama asks, wiping a spot of mud off my white eyelet blouse with puffed peekaboo sleeves and rabbit-fur-lined 100 percent wool vest. "That sure is a nasty fall you take, Lorraine."

The tall girl in front of me starts to laugh and then

hides her face behind a grimy hand. And before I know it, the boy is giggling right along with her, not even having the good manners to pretend otherwise.

"What in heaven's name are you two laughing at?" I ask, feeling mighty annoyed. "It could be that I get a serious disfigurement from a fall such as this. Might even be a spinal injury of special note. I do believe that I wouldn't find anything the least funny in someone else's misfortune."

"Now, Lorraine," Mama says calmly, "I'm sure these two children don't mean anything at all. Seeing as you're all right, I must agree that you do look pretty comical rolling right over on your back and all. Don't know you can manage such a fine-looking somersault."

The children start to laugh again, and the boy points to my feet. "Can't even see your shoes, lady," he says. "So much mud covering your feet. Looks like you ain't got any shoes at all."

The girl pokes him in the ribs with her elbow but keeps grinning like there's no tomorrow.

"Well, I'll have you know," I reply, "that I am wearing simulated alligator pumps that we order all the way from down south and it appears that they're ruined. Seeing as my mama works two jobs to keep us clothed, I surely fail to see the humor in that."

The children look down at the ground, but I can see them still shaking with laughter.

"I don't think it's a tragedy, honey," Mama says, smiling

and putting her arm around my shoulders. "I bet we can get these shoes back to normal in no time. Don't you be worrying about your wardrobe or nothing—your mama's gonna take care of that for you."

"Hey, lady," the boy interjects rudely, "isn't this the jailhouse or something? You just getting outa jail?"

The girl begins giggling all over again.

"Jimmy Pete," she says, "maybe this here lady's in jail for wearing dirty shoes."

Just as I'm fixing to haul off and deck that snotty know-it-all girl, Mama squeezes my arm and starts asking the two juvenile delinquents all kinds of personal questions. She acts as if these two creatures require special candy-coated treatments.

"You two children don't look familiar," she begins softly. "Your folks from Bethel?"

"Don't got no parents," the girl answers. Her head stays up and she looks directly into Mama's face. I notice how thin she is, how you can almost see through to the bones of her pale face, her skin like some kind of clear plastic wrap pulled tight over a skeleton head. I also notice that her eyes are two different colors, one light blue and the other brown. Kind of creepy. Never see eyes like that before.

"Evelyn here's a shaman," the little boy announces proudly, as if reading my mind. He gazes over at his friend like she's made of pure gold. "She can put the curse on anybody she don't like."

"Oh she can, can she?" I roll my eyes and sigh, somehow feeling particularly irritated at the boy's obvious admiration. "Well, why don't she put a curse on me right now? Let's see what her shaman powers can work on someone like me."

"Come on, Jimmy Pete." The girl tugs at the boy's shirt. "Ain't got the time to bother with the likes of this fool. Let's finish what we come here for."

"We're going to see real, live prisoners," the boy says as he's being pulled up the jailhouse stairs. "Betcha never see a real fire-eating crazy prisoner before." But before Mama and I have a chance to say anything at all, they both disappear into the Bethel jail.

"Do you expect those children are really without a home?" Mama asks as we walk back. "Hate to think of any young'uns without parents or a home."

I shrug. I'm really not the least bit interested in the goings-ons of those two brats. The girl don't look much like a child, not much younger than me, anyways.

"I rightly don't much care about the personal facts of those two rude individuals," I reply. "And I can't believe that anyone could be so absolutely impolite as to laugh at a serious accident such as the one I just experience."

"Oh, Lorraine." Mama smiles, trying to grab and tickle me under my arms. "Loosen up, honey pie. Ain't no one gonna laugh at you when you can laugh directly at yourself. Those two kids don't mean no harm, child. And it does concern me that they're hanging out at the jail with no adult supervision to be seen. Never see them two around before, do you?"

I shake my head. "Maybe they're just visiting Bethel. Or staying with family. Maybe they're living up at the receiving home. Never recognize half the kids from up at the receiving home."

"That's probably it. You're right, Lorraine. They probably get themselves loose from the home and is looking to raise a little devilment. Wonder if we should stop on up there and let those receiving home folk know what we see."

"Oh Mama, don't we have enough to worry about without traipsing all over town after some filthy orphaned children? I'm sure they'll find their way back to wherever they're from. Let's go on home now. Seeing as I got to clean myself off and don't want the mud to harden all over these shoes. Surely need to get myself fixed up before anyone else sees me in this particular pickle."

"And who is it gonna see you, anyway? Don't think you have to worry about keeping yourself all dolled up in a town such as Bethel, Lorraine. That's one of the things I like about being who we are and living the way we do; you can just be yourself and don't have to put on any doggone airs." She stops for a minute and looks at the darkening sky. "Well, maybe we should head on back anyways. It's coming up a cloud and I sure don't feel like walking home in the rain."

I look at Mama, who's trotting at a good clip in the

freezing drizzle, her hair pinned up loosely at her neck with all kind of strands flying every which way. Her face is flushed up pink and she swings her arms back and forth just like she's a soldier marching in a parade. One of the straps from her stained overalls falls open, and the top flaps back and forth over her plaid flannel shirt. I gotta admit, as peculiar as she dresses sometimes, no one's gonna mess with the likes of this woman. Maybe she ain't as pretty and dainty as I might like, but you got to admire a woman with her kind of spunk ("Self-Confidence: Find It, Fake It, Flaunt It," *The Contemporary Woman*). Not all the time, mind you, but every once in a while I wouldn't mind growing up just like my mama. I sigh to myself and follow her all the way home.

It's a good thing that my job cooking for the jail keeps me so darn busy, because try as I may, I just can't seem to keep away all deep and disturbing thoughts of poor Dove Alexie. But losing myself in my demanding culinary tasks helps, and one of the best things about a certified position in the field of cuisine is that nobody orders you around and you can be absolutely, positively as creative as you like. Ain't no one standing there to watch what the heck you do, or to tell you what ingredients to include, how long to leave your Glazed Spam Pineapple Puffs in the oven, how to ice your dinner rolls or decorate your Ritz Cracker Quick Mock Apple Pie. I absolutely find cooking the perfect opportunity to try things out and take the most daring of risks; figure there's no sense at all in playing it safe. Why, Betty Crocker herself would be impressed with my original and thoughtful experimentations, and nobody cooks up a mess of reconstituted potato flakes like Lorraine Hobbs (use two drops of red food coloring for a surprising visual effect).

But every time I trot myself up to the jail with my trusty Carry-O-Meal brimming with delectable morsels of every kind, I can't help but think on Dove Alexie and get kinda down in the mouth. I try to stall for time, just in case I might get a glimpse of the back hallway where I see him for that one short minute, but Arnie won't have none of that. Seems like ever since me and Mama go up to the jail and question him, Arnie keeps an eagle eye on all of my doings. It used to be that I'd often leave my specially cooked meals right on his desk because no proper official is never much around, but these days, things take an entirely different turn. Every time I set foot inside, Arnie's right there to meet me at the jail door. It gets me to wondering exactly what's going on. Maybe there's something that he don't want me to see.

But then I think again and try to wipe all those negative vibrations right out from my picture imagination, which sometimes is known to work just a little overtime. Sensitive as I am, every once in a while I tend to make a big deal out of nothing and overreact just a tad. I'm trying to work on that particular weakness of mine which gets me into a heap of trouble in the past, I can tell you that. It surely seems, with all of my tireless working 'n' all, I wouldn't have the time or energy for worrying about some locked-up stranger, anyway, but every time I try to think on something else, that boy's pretty, cut face comes back to mind. I close my eyes and see his dark ones staring right back at me; I can almost hear him call my name.

But facts is facts, no two ways about it, and things sure do look like poor Dove Alexie is long gone. I try to forget what I see and try to concentrate on developing my recipe file and on refining my flour piecrust technique. But one day when I'm at home, finished making Barbara Mandrel's Rainbow Icebox Cake with extra lime and cherry Jell-O, I find a crumpled piece of brown wrapping paper stuck in the bottom layer of my Carry-O-Meal.

At first I don't think nothing. Figure that some inconsiderate type of some sort or another at the jail just throws down a piece of trash inside. But when I take a closer look, I see that it's not the case at all. I wipe my hands on my apron and flatten out the paper real smooth; I see someone writes something that looks like my very own job title in small, carefully formed letters: "Cook" is written neatly in cursive, and some other word (probably a mess-up) is covered in a big blob of black ink.

I sigh to myself.

Maybe my most worst fear is realized. Maybe one of

those wild, mouth-frothing, murdering prisoner types gets so ticked off at his dinner that he writes me a nasty hate letter. No, I just can't bring myself to believe that, seeing as my meals have been particularly succulent these past few days. Maybe one of the nicer prisoners, stuck up there at the jail on account of a crime of passion—loving your woman too much can't be all that bad in my book—decides to answer one of my Carry-O-Meal letters. Maybe he spies me from behind them iron bars when I'm dressed up in my white vinyl (looks just like leather) go-go skirt and ruby-red knit shirt with silver lapels; maybe he learns that he can love again—could be. I think for a minute more. The go-go outfit is particularly alluring, but I really don't know. . . . It's probably more likely that those dang receiving home kids, the grubby ones who like to tease me to death when I fall down up at the jail, decide to play me for a fool. Those two would surely get a kick out of toying with my mind and could easily find a way to slip a message inside. There ain't no one can pull the wool over this girl's eyes.

I look at the note for a minute and sigh again. Then, somehow, I slowly start a whole barrelful of willies in my belly and am suddenly scared to even budge. Feels like something real evil creeps into my bones, almost like I get one of them bad kind of premonition things I read about ("Can the Future Be Told? Candid Interviews with Six Physician Psychics from the Midwest," *Family Life*). Suddenly I know that the note isn't from those receiving home brats at all.

Suddenly I know that something real bad happens and there ain't nothing in this world Lorraine Hobbs can do to make it stop. I don't know what and I don't know why.

I feel my forehead break out all sweaty and cold.

I look around for my mama but remember she ain't home. Even Mr. Samuels ain't nowhere to be found.

I breathe deeply a few times and sit myself down at the kitchen table. "Get a grip, Lorraine," I tell myself firmly. "This ain't no time to lose hold." I rub my eyes and open the note real slow, as if something scary is about to pop right out all over. The note is written in the same large, scrawly print. This is what my note says:

COOK,
CAN YOU HELP ME OUT OF HERE.
NEED TO GET HOME.
TELL HER TO HELP TOO.
FROM
DOVE ALEXIE
MAY 16

At first I don't understand anything I read. I blink and quickly look at the note again and slowly the words sharpen into focus. Even though the punctuation's all wrong, even though it's dated almost sixteen days ago and the handwriting's real shaky, it's finally clear just what the note says.

Dove Alexie needs me to help him get home.

I take a deep breath in. You can't imagine my surprise.

Why, with all my whining about this particular individual 'n' all, you'd think that I would be ecstatically delighted about receiving such a greeting, but I'm not feeling that way at all. Instead, I'm wondering again how a young boy of sixteen would end up in jail, far away from home. I'm also wondering what he means by writing "tell her." Who could "her" possibly be? And I'm wondering why in the heck the note is dated May 16 when it's already May 29. It must have been sitting, hidden away in the Carry-O-Meal all this time. I'm also not exactly sure why I'm feeling that somebody's knocked me over square in the jaw.

Seems like the walls around me grab my shoulders and slowly turn me upside down, inside out.

I hold my breath.

I feel my scalp tingle and the tips of my fingers get cold. It's as if someone has reached out and squeezed me by the throat, my heart beating so fast and my insides stirred up crazy all together, spinning out of control.

Is some nasty person playing some kind of mean trick on me, trying to make fun of my fiery, caring feelings for Dove? Does Arnie write this note his own self, looking to find a little merriment on account of some foolish lovesick girl? Or is Dove Alexie holed up somewhere, chained and gagged, and itching for my help? Maybe that's why the handwriting's so peculiar, why the punctuation incorrect, why I get this sick feeling all the way through to my toes. . . . Why, maybe that boy's hands is tied up and his mouth all covered with Johnson & Johnson white adhesive tape. . . . Maybe he's held hostage in some one-eyed murderer's attic room where the light's no more than a naked bulb and the bats swing, squeaking, over his head. . . . Maybe he don't eat or drink nothing for days and days. . . . Maybe he's being tortured by a crazy love-jilted woman with teased, peroxide-bleached hair and a neat little mother-of-pearl-handled pistol slipped inside the waistband of her flared-at-the-hem miniskirt. . . .

I try to pull myself together. I try to get my picture imagination under control.

For a minute, I don't even know why, but for a minute I suddenly think I might actually throw up my very favorite breakfast of cornbread-in-a-glass and fried cinnamon toast.

A gigantic chill smacks me in the heart.

I either suddenly get that Chinese flu bug flying around town or something real bad happens somewhere. I don't even understand how I know.

I put my head between my legs, just how Mama teaches me that time we go upriver in the Swansons' fishing boat. I get the same gut-tossing, face-tingling stomachache as then, the same hot-cold prickling all over my skin.

I read the note again and lay my poor head right down.

I begin to cry.

✦ ✦ ✦

June 3, 1969

Dear Miss Hobbs,

Thank you for your visit of May 30 and for your letter of May 31. As my secretary told you at the time of your visit, Bethel Social Services has no record of a Mr. Dove Alexie from Stony River, Alaska, in or near our facility on the dates in question, Tuesday, April 29, 1969, or Wednesday, April 30, 1969.

I would also like to reiterate that it would be impossible for a Mr. Alexie to be jailed at any prison or detention facility as, according to your information, he is underage. Additionally, if your friend had been entered into the social service system, we would have full records on him.

I imagine that you have made an error as to this individual's age or location.

Thank you for your interest in Bethel Social Services.

Sincerely,
Audrey Turner
Executive Director
Bethel Social Services

June 5, 1969

Dear Miss Hobbs,

We have received your letter of June 2, 1969. The Department of Corrections is not at liberty to release any information regarding inmates, except to family members and officers of the court.

Thank you for your inquiry.

Sincerely,
Marshal Cooker Nicholsen
Town of Bethel
Department of Corrections

June 11, 1969

Dear Miss Hobbs,

The State of Alaska Department of Corrections has received your inquiry regarding Mr. Dove Alexie of Stony River, Alaska.

Please be informed that no reports of this individual's entrance into the system have been forwarded to the state. As this individual is underage, according to your information, I suggest that you contact the State Department of Social Services.

If you have additional questions regarding the Department of Corrections, please contact Marshal Cooker Nicholsen at the Bethel Town Jail.

Sincerely,
Elise Dobson
Program Officer
State of Alaska
Department of Corrections

June 17, 1969

Dear Miss Hobbs,

The Alaska State Department of Social Services at Anchorage is in receipt of your correspondence dated June 10, 1969.

I regret that we are unable to respond to your request for information and recommend that you contact your local Department of Social Services. According to our records, you may write Miss Audrey Turner, Executive Director, Bethel Social Services.

Please do not hesitate to contact us if you require any other information.

Sincerely,
Christine Keaton
State of Alaska
Department of Corrections

June 19, 1969

Dear Lorraine,

Thanks for your letter about the Bethel prison.

While this could be an interesting story, I'd need some verification of your facts from the marshal or from Arnie. It's easy to get the facts of a situation confused, and this can lead to all kinds of problems for the paper. I'm not comfortable publishing anything without being able to check all the information myself. As far as I can tell, Arnie is the only one who can corroborate your claim, and it doesn't sound as if he's willing.

Are you sure you've got your information straight? Let me know if anybody can back you up.

Thanks,
Steven Roberts
Editor-in-Chief
Kuskokwim Kronicle

June 24, 1969

Dear Miss Hobbs,

It is my obligation to inform you that the Bethel Town Department of Corrections is within its rights to (and will) take formal legal action if you continue to harass this office regarding a missing child.

Steven Roberts of the <u>Kuskokwim Kronicle</u> has contacted us about this issue, and I have provided him with the same information I have provided you in writing on 6/5/69. The Town of Bethel Department of Corrections did not admit a Dove Alexie into our system on April 29 or April 30, 1969, or at any other time. No individual sixteen years of age has ever been or will ever be restrained in our facility, as it is against state law. It is not clear to me why you continue to make this unfounded claim, but any further slandering of the Department of Corrections will be handled by our attorney. I am formally cautioning you to halt the spreading of rumors regarding the department and its employees.

I am copying this letter to your mother, Mrs. Lucille Hobbs. If legal action is to be filed regarding libel of the Department of Corrections, your mother will be contacted directly.

Sincerely,

Marshal Cooker Nicholsen

Town of Bethel

Department of Corrections

cc: Mrs. Lucille Hobbs

Mr. Steven Roberts, <u>Kuskokwim Kronicle</u>

June 30, 1969

Dear Lorraine,

Just got off the phone with the mayor. Seems like Arnie has taken a position up north and no one is able to back up your story regarding Dove Alexie.

The mayor is talking suing for slander if you and your mother keep making waves about this situation. I know you mean well, but my guess is that you've got your information confused.

Stop by the office if you're interested in making a little money. I've got a few delivery routes still open.

Best,
Steven Roberts
Editor-in-Chief
Kuskokwim Kronicle

P.S. Thanks for your suggestion about my wardrobe. Nehru jackets may be in fashion these days, but I'll stick to my sweatshirts and jeans.

# ANNETTE WEINLAND

*Bethel, Alaska*
*Summer 1969*

"The Town of Bethel Department of Corrections did not admit a Dove Alexie into our system on April 29 or April 30, 1969, or at any other time. No individual sixteen years of age has ever been or will ever be restrained in our facility, as it is against state law."

The letter I have just finished typing is addressed to Lorraine Hobbs, and I lean back in my desk chair at the Bethel jail and wonder why that name sounds particularly familiar. Lorraine Hobbs. Then I remember; she's the girl who cooks and delivers the meals to the jail every day, a thin, pale, freckled teenager usually wearing a peculiar outfit of some kind.

The word around Bethel is that her mother appeared in town about ten years ago with one little kid and no money to her name. In fact, I often run into Mrs. Hobbs at the Northern Commercial or sometimes waiting on the barge. She's a solid kind of woman with wide, clear eyes, and there is a quality about her that is almost comforting, the set of her square jaw, they way she holds herself, back straight, no slouching or head down. Unlike her daughter, usually fancied up in flounces and frills, the mother wears the simplest of clothing, pants and sweaters, fisherman boots or old sneakers, the backs of their heels rubbed off by wear. She's earned the respect of some town residents over the years, a hard worker, and someone who seems to care well for her family, even if they do live in one of the Oscarville shacks. They're not church people at all, and Father would never give them the time of day, but something about the way they go about their business, confident and proud, well, I almost find myself admiring them, even that silly Lorraine girl.

And she sure is silly. Sauntering up to the prison in some short fancy dress and party shoes, usually carrying a purse or wearing a hat to match. People in town laugh behind her back, imitating her high Southern drawl and that little skip in her walk. But I feel a little sorry for her, always alone, never with any friends at all. I know what that feels like, being confined to the house, never able to meet girls my own age. I often stare as Lorraine drops off lunch or dinner at the jail and wonder how she has the nerve to be such an odd character in this little town. Then I look down at myself, dressed in any old rag, without any friends of my own, a minister's daughter who can't even control the sin in her own heart.

And the letter to Lorraine from the marshal does strike a chord. I'm somehow bothered and don't quite know why. Then it all suddenly comes back to me, something I would have otherwise not even given a thought: that Tuesday several weeks ago when Arnie dragged in that frightened boy, locking him up with no paperwork at all. By the next week I had forgotten all about it, never involving myself in any real aspect of the prison administration. And yet, now that I've typed the marshal's letter (and I thought he was still out of town), it occurs to me that something isn't right.

Quickly I do a little math and sit back in my chair. It was exactly on one of the dates mentioned in the letter that Arnie had brought in that boy, who could have easily been just sixteen. Tuesday, April 29, just eight weeks ago. The intake log lies open on the shelf behind the desk, and I flip through it, trying to find the same date. And there it is, April 29, with no record of the boy at all.

Why would Arnie, usually so meticulous with his record keeping, sometimes reminding me of Father with his almost compulsive precision, omit entering any record of this one particular inmate? How could the marshal, out of town on extended business, even write two letters dated June 5 and June 24? And why would Arnie bother to lie to someone like Lorraine?

I flip back in the file and read the carbon copy of Marshal Nicholsen's June 5 letter. Then I look at the handwritten copy of the letter I just typed and study the handwriting. I take a deep breath. Something is definitely not right.

The next time I see Lorraine is the following Tuesday. She stops by to deliver dinner and hesitates at the desk before turning away.

"Miss Annette," she says slowly, winding her pink satin belt around a freckled finger, "you wouldn't happen to know anything about them prisoners the marshal brings in, would you?"

I look back at the typing in front of me and don't say anything for a minute. "I'm only here on Tuesdays," I finally reply, looking down. "I really don't know much about anything that goes on."

"Oh," she says as if disappointed. "So you wouldn't even remember a particular prisoner if I was to describe him or mention his name?"

I shake my head and feel my stomach tighten.

"Oh," she says again. "Thanks anyway." And then she spins herself around toward the front door.

"Lorraine," I call after her softly. "Lorraine?"

She turns around again, her eyes widening with anticipation. I almost lean across the desk toward her, but then abruptly pull myself back.

"It's nothing," I finally say. "I just wonder if you could give me your recipe for Red-Eye Gravy."

Her face brightens and she almost chuckles with delight.

"I most surely will." She grins, hands on her hips. "Get it out of some new fancy magazine special recipe insert: 'Easy, Easier, Easiest Sauces and Gravies.' Funny. That's one of Arnie's favorites too—he likes it over a mess of Minute rice or bow-tie egg noodles."

I take a deep breath, finding it suddenly difficult to speak at all.


I walk slowly into the front room with a cup of tea. Father is sitting on the couch, reading yesterday's paper. He takes off his glasses and wipes them with a hand-kerchief; he smiles. "What's this?" he asks, stroking the top of his head with one hand. "I didn't ask for anything to drink." I nod and place the cup on the table beside him.

"Just thought you'd like some tea after dinner. Father," I continue slowly, looking at my hands, "is it possible that something could ever go wrong up at the jail? I mean, do you think it possible for an intake error of some kind to be made?"

"What are you talking about, Annette?" He takes a sip and then grimaces. "Is this the English Breakfast tea I ordered from Outside? Tastes more like Russian, and you know how I hate that kind."

"You've finished the special tea. Sorry. But listen, Father, I think that something criminal could have happened up at the jail. I'm worried that something bad might have happened to a young boy."

"What are you talking about?" he asks. He sighs and puts his glasses back on. "Of course something criminal is going on at the jail—that's what prisons are there for. Can't you just get to the point and explain what it is you are talking about? See here, I'm too busy right now to be bothered with idle gossip."

"It's not gossip."

"Then what?"

I squeeze my hands together and look away, terrified to even bring up Arnie's name. What if Father were to talk to him or accuse him of wrongdoing? There's no question what would happen; it would take my jailer exactly one minute to tell what I have done while working at the prison, one second to tell my father that his daughter is a thief and a liar. My stomach turns and I feel my skin burn all the way from my face, down my arms, to my shaking, heavy hands.

"Nothing," I finally say, head down. "Nothing, really. I was just wondering about something someone said. Something about maybe seeing a young boy detained at the prison, you know, kept behind bars. It's not, I mean, it's not possible at all, is it? Even if the boy could pass for being of age? That couldn't ever happen at all?"

"For goodness' sakes." He shakes his head and frowns. "Sometimes I don't understand what goes on in that head of yours, Annette. Of course a child couldn't be locked up as a criminal. Anyone younger than eighteen would be tried in a juvenile court. Probably sent to Chimawa in Oregon or placed in a foster home. What's come over you, anyway? Reading too many fiction books, that's your problem, too many of those books that have nothing to do with the real world. Social services takes care of the underage. I'm sure you're aware of that—no one would let a child even near an adult prison."

"So it's not possible?"

"Not possible."

"Oh." I sigh with relief. "Then I must have misunderstood. Just probably overheard something incorrectly. Sorry about the tea, Father, I'll make sure that I order more."

"See that you do. I'd appreciate your doing exactly that as soon as you possibly can."

He looks down at the paper again, and turns to the next page.

The next Tuesday I pull out copies of the marshal's letters to Lorraine and read them again quickly. I note the dates mentioned again, April 29 and April 30, and try to picture the face of the boy dragged in by handcuffed wrists. His face is hazy to me, the features blurred, but I can picture his terrified eyes, and I grip the desk tightly with both hands.

It's clear to me now that the boy Arnie brought in could easily have been sixteen years old.

The odor of stale coffee drifts up from Arnie's coffee

mug balancing precariously on the desk's edge. It is black with large red letters: JEST A GOOD OLD BOY written across the front. I softly nudge it with my finger and watch as it sways, then shatters on the prison's hard, cold floor. The large old school clock on the wall behind me strikes two, and I realize that I've already missed Lorraine's lunch stop. Unless I stay until six o'clock for the dinner delivery, I won't run into her until next week. It'll wait until then, I say to myself, oddly relieved. Nothing's all that important that it can't wait seven short days.

But at night I have trouble sleeping. When I first close my eyes, I see Arnie's face blown up like a balloon, his features huge and distorted. Different-size coins, silver, gold, and copper, swing across the sky like small planets and I try to pick out the Milky Way. The moon drops its silver glare, whitening the sky and illuminating Arnie's hideous face.

And then I hear his voice, soft and cajoling, "Don't worry, honey, I'll get you come next week."

The boys and the babies moan together in their sleep.

I am lying on the very edge of my bed, trying to keep from falling.

And so it turns out, to my surprise, that seven days is too long to wait after all. Somehow I can't seem to think of anything else but that boy, locked up behind bars like a common criminal. As hard as I try, I can't get the marshal's letters out of my head or forget the fear in that boy's eyes. Why hadn't I said something before when he was first brought in? Why hadn't I pulled myself up right in front of Arnie and the whole world and asked how dare he imprison someone so young? Wasn't it enough that I was already his prisoner? Didn't he have enough power, making fun of the few inmates who were already under his thumb? But then I just have to laugh at myself. What makes me even think for a moment that I would have the courage to stand up and demand the truth? My whole life was a lie, elaborately carved into small pieces and hidden away far from everyone, especially from Arnie's hungry mouth.

When you are a little child, you wonder who you will eventually be; here I am at eighteen, and still don't know anything about who I am.

My secret rots in its small cupboard, growing larger and larger with mold and rind.

The days, the weeks, the months line up one by one, turning on their backs and floating, directionless out to sea. Ponds, lakes, rivers, oceans connect each day, then drift away.

I lay my head in my hands. I am sitting on my bed, in my very own room, but even here, the Bethel prison walls shrink around me and I can feel its ceiling graze the top of my head.

The big boys are playing downstairs and the babies whine softly in the playpen at my feet. I lean over and they both lunge for my hands. Their grip is slippery and I watch them fall backward, one by one, far away from my outstretched arms.

My father tells me that his parents taught him well, how to grow up to be a man, how to know God, rid oneself of laziness, of carelessness, of impure thoughts. He tells me that he demands the same for his own children, and asks me if it was too much to ask his wife for a clean home, a household maintained with dignity and order. We speak rarely of my mother, and I am frightened to ask him anything, fearful of the anger lodged deep in his throat, behind his eyes. I think that if we speak of my mother, he will explode.

My father tells me that when he comes home at dusk, he expects to see the boys bathed and fed, his dinner cooked long and hard, his meat braised through and through, not a trace of blood there. He expects each room to be perfectly neat, the couch exactly where it was when he left in the morning, set even against the left wall and not turned sideways, the pillows not piled high in a play fort, not pressed to the coffee table, not moved at all. When he comes home, he doesn't want to find his books falling off the desk shelf or have to remove my knitting needles from the window ledge. These things should be in their place, identical to when he leaves each morning. Is this too much to ask?

He shows me how to wash the broom so as not to sweep

grime back into the house and asks that the boys not eat crackers in the front room. They may not put their blocks in their mouths or suck on fingers that have not been recently washed. The sheets must be changed daily, the towels and napkins ironed, sinks steamed clean with pots of boiling water. He tells me to store the sugar in plastic bags and insists that the sponge must be rinsed each time so germs will not grow.

He sees how I tap my foot at church. He sees how I am restless, yet always tired. I order fabric from Anchorage and leave it sitting, nothing ever finished, nothing ever made. There is a freezer crammed with deer and halibut at home, yet I ask him for ground beef and fresh apples from the store.

He notices that I bathe the babies once a day instead of twice, using warm water instead of hot. He notices that I dry them with unironed towels, touching them without looking away as instructed, allowing them to stick steamy fingers into their full, wet mouths.

He sees me wipe my face with the back of my hand. I am bathing the babies and they are bouncing up and down, back and forth. My sleeves are rolled up, my shirt open at the throat, a ring of wet under both of my arms.

Something he cannot recognize pushes him back out of the room while his daughter and his babies are washing and singing all together.

"Annette," he finally calls to me from another room.

"Hurry up and get those boys to bed. I need to work, and this house is too noisy to get anything done."

Why don't I ever listen? I hear his instructions but am so tired every single day that I am unable to rush, my eyes burning, my limbs heavy, my stomach full of children's meals: tepid macaroni and cheese, thick grape jelly sandwiches, lemon pound cake, iced animal crackers, orange pops, apple juice, canned vanilla icing eaten with a spoon. My stomach is distended and full, but I lick my lips. I need something more.

It's not as if he's a bad person, rough with any of us. Always in control, never losing his temper, he absorbs the world carefully, bloated with the mistakes and sins of others.

His load is heavy, growing larger and larger each day.

He tells me that he prays for answers; he asks the Almighty Lord to teach his daughter the way his parents taught him.

I stay at home with the boys all day, trying to keep up with the house and laundry but somehow getting nothing done. I feel my every movement a challenge: I shuffle about from room to room, picking up toys, and then watch them get thrown on the floor again. The minute I clean the front-room table, his desk, the windowsills, a murky film appears again, thicker than ever.

It's as if the dust is magnified, engorged, each particle blown up heavy and full, containing a liquid secret; it rests in the air, stagnant, always returning no matter what I do.

The dark bats its enormous eyes and hovers over me, blackening each room.

I tire easily and find myself napping when the babies sleep, awakening disoriented and dizzy, my mouth full of a bitter and terrible taste.

In the mornings, I can't move. The boys surround the bed and pull at the covers. The babies are crying in their cribs.


One day soon, I will awaken early, long before my father or any of the boys. I will bathe in the old iron tub, shaving off all of my body's dark, bristly growth. I will not cut myself.

The rose body lotion, given to me by my mother, sits on the bottom bathroom cabinet shelf, its perfume evaporating from day to day. Her sponge hair rollers, untouched for years, tuck themselves around each other in a cardboard box like fat, pink worms. My mother's makeup congeals in the old suitcase, thick as cooking grease or paint.

I will gather her cosmetics around me like weapons. I will twist my hair and decorate my face.

Look how proudly I walk out the door in my new, pressed blouse and skirt.

I will stroll slowly through town and greet everyone in my path.

But then I remember how they look at us. The church-women whispering in groups while shopping at the store or while congregating after church. I know what they are saying about our family, and wonder at their composure, perfectly groomed and full of calm, steady breath. I can't imagine how they remain impeccable, their clothes always ironed, their skin soft, their light hair pulled back tight in a ribbon or a bow. If you look closely, you can see their translucent temples quiver.

They will look up and smile. These are the women who were once my mother's friends, who would bring covered dishes to our house after each baby was born: heavy, brown, ceramic casseroles filled with wide noodles and tuna, steamed puddings sprinkled with sugar, potatoes whipped yellow and thick. Whenever a birth or death, whenever an illness or emergency of any kind, the churchwomen come to your door with covered casseroles balanced carefully in their gloved hands. Their faces are plain, wiped clean of distinct feature or expression, as if all related. They stand on your threshold with their offerings, the food already cold from the frigid winter air.

This is a ritual between churchwomen, food passed from one to another. They travel in groups. No one comes alone.

Bethel is a town of covered dishes.

When my mother left, no one was standing at our door.

✷

172

In the morning I lie in bed, my head throbbing. I can barely open my eyes, so swollen and glued together with sleep. I touch my face carefully, feeling it puffed with fluid, with shame. I hear the boys talking in their bedroom, but the babies are quiet, probably still asleep.

I sit up slowly. I lick the dryness from my mouth.

The morning light drifts through my window and grazes a path to my face. I blink, surprised, and feel my eyes burn. I can barely turn my head, my neck stiff.

I know that something must change.

I know that something must be done.

I cannot change the mistakes I've made in the past, but maybe I can help right a horrible wrong. Maybe I can actually help someone else in need.

Maybe I can be redeemed.

I slowly swing my legs out of bed and try to stand up straight, but am dizzy and must lean against the wall. The boys call my name and I answer softly.

I will get dressed and feed my brothers.

I will sweep the kitchen and dust his desk.

I will leave the house and go for a long walk.

The boys run out the front door after breakfast, yelling happily to their friends in the next house over. They will stay there all morning, playing until late afternoon. I force myself to dress the twins in matching playsuits and load them into the double stroller my mother bought at a church bazaar. They wiggle cheerfully, an animal cracker in each hand, and we bounce down the rocky path over the slough's shaky wooden bridge.

My mind wanders. I walk faster and faster. Once again I think of Lorraine and the marshal's confusing letters. Once again I am troubled by the thought of a young person imprisoned in the Bethel jail, and wonder how such an injustice was even possible.

I begin to tire, the dampness of the morning leaving me chilled, and I wish I had brought along a warm sweater or a coat. Suddenly I realize that the houses have become smaller and that I have pushed the stroller across the slough bridge, almost all the way to Oscarville. I see the small Oscarville shacks through the fog up ahead. They are built close together, some of plywood and some of tar paper or tin. A few are built on common pilings to avoid the river's flooding and the erosion of the permafrost, but most balance on old, corroded oil drums for the same purpose. The village children run outside, calling to each other, laughing. The path is littered with trash, empty beer cans, candy wrappers, soda bottles wedged into the ridges of dried mud. Small dogs chase each other in circles, barking and nipping at their own tails, and large puddles spray around us, glazing the babies' faces with black. I have to stop every few minutes to dislodge the wheels from the mud, and the hem of my dress darkens; I can feel it stick to my skin, not a single boardwalk to be found here.

A large, white husky suddenly appears before us and I stop: I stay perfectly still. It stands there panting only inches from the babies' faces and they both squeal with delight.

"Shoo," I say, frightened. "Shoo, doggie, shoo." And it raises its head to me, each eye a different color, one brown and one blue. A small girl, maybe three or four, runs past us and then circles back quickly to swing her arms around the dog's thick neck.

"Quimuckta." She laughs, squeezing the animal tightly. I smile nervously and steer the stroller around her, hoping the dog will stay put. When I turn around to check, nothing is there. The dog and girl have vanished right into thin air.

"Miss Annette, Miss Annette!" Lorraine is waving to me from the doorway of a plywood shack across the road, and to my surprise I see the husky sitting right at her feet. "Hey, Miss Annette, what are you and those babies doing in our neck of the woods? Ain't used to seeing you up our way."

I smile and push the stroller toward her.

"Is that dog okay with children?" I call. "It's awfully big."

"What, Quimuckta?" She laughs and rubs the top of the dog's head. "This puppy here won't never hurt nobody. I can practically, absolutely guarantee that myself. And, by the way, he's a he, not an it. Don't belong to nobody in particular but kinda shows up when he wants to and where he's needed. I'm not exactly the type myself to be fond of

175

animals, smelly as they are, but this fella here's not hard to admire. And some of the Natives say he's even part wolf."

"Part wolf?" I brake the stroller in front of Lorraine's house and try to catch my breath, as I'm not used to walking much or getting any kind of exercise for that matter. "I think I'll just keep my distance."

She shrugs and gives the red lollipop in her hand a quick lick. I notice she is wearing one of her typical outfits: a sleeveless purple top with large silver studs around the neck and a short shiny black skirt that almost covers what looks to be a cropped black crinoline petticoat.

"Them wolves way out in the tundra probably might be dangerous," she finally says. "But this old mongrel here wouldn't hurt a fly." The dog looks up as though he knows that he's being discussed. He nuzzles Lorraine's hand softly. "Now don't you be cozying up to me just to get a lick of this here sucker, Quimuckta. Don't you know that sugar ain't good for dogs and wolves?" The dog stretches and yawns, then looks straight at me.

"Well," I say nervously. "It's not that I don't believe you, but I've always had a thing about big . . ." but before I finish my sentence, the animal leaps off the front steps and disappears around the back of the house.

"See?" Lorraine laughs. "You done hurt that puppy's feelings. Don't do to be talking bad about animals in front of that dog."

I take a quick breath, relieved, and smile. "Do you mean

to tell me that you think that dog understands what we're saying? Why, Lorraine, I'm surprised." She shrugs and laughs again.

"Sometimes things around us don't make a heap of sense, Miss Annette. I know you and your father is real religious folk, but sometimes you just got to keep an open mind. Last week, I read me an article about life on Mars. What do you think about little green folk living on Mars?"

This time it's my turn to shrug.

"I guess I don't believe in life on other planets. Life right here, right now on this planet's hard enough to figure out. And not to change the subject, but I'd like to talk to you about something important. Do you mind if we come in for a minute?"

My nervousness suddenly comes back and I feel my hands shake. A worried expression flashes across Lorraine's face and she looks away.

"It ain't that I don't want to invite you in or nothing, but Mama and me, we's just beginning a real serious redecorating of the house. I would hate for you to see it, all messy like, with everything out of place. Your house probably is looking perfect all the time. . . . Oh, what the heck, come in, what am I saying, of course you can come in. You must be tired from that long walk, and I surely don't mean to be impolite, just that we're not used to a visit from the minister's family, or much of anybody, truth be known. Mama and me keep planning to extend some party invitations one day, you know, nothing fancy, maybe for afternoon tea with little cherry jam cakes or something for the ladies, but to tell you the truth we both are so busy, what with cooking for the jail and receiving home and other social obligations, why sometimes I just think we'll never get to our own invites, after all."

"Please don't consider this a formal visit," I say, reaching to lift the babies from the stroller, "and I hope it's not an imposition to bring in the twins. I'd thought I'd just stop for a minute to talk to you about something that's been on my mind."

"Come right along in." Lorraine reaches to take one of the babies and then pulls back suddenly. "I'd offer to help with one of your little brothers, but to tell the truth, I never do care much for babies, seeing as they're always getting ready to drool or spit up or some such thing. And I do have on one of my favorite summer wardrobe selections. Them silver beads you see sewn around this here neck, well, Mama stitches them on one by one by hand. She has to order them all the way from Chicago, Illinois, seeing as they don't seem to have these particular beads down by Prince Rupert or even Seattle, and you know that nothing of this high quality can ever be found in Anchorage or Fairbanks."

She sighs heavily. "Sometimes I think that I'm not meant to be living here in the way north, that a girl like me's not meant for small town life. I'm more of a big city type, don't you think? And I surely ain't planning to whip myself into a froth over this moon thing, going to the city and watch the TV and the like. As much as I admire city living, I do think folks 'round here is going a bit too far with this moon walk nonsense. Personally I think the whole thing's made up by some crazy folk in Washington, D.C., trying to make a buck or two on income taxes. Why, most of us folks here in Bethel can't even get ourselves a flushing toilet, so how am I gonna believe that there's men up there walking on the doggone moon?"

I smile, not exactly following her logic, and follow her into the little house, a baby on each arm. There is hardly any light inside and it takes a minute for my eyes to adjust. And when they do, I take a step back in surprise.

Lorraine's house is smaller than any house I've ever seen, basically just one large room with a tan sheet hung up at one side. The kitchen, or what there is of it, lines the back wall, a large rusty refrigerator and a square metal sink hooked up to a warped countertop. A tin cupboard hangs crookedly over the small black iron stove, and I notice that there are two cots made up neatly with brown and orange striped blankets, and set up in one half of the room. A black and white speckled Formica table crowds the other half, flanked by two chipped metal folding chairs along with four huge cartons marked CUP o' NOODLES. More cartons are stacked by the refrigerator and two are placed side by side, as if used for a small table, with a tall stack of magazines and newspapers piled on top.

"Well, don't be shy for goodness' sake, come right on in, why don't you?" Lorraine's voice takes me by surprise. "Why don't you just have a seat right here in the kitchen and I'll make you a cup of Russian tea stirred up with Mama's own special mix of Tang and sugar."

"Oh, no thank you, Lorraine." I walk over to the table and sit down, my arms aching from holding both babies. They slide off my lap the minute that I'm seated and stand there, hanging on to the bottom of my skirt.

"Are you sure? I don't feel like much of hostess without offering my guest some refreshments of some kind. How 'bout soda pop or a cup of coffee?"

"No thank you, really." Suddenly I feel awkward and wonder what I am doing in this little shack, talking to a very strange young girl. And it doesn't escape me that she is eyeing the babies suspiciously. The bigger one tries to cram a piece of her dress into his mouth. She swats at his hand.

"Well, I'm sorry that Mama isn't here 'cause she'd be happy to help out with those little ones you got there, but is there something that I can assist you with? Another recipe?"

I shake my head.

She taps her fingers on the table and her feet scrape the floor. Her nails are bitten and painted a shiny pink, and her long freckled arms are noticeably skinny and white. I can almost see the bones shift quickly under her skin as she moves.

"Lorraine," I say slowly, "remember when you were asking me about some boy who was locked up several weeks ago?"

She stops moving suddenly, her feet and hands frozen in place. My stomach tightens. I think about Arnie; I see Father's angry face.

"Now, I'm not sure about this or anything," I continue, my voice quavering, "and I don't want you to think that I have any real proof, but it seems to me I might remember a prisoner who looked a little younger than he should."

She doesn't say anything for a moment, her narrow brown eyes glued to my face. The air between us stretches until I can almost hear it snap.

"Miss Annette," she finally says, "if you know anything at all about him, if you remember anything at all about that particular boy, why me and my mama, we would be beholden to you forever. That young boy, for sure he's in serious trouble, and without your help, well, I'm not certain what's ever gonna happen to him. It would mean the world to me if you could just remember."

I sit back in my chair and feel my throat fill; suddenly it's as if I can't speak at all. I look at Lorraine's face, her light, smooth skin unblemished by a a single line, a single mark. A few freckles fall over the bridge of her nose and her bright eyes stare at me, unblinking. I see her full lips open and close, but she doesn't speak at all. I try to say something. I want to tell her everything I know, but fear digs deep into my throat.

"You okay, Miss Annette?" I finally hear Lorraine whisper, reaching out her arm to touch my wrist. And then all of a sudden, before I even know what I'm doing, all that has been left unsaid for months and months, all I have hidden way deep inside, rises up and my eyes fill with tears. I take a quick breath and try to regain my composure but find that my voice still quakes when I try to speak. I wipe my eyes quickly and look away. One of the babies pulls at my skirt and coos.

"You okay?" she repeats, this time walking around the table to put her arm around my shoulder. "Do I say something wrong, do I say something to make you sad?"

I shake my head and lean back so that my shoulders are supported by her hands.

"It's nothing, Lorraine, nothing at all. Please, I don't know what's wrong with me today. It's really nothing at all." She's quiet for a moment, and I feel her pat the top of my head awkwardly.

"You're shaking, do you know that? Why, you're shaking all over. Is it the time of the month for your womanly visitor? Some females get all aching and quivery and the like, don't you know. Or maybe you're coming down with that flu bug that's going around."

I shake my head and smile weakly. "I'm fine, Lorraine, thank you. I've just got some things to work out on my own. Some things that have been on my mind for a long while now."

"Guess your own mama leaving's gotta make you sad time to time."

I nod. "Guess so."

I look at Lorraine and see that it's her time to cry. Her eyes fill up suddenly, and I reach across the table to take her hand. It feels small and cold.

"Listen," I say evenly, taking a deep breath, "I think I may have seen that boy you've been asking about. On Tuesday afternoon, April 29, I saw Arnie bring in someone who looked to be underage. But that's all I saw, Lorraine, Arnie dragging in a tall boy who might have been pretty young." I hear my own voice echo, strong and firm.

"You say he's real tall? That's him, I'm sure of it, Miss Annette, that's the same boy. Can't believe you actually see him, can't believe that you see him too! Do you have any idea where he's sent, I mean after you leave that day?"

"I'm sorry, no. I didn't even think about it then, to tell the truth, other things on my mind at the time. But I do remember the date, the Tuesday that I work, and I remember that boy's scared face."

"Dove Alexie," Lorraine says softly, wrapping both her

arms around me. "His name is Dove Alexie from Stony River, Alaska, U.S.A."

By the time I get the twins back in the stroller, it's already afternoon. Although it is getting late, I decide to take the long way home and stop by the river to think. I lift the babies out of the stroller and watch as they crawl on the rocky beach, pulling at shells and pebbles with their chubby fingers, stamping their little fists in the sand. The wind picks up and I sit by the river's edge, trying to imagine the way to Stony River, the long, circuitous route to Alaska's enormous, mysterious interior. I close my eyes and picture the deep, rich forest, the woodland animals: the owl, the bear, the fox. Strange, how the land changes from flat to mountainous, from bare to forested, all within the same river's route, and I feel a sudden, surprising pressing urge to follow the Kuskokwim's path as far as it will go. I know the journey to the interior is a long one, filled with surprising twists and turns, but realize that I can no longer remain where I am right now.

I stand on the circumference of a distant center, tracing the outer rim but never actually stepping inside.

I look up and lean back, dizzy with the expanse of sky above. The aurora borealis is due next week, and I can almost make out its arc and almost see its vibrant color. I close my eyes and open them again, noticing how the sky is reflected in the river and the river in the sky. Suddenly I am comforted by what amazed me as a young child: that no matter where you stand or where you're going, everyone in the entire universe looks at the very same moon and the very same sun.

The walk home is longer than I remember, and Father is waiting in the kitchen, DeWitt and Garrett at his side. They are sitting at the table with the lights all off.

"Where have you been?" Father asks, not getting up. "Where have you been with the twins? They're filthy. Haven't they had their baths yet today?"

Garrett runs up and hugs my knees.

"Daddy says we got to wait for lunch, but I want a cracker, now, Nettie, can I have a cracker, please?"

"Just a minute, Gary, give me a second." The babies are both sleeping in the stroller and I roll them to a quiet corner of the room. "I'm going to wash up for a minute and then I'll get to making your meal."

"You haven't answered my question, Annette. Where were you all day?"

"Nowhere special or anything. Just doing some visiting around town. Just visiting." I wash my hands in the sink and splash my face with cold water. My skin is covered with a film of mud and dust.

"Well, next time you decide to do your visiting, confine it to the early morning, will you please. Your father and brothers have been waiting."

"Forever." DeWitt suddenly pipes up. "It's not Daddy's

job to cook and we've been waiting forever."

"All right, son, that's enough." Father stands up and crosses his arms. "I'll be reading in the front room—call me when my meal is ready."

"It might not be for a while." I am suddenly feeling irritated and tired. "You just may have to wait for a while."

Nobody says anything then. Father turns slowly around, his back toward me and the children. Gary reaches for my hand and DeWitt's face looks startled, frozen. The babies lie perfectly still in their stroller, and I feel the floor under my feet shift and then settle, reconfigured, into place.

# PART
# THREE

*The most beautiful thing
we can experience
is the mysterious.*

—Albert Einstein,
*What I Believe*

# LORRAINE HOBBS

*Bethel, Alaska*
*Summer 1969*

" Lorraine," Mama says to me one boring, rainy Sunday afternoon, "you just gotta get your mind off all that serious prison business and find yourself a change of scene. You can't go on, sulking around like your best friend dies—it ain't good for you, child. Maybe you should think on trying that new teen center out by Northern Commercial; all the kids from school seem to be meeting up there these past few months. You need to find yourself some old-fashioned fun, daughter. I can see that all your worrying about that locked-up child is wearing you out something terrible."

I'm sitting at the kitchen table, giving myself a deluxe combination manicure/pedicure overhaul, and wondering if spending a full half hour on my feet is the very best expenditure of my valuable time ("Finally, the Truth About Organizing Your Life," *The Professional Woman*). Somehow hunching over my little toes with a tiny vial of red polish seems a tad foolish these days when more important issues is facing me whole hog. For example, nosing around for Dove Alexie might be more worthwhile, but I can't figure how in the world I can find out much of anything at all on that particular subject. It seems like the whole thing is practically hopeless. And I surely don't feel like listening to my mama think on what's best for me, or discuss my very own personal business. Recent events are just too private to talk about over nail polish and Grape Jelly Chunk Muffins.

"I don't want to say a word about it, Mama," I say, trying my hardest not to be rude. I start to take a bite out of a muffin, but put it down again as I remember there ain't no eggs for the batter and them muffins taste like sawdust. Lately, it seems like my words slip out all mean and sharp without my even knowing it. I don't mean to sass Mama or Mr. Samuels none, but all that sad weariness weighing heavy on my heart turns everything I say into something nasty and cruel.

These days the world seems a pretty disappointing place to me. There's still no word from Dove Alexie; nobody else besides Annette Weinland even seems willing to admit he exists at all. I get myself all in a dither over Miss Annette's recent tidbit of information, but it turns out that she's the only one to ever see him. And she sees him only that once, if at all. And no explanation for that note asking for help. No explanation for the way I feel when I read the note, either, can't figure why that little piece of paper makes me so sick and scared.

Sometimes it feels like I make up the whole dang thing and my picture imagination has taken full hold of my overactive, feverish brain. I get a crumpled note in my pocket and a blurry memory in my head—that's all that is left of a sixteen-year-old boy from Stony River, Alaska.

And I hear that Arnie leaves town last month for a fancy job up Prudhoe Bay, so one of my only two living witnesses ain't even available anymore. He sure hightails it quick outa here—guess he's counting on them old pipeline bucks—and leaves poor Bertha Sam all alone at home and Annette Weinland with a load of work at the jail. The marshal being out of town so much and all, seems like Miss Annette's gonna have her hands pretty full. Oh, well, I'm sure they'll fill Arnie's job right quick—there's probably a whole boatload of men eager to get their hands on a badge. Why, I even hear that them Norichinka boys got some irons in the fire.

Don't you know that even Mama thinks I should drop the whole Dove Alexie thing and concentrate my energies on another of life's many exciting arenas. With school starting come September, she tries to get me interested in a new fall line of back-to-school clothes. I don't know what's wrong with me, but even a swatch of aqua silk brocade with coordinating chiffon welting don't perk me up nothing substantial anymore at all. No matter how hard I try, I keep wondering about that strange note that somebody writes. Seems like if it is from some kind of mean jokers, well, then they would make themselves known by now. Seems like the note really is from Dove Alexie, his own self. But if that's the case, then why does he write me and what can I do to help? And why do I feel so sad and desperately dejected every time I look at them words:

**CAN YOU HELP ME OUT OF HERE. . . . TELL HER TO HELP TOO.**

Does something real down dirty evil take place and is he really held somewhere against his very own will . . . or is it my picture imagination just kicking in again? And who in God's name is "her"? Ain't no other females around the prison that I know 'cepting Miss Annette, and she never would be messing with any prisoners in the back. She just ain't the type. Although Mama ain't so sure when she reads the message, it's clear as day to me that Dove needs my help. I try to remember what Arnie says about the boy—some talk about Dove being crazy in the head, not knowing his own name. Could it be that something is wrong with Dove Alexie, something wrong with the goings-on of his brain and his heart? Could it be that the handsome young man I see in prison is no more than a crazed barbarian brute? I just can't even begin to bring myself to believe that.

"The young girl working up at the receiving home has

to head back east to college," Mama suddenly says, waking me from my absorbing reveries with a jolt. "Audrey Turner from Bethel Social Services asks me to take over for a while."

"You mean cook plus live there and everything?"

I put down my bottle of Reckless Red nail polish by Max Factor and smudge my big toe.

"Lookee here." My teeth are grit together real hard. "You ain't gonna find Lorraine Hobbs bunking up at that crummy orphanage."

"Shucks, girl, not move in. They got some other lady who works days down at social services to sleep there nights. I'm just gonna stay there during the day, you know, cooking, cleaning, and watching all those little children."

"Little children, humpf." I think of those two juvenile delinquents I run into up at the jail a while ago. Those two surely don't look like little children to me. More like hardened criminals. Especially that Evelyn Sugarbush with her strange different colored eyes. I still ain't even absolutely sure them two don't have something to do with sending me that note signed Dove Alexie.

"Lorraine," Mama says kinda carefully as she folds some nubby yellow fabric into a neat pile, "there's something else, too."

I cap my nail-polish bottle and sit up straight. I can always tell when Mama's going to drop some unwelcome news.

"How would you like to make some extra cash? Turns

out old Mrs. Turner wants you to help out as my assistant up at the home, seeing as they get a new truckload of children coming in this month."

"You got to be kidding."

The nail polish slips out of my hand and goes spinning across the table. The top looks loose.

"You mean to say that you done hired me out as some kind of baby-sitter? I'm sorry, Mama, but there's no way that Lorraine Hobbs is ever gonna take a fool job like that. I got my own work as it is, cooking for the prisoners at the jail, and I'm not about to start changing diapers and playing house, too. No, absolutely not, Mama, there's no way at all."

"No need to work yourself up into a dander," Mama says calmly. She stands up and stretches out her back. "Whew, I sure am not the woman I use to be. My old bones start creaking something fierce before I even move a single muscle."

I look at Mama sideways.

"Come on, Lorraine, let's you and me walk over to Northern Commercial and collect a few groceries. I hear tell that a new shipment of Golden Delicious come in. Let's splurge and pick us up a few."

"What about the receiving home job?" I ask suspiciously. "You mean to say that's all you're gonna harp at me on working up at the home?"

She smiles sweetly and sticks another pin into her

hair. "Nothin' else to talk about, child. You're old enough to make up your own mind. And it don't matter nohow anyway, seeing as that the receiving home job pays fifteen dollars an hour. I don't think it's gonna be a problem finding some other young girl."

I slam both freshly pedicured feet down on the floor and watch as the shiny bottle of polish tips open and spreads itself right over the table. It don't take a lot of brains to figure out that Mama knows exactly how to get me to do any darn thing she likes. It ain't fair, it ain't rightly fair at all.

"Have a muffin, Mama," I offer, passing the full plate of eggless delicacies over to her side of the table. "Think you're gonna like the newfangled recipe I make up just last night."

Don't you know that my mama just looks at me and laughs right out loud.

And so, before I know what's what, Mama and me's trudging over to the receiving home every single day, Mama working like a slave from eight A.M. all the way to six P.M., and me joining in the afternoon at three-thirty. And at first I don't think I'm going to survive, what with all the cleaning up and generally unpleasant work to be done. Sometimes I get so fed-up plain tired that I feel as though I'm about to scream. I can hardly believe, with all my studying of beauty secrets 'n' all, that I suddenly find myself doing run-of-the-mill housework—washing dishes, folding laundry, even mopping a floor every so often—and basically supervising a bunch of rude and very dirty children. All at once I realize that no matter how many Vaseline treatments I give my poor, sweet hands, they're gonna eventually pucker up like no nevermind. Makes you think on why we women bother in the first place—all that time spent trying to look fetching when the work of the world's gonna catch up with you anyways and leave its permanent calling card before you can even turn yourself around.

I try to wear my yellow Playtex gloves, in any case ("new super-long length"), to protect my extra-sensitive skin whenever I can, tie Mama's blue apron around my waist so as my custom-made outfits stay clean and pristine, and make sure that I avoid inhaling harmful cleaning fumes—potent chemicals can damage unsuspecting skin—but I just know that this kind of work is not meant for me. Not with my fragile constitution and delicate sensibilities. And I also somehow understand that no matter how hard I try, my work at the receiving home will leave its unforgiving mark in ways I can't even begin to expect.

But what particularly alarms me from the start are the children. Never, ever in my whole entire life do I see such a mess of pitiful ragamuffins as those receiving home kids, some covered head to toe with filth deep enough to grow carrots, wearing torn pants or tattered shirts three sizes too big or too small. The kids are from villages and towns all over the state, up- and downriver, as well as from way up north and even from the south. Some high school kids too, fresh out of Mt. Edgecumbe; those who can't go back home are sent to the receiving home for the summer, then back to Edgecumbe in the late fall or next semester. But all of them kids are Native, mostly Yup'ik, and some are real young, anywhere from scrawny little infants to real old, big, hulking boys, one almost a full eighteen years of age.

That particular almost-eighteen-year-old specimen is a piece of work, I can tell you, and I surely see him checking out Lorraine Hobbs as I brush my altogether natural blond hair out of my eyes or massage the fragrant skin at my temples after a particularly challenging day. He's definitely a criminal type, that one, and you can be sure it won't be long before I'm serving him meals up at the prison. And it also won't be long till he gets himself all tangled up with the law, seeing how he's got no respect for authority, always sassing Mama, and sometimes showing up late at night, liquored drunk as a skunk. And you can always find him skulking around, sneaking about in those beat-up old two-tone cowboy boots of his, the ones with the pointed metal tips, and those worn-out tight jeans plastered right to his skin as if he glued them on his own self. It might be that the boy does happen to be put together right, and I ain't saying he don't move pretty, but that's no reason to dress like a common hoodlum. He wears his black hair greased and slicked back long, and he cinches in his T-shirt as tight as can be.

"Hey, Edgar Kwagley," I've been known to call, "you still breathing okay or what? Sure don't want any of these here children under my care suffocating themselves to death on account of extra-tight clothing." But he just squints up those black, evil eyes of his and takes another puff off his cigarette, even though Mama don't like any of the kids to light up inside.

The way I see it, no one really cares for Edgar Kwagley at all, not even the littlest, most pathetic kids, and you can be sure that he's mostly by himself, tapping those dumb cowboy boots on the receiving home floor or standing out on the front steps, just looking and looking for I don't know what. That is at least when he's not up at the pool hall, partying 'n' all. Mama tells me that Edgar Kwagley grows up in Hooper Bay, a tiny Yup'ik village up north. She says that his father just hightails it outa town one day last year to sign up with the army or navy or some darned thing. Old Edgar is pretty much left on his own until social services brings him to Mt. Edgecumbe last winter. He's here at the home for another month until school starts up again.

Nobody really knows that much about Edgar Kwagley, only that he's some kind of troublemaker and don't got family nowhere. I even hear tell how he's a drug addict and smokes that marijuana pot till he can't walk straight no more. I can't absolutely verify to that fact as I never really see him in an actual certifiable drug conniption. But I look at Edgar and shake my head; guess he does manage to get under my skin sometimes, but I really don't have time for the likes of him or any other receiving home brat, I really don't.

The only time I ever see old Edgar act like an ordinary normal human being at all is when he sets his beady eyes on this pretty new girl just come in from Mt. Edgecumbe few days after him. This kid, Thelma something-or-another, ain't really so bad on her own, she's quiet enough and don't make no trouble, 'cepting she has a pain-in-the neck little sister who lives at the home all year 'round. You should see this brat when her big sister comes up from Edgecumbe. Looks like the little bugger's gonna split a gut; she's squawking, hopping around on one foot, squeezing tight to her big sister's leg all day.

Anyway, Thelma just smiles real quiet and acts as if nothing's outa whack at all. You kinda almost gotta admire someone like that—nothing seems to bother that Thelma girl much at all. Thelma Cooke, that's her name. Even Edgar's following her around don't seem to give her no nevermind.

The thing is, it's surprising how the number of receiving home kids changes day to day, anywhere from three to sixteen, so you never really know what it is you're up against. I can leave behind five or six children one evening and be faced with fifteen the next day. Social services moves those varmints in and out like some kind of ordinary ship-ment of dry goods or something, and I get to wondering where in the heck do these kids come from and whatever happens to their very own mamas and daddies. But I try my very darnedest to stay away, mind my own business, and keep my distance from those poor excuses for children.

The minute you get too close, they start hanging on to your legs, snot running right outa their sored-up noses, and Lorraine Hobbs surely don't need none of that disgusting business. I got bigger fish to fry than wiping up after some crummy little orphan's grimy face. But sometimes, when Mama's got her hands full, I do have to help the kids get dressed or set them up with an afternoon snack. They circle around me like tiny little vultures, pecking around for whatever strawberry-flavored Kool-Aid and pilot bread (spread with marshmallow fluff) I have on my tray, and I need to raise my arms way up high so nothing spills.

But I don't take any nonsense from nobody, that's for sure, and know exactly how to keep everyone right in line ("Make Children Behave in Just 20 Seconds," *Home, Health, and Hearth*). My own personal treatments, not exactly endorsed by any magazine at all, are most effective: When the little monsters start messing with me, I just give them the evil eye. I open my big eyes as wide as I can and roll them back into my head as far as they can possibly go. Those kids don't say nothing, but they surely scamper away as fast as their stubby little legs can take them. Soon all's I gotta do is say the words "evil eye," and they scurry off like scared baby mice. You ain't gonna find Lorraine Hobbs pushed around by no stupid little kid. There's no godly way that's ever gonna happen, I can tell you that.

And you can be certain that Mama's enjoying herself plenty, what with all the ragamuffin children always needing some such thing or another all of the time. Nothing Mama likes better than to take care of someone, and now that I've gone and turned into a fully blossomed growed woman, she's missing having a little child baby to fuss over to her heart's content. I'll see her sitting smack in the middle of that old torn-up receiving home couch with four children squished up her lap, and another four standing around, waiting for a space. And she's grinning like they is born right out of her very own self, not an altogether appropriate demeanor for the important position of home supervisor, if you is to ask me.

"Mama," I say, somehow plain irritated at seeing her help some little savage get dressed or find a toy, "with the exception of a few babies just come in the other day, these children are old enough to button their own silly little coats, and surely don't need you messing in their business every minute." But she just laughs and keeps on doing what she's doing, and I can see her whole face go perfectly soft with whatever giant-sized maternal hormones are shooting through her system at that particular time. It's almost as if she don't even hear me at all.

So it turns out Mama takes over most of the child-care activities and I handle the kitchen duties now that I am an experienced gourmet cook. I can thank my lucky stars for that, I surely can. I must admit, however, to some-times making a few minor mistakes in my expert cooking and fancy recipes, nothing important, mind you, but def-initely a few small errors. Why, just the other night I serve up a golden roast chicken dotted with Parkay margarine, the paper-wrapped innards cooking right along with my real soda cracker and spam stuffing. It wouldn't be quite so bad if little Tessa Michaelson don't chew up the paper real good and spit it out right in the middle of the supper table in front of Mama and everyone in the whole wide world. Mama and the rest of the kids sure has a few chuckles over that one and my whole dignity is insulted, I can tell you that.

But in a way, I'm grateful for this particular minor incident as I immediately squeal out loud, drop my Bounty quilted napkin on the floor, and race straight on up to the jail before the prisoners' evening meal is served. I manage to quickly pry open the Carry-O-Meal right on Arnie's old desk before his replacement has time to serve anything up. Utilizing exceptional dexterity, I dig myself a neat little hole right in that chicken's rear end with my cracked tortoiseshell compact cover ("Be Resourceful— How to Manage in Unmanageable Situations," *Family Life*), pull those innard papers right out, and then throw back in all of my homemade stuffing. Quite a sight to see those crumbs flying every which ways. But once I delicately pat all the stuffing crumbs back inside, that old bird looks good as new. Nobody has to be none the wiser. Sometimes I surprise myself with my own wherewithal, I really do.

And, of course, who should laugh the loudest at my minor cooking mishaps and make themselves the most nuisance of all but that rude boy and girl who see me almost seriously injure myself up by the Bethel jail. Every time the boy, Jimmy Pete, passes on by, he has to make some unpleasant remark or another about my unfortunate accident or the condition of my poor, ruined shoes at the time. And Evelyn Sugarbush, the girl, just sneers up her little, pale, bony face whenever she sees me as if she's something special and I'm the pathetic one, all holed up in this poor excuse for an orphanage with no family, with nothing to call my own. And when she bats those two different-colored eyes, looking right through me like I ain't even there, well, I can tell you I might get a pinch nervous. I know she really can't put any stupid shaman curse on me, but then again, you never know. You really never do.

I can tell you that I have absolutely no sympathetic feelings for these two, orphans or not.

"Just take a minute and imagine, Lorraine," Mama says whenever we get a minute together, "just imagine what it must be like to be a child and all alone in the world with no parents to speak of. Living all on your own, outcast from your own home. Wouldn't wish that on my worst enemy."

But imagining or not, nothing's gonna convince me that those two juvenile delinquents deserve any down-deep feelings of any kind at all. They strut around with their noses up in the air and whispering secrets to each other whenever they see me coming. None of the other kids seem to like them either, they really don't. Who could care for pitiful brats like those two anyway? Even with them being some of the oldest of the receiving home children, you never see them offering to help with anything or setting an appropriate example for others. Mama says that they've both been at the home for a real long time, longer than any of the others.

And it's not as if I really do ever manage to forget about Dove Alexie. Funny how someone can suddenly hitch up to your heart without no warning at all, without your even understanding why. Time passes, endless summer nights stretching out damp and cool, days all windy with the stinging of sand and dirt smack dab in my poor eyes. I sit in the receiving home trailer, straightening up a pile of toys or reading through my magazine recipes, and thinking about that boy's pitiful face. But nothing to be done about it now, that Arnie fella already leaving town for a pipeline job up north and nobody anywhere willing to help find out whatever happens to poor Dove Alexie.

Sometimes I get real sad just thinking about it, thinking

about how I can't make right what's wrong, that I can't even change anything at all. I get real down-in-the-mouth when I consider that there's nothing I can ever do to help that sorrowful boy, and I truly wonder about this here world—do we each just go about living all alone, just doing for ourselves, split apart into tiny river islands like Kuskokwim River villages, or do we cross some bigger bridge together, each of us holding the other's hand?

I look out them tiny receiving home windows and wait for the whole universe to just up and vanish; I watch for them misty rings of collapsing stars.

I ain't much for believing in the Almighty, but I do wonder about how the moon and them crazy planets all hold together just so, and I just can't figure what keeps the galaxies linked up strong and in their rightful place. Why, I learn at school that this here world's beginning's still a mystery, that back then there ain't no time or even no space. Our world don't got no rhyme or reason at all for being, and maybe there just ain't any kind of making sense on how things work out the way they do and folks act the way they act. My daddy leaves me, my grandpappy dies, my mama and me, well, we just don't have much of anything to call our own, and I just don't seem to fit into nowhere nohow.

And yet things just go along, day to day. Mama keeps working, I keep dreaming of something more, and them receiving home children, well, they keep waiting for a home to call their own. But nobody comes for them, nobody calls them back from the edge of this here lonely world, ain't nobody around to show them the way home, and I secretly wonder how they ever get on after having such a crummy deal, all by themselves in a big, lonely, mysterious universe.

Not that I really care or nothing, don't give an owl's hoot about any single one of them, but just thinking on it makes you wonder about the way things are; it really does make you wonder.

And the whole moon walk hulabaloo gets on my nerves, it surely does. I just can't see how it's got anything at all to do with my life or how in heck it's gonna improve the pitiful lives of all them little children with no place to go. And when snotty Evelyn Sugarbush keeps on and on about the details of July 20—the actual date of the blessed event—as if she's the only one smart enough to understand it all, I find myself getting particularly annoyed. Why can't she keep her big mouth closed down for once? She ain't the only one with a brain in her head, for heaven's sake.

"Guess since you don't believe that the astronauts gonna walk on the moon, you must not believe in the planets revolving around the sun?" she asks me one afternoon just as I'm getting ready to set the table for lunch.

I'm wearing a red and black bandana tied jauntily over my head so as not to get any particles of receiving home grime in my recently washed and conditioned plaited hair, and an old midnight-blue apron of Mama's that says

"Heavenly Body" with a silver profile of a woman's enormous, pointed chest. "Maybe you don't even believe in the whole entire solar system?"

"Oh, be quiet." I'm trying to experiment with folding the white paper dinner napkins into tulip flower petal shapes, but keep ending up with something that looks like plain old squares. "I can believe anything I like. How do you know so much about outer space and all that? Especially since you don't bother going to school all last year."

Evelyn tells us that when her pop dies up Emmonak, she stays with an uncle who keeps her home to take care. Nobody bothers her about a proper education, for goodness' sakes. That's how she ends up in the receiving home; social services takes her away from home. Mama says that Evelyn's so smart that she skips a grade and is going to start in Mt. Edgecumbe soon.

"You don't gotta go to school to learn, stupid," she practically spits right at me. "If you're smart like me, you can learn all the things you want from books. Betcha I know more about the great beyond than you do, school or no school."

She plops her scraggy rear right down on one of the card table chairs and starts on huffing on her bitten fingernails and polishing them like crazy.

"For example," she continues, as if I'm even listening, "do you know what the aurora borealis is, the northern lights we get to see up north?" Evelyn's talking about them colored lights that take over the skies some certain Bethel nights, and I ain't impressed even a little.

"Of course I know," I reply smugly. "Everyone knows about the northern lights."

"Yeah? So what are they?"

"What do you mean, 'what are they'? The northern lights are lights color up the sky. Now will you shut up?"

She shakes her head and smiles. "You don't know, do you? You don't know what the northern lights is and you don't know nothing about outer space. Them northern lights, for your information, is what comes from a whole mess of charged-up pieces of the sun blasting along the edge of the world's magnetic force. Betcha don't even know what the planets are and what they do."

I shrug. I must admit I'm feeling just a little embarrassed. And pretty impressed, despite myself, at Evelyn's show of smarts.

"There are nine planets," she continues, "that revolve around the sun. And even though there are thousands of minor ones, asteroids, as some people call them, there's just one that exists outside the solar system."

"Just one?"

"Yep, one. Most people don't know a thing about that particular planet. Don't even got a name. Why, they just discover the thing back in '63, just before the big Alaska earthquake. And no one can ever see this one planet, but we still know it's there."

"How do they know it's there if nobody can even see it?"

"They can tell it's out there because of this funny behavior of one wild star, called Barnard's Star, though I don't know why it gets that name. This crazy Barnard's Star throbs some peculiar way, not like any of them other ordinary stars, all the while keeping time with its hidden planet. Guess it beats just like a human heart. Anyway, that invisible planet don't even got itself a name; they just call it Barnard's Star's Unseen Companion. Ain't that strange?"

I nod.

I close my eyes and try to imagine Barnard's Star and its invisible, solitary partner. The enormous blue-black sky deepens under my eyelids and I feel myself drawn inside. I feel my whole body lift off the ground and slip, piece by piece, atom by atom, molecule by molecule, into the endless dome of space. I squeeze my eyes real hard and see Barnard's Star, silver and angular, tilting its lonely head in the darkness toward some compelling force, something familiar yet unrecognizable, something glowing yet unseen.

I open my eyes and look into Evelyn's gaunt face, into her two extraordinary eyes. There's one planet, only one in all of space, that exists outside of the whole, entire solar system.

All by itself and don't nobody even call it by name.

# THELMA COOKE

*Bethel, Alaska*
*Summer 1969*

Even before, I know.

Even before, I put my things in the brown cardboard box and sit on the bed waiting for them to call my name. Zena pats my arm then hugs me tight. Her yellow suitcase is packed and she leaves without no words.

Soon I will see Rosie and kiss her dusty mouth. Her lips will be pursed up tight in the shape of a little flower. I will bundle her, gathering each arm and leg in my arms like kindling, like the long, hollow weeds grow outside our small Sleetmute house. I will take care.

Even before I feel sick mornings, even before my zipper don't close, even before.

Rosie stands on them swaying receiving home steps, her *kuspuck* blowing in the watery wind. She holds out her little arms to me, the tiniest body just a little bigger now, one leg stretched forward as if she's about to leap. "Thelma," she calls in that croaky high and low, funny voice, "Thelma, I see you, I see you now!" And then she blows herself toward me, that old whoosh of thick summer air just picking her up in its thick, sticky fingers and tossing her right to me.

Suddenly she is holding me tight, her wet cheek against my cheek, her little heart pounding against my heart, her chalky, silty smell rubbing itself onto my chest, my arms, my face, until I can't smell anything else at all. Just my little sister Rosie rubbing her whole self through and through, all the way into me.

Old women, they say, when it's your time, you don't feel no pain. Your time will bring peace and we will stay there with you then. We will hold your hand. Tea made from dried lichen, cool grasses on your brow, our songs, our prayers. Cover fish eyes with ash. Spit in the air, then toward the ground. Scraps of caribou skin to bury underground. We are true by your side.

But all of my old women is gone. They sleep together in someone else's forgotten bed. They sweep out the corners of dream.

Rosie climbs into my lap and lays her small head against my chest. She smells like ocean this day. Her hair, black and shiny as seal, spreads. She takes my hand and pinches each finger as if to be sure that they are all there. I hear her little-girl voice counting.

At night I lay on my back and watch for the unseen. I listen to the gurgling of my other, smaller heart. They say you cannot hear, but this is a lie. My other, my tinier heart sounds like water; I can hear the rinse of sound.

Rosie says, "Thelma, why you so quiet nowadays?" Rosie pulls at my tattered sleeve. She looks up at me real hard, her sparkled eyes all squinty black, and I can hardly believe that she don't know. But nobody knows. Nobody will until it's done. Then I will lay my tired head down on my own mother's cold lap. I will close my eyes and feel nothing. I will turn my head when they take my other away.

Old times, the girls keep their babies home. The villagers bring fur blankets and reach out their arms wide. Old times, the babies belong to each of us, and we pass them house to house days and nights, too. But soon, these years, things change and the missionary women come to write down your name and whisper into their little books. Your own mama dead, your papa too, aunties gone, nobody left to help you take care. These years, the young girls watch, mouths drop open wide, empty hands fluttering; their other ones are someone else's now. We're too young. What is once ours disappears.

Some girls, they don't grow big, and this is how it is for me. I feel my belly harden, widen, but no one can ever see. My breasts are sore, my back aches, and the vein that runs up and down my neck trembles. Sometimes, if I touch it gently, I can feel my whole body quiver.

Rosie says, "Thelma, come end of summer, do you go back to that school down Japonski all over again?" I shrug.

"Do they take you away again?" Her warm cheek damp against my chest, her fists tighten then open then tighten again like some kinda small somewhere tundra bud trying hard to breathe.

My unseen breathes now. Her little puffs tickle. I turn on my side and feel her slide.

She will have my sister's name.

They will send me back to Sleetmute but Rosie will not come. She will find another home, other sisters, another chest where she can sink her sweet seal head.

I will close my eyes and see her diving through blue water, dipping her slippery, soft, smile suddenly away.

Even before, I know.

# EDGAR KWAGLEY

*Bethel, Alaska*
*Summer 1969*

Ain't no place here for me. School ends, I'm ready to move on, wanna get back to Hooper Bay for the summer to see some friends or maybe go to Anchorage. They say there's good cash to be made by Anchorage, and some cousins sell down by the Westbard Hotel, right by that Earthquake Park. I'm gonna make me some cash soon, once I figure how to get outa this damn place.

But for now, they stick me here in this receiving home, like some dumb kid, like somebody don't even know his own name. Them little children, they run around all day and I can't even get me no sleep. "Go away," I spit at them kids, "shut up and go away." But they just stare me down with their little children eyes like they's frozen or don't talk at all. When I tell them shut up, you can see them stop dead in their stupid little tracks. Ain't they hear anyone speak to them like that at all?

Me, I'm used to it. Call me any name you want and

I'll just spit it back in your face. Don't make me no matter. I know what I learn down Edgecumbe, I know what I learn about taking care of myself. Ain't nobody else gonna watch out for no one. You just gotta keep an eye out for yourself. And ain't no one gonna make me do nothing I don't want. Ain't no one gonna make me feel bad, gonna make me feel anything at all.

Until I see her again, that damn Thelma Cooke girl from Edgecumbe. The one wears her black hair sliding long down over them glossy shoulders so you just gotta stare. She shakes her hair offa that quiet face and it scatters down her back: black birds running over ground. It ain't easy not to stare, ain't easy not to look. Who cares anyway, who needs to watch some bush girl got no home, got no folks, got no cash. Nothing. That's what Thelma Cooke got. 'Cepting one little sister loud enough to make your head hurt.

So nights, days too, I go up the pool hall and try to hustle for some cash, gonna get me some booze, gotta get me high. Them old men, too drunk to care, let me use their old sticks and sit down as I shoot one ball, then another, into each corner hole. Them old men don't even care, just giggle their toothless smiles and sink themselves backward, stuffing their monies into my hand. Then I get me a beer, maybe a shot or two. Sometimes a bottle, best if it's a bottle, and sit myself down right outside. That pool hall's so loud with people yelling, feet stomping, things falling down and breaking, even the wall outside shudders against my back.

I sit there in the dust, sometimes in the black mud, my shoulders hunched up real tight, my jacket pulled up over my knees, and I take that bottle close to my ole heart. Even through my clothes I feel it get me warm, even before I pop off that damn cap. Then whatever's cold and empty down inside gets filled up real quick. The hot leaves a path right from my mouth down through my chest, my legs, all the way to my damn freezing toes. I close my eyes and lay my head against that old pool hall wall. Them old men, them women inside raise their voices and cackle loud. Glasses fall to the ground and crack open wide. Someone yells, "Shit," and "Hey stop it, damn you," and "Stop him," and "Quit it." "Gonna call the marshal." "Watch it, you. Watch it."

But I ain't watching nothing, nobodies. I close my tired eyes, light me a butt right from the ground, and breathe in real deep. Nobody and nothing gonna make me feel anything at all.

Some nights I end up at the Sleep-Off. Can't do nothing about that. Someone calls them Norichinkas and they throw me in the back of the truck, that truck sure stinks from honeybucket haul, and they dump me right off at that damn Sleep-Off.

It ain't always so bad when I get to lay me down, but don't like them women up at the Sleep-Off pushing me around. They cluck their fat tongues and pull at my clothes and even my boots. Gotta watch out or you don't get all your things back. Gotta make sure no one's hands stick to your stuff. All these other folk, men and women, too, they lie on their backs lining up on them stupid cot beds, mouths wide open, heads back, snoring, sometimes sitting up in their sleep and calling out real loud. Nights I'm sloshed real bad I don't even care. Just roll myself into that blanket and forget to even be awake. But some nights all that snoring and yelling and bawling make my skin crawl. Some nights you can't even sleep at all.

So that one, that first time I get stuck up at the Sleep-Off, I think I ain't ever going back. I sit there on some broken metal chair, trying to tell some stupid lady to shut herself right up.

"Gimme back my boots," I yell, waving at the air. "I know you got my boots back there."

That lady got a mustache thick as a man and her black hair's tied in two pigtails full of white string.

"Shut up, Edgar Kwagley," she sneers, her fat face shaking itself all around. She sits her big fists on the desk and closes down her small eyes. "I know your uncles up Hooper Bay, and them guys ain't gonna be happy about you yellin' them words all around."

"You don't even know any uncles." I try to open my eyes wide, but that Sleep-Off room keeps spinnin' itself around.

"Sure do. Don't you remember old Lucy Sam?"

I slide my chair up closer and try to hold my head still. "You ain't Lucy Sam from Hooper Bay. Lucy Sam's up home with her little childrens and husband Ben."

She giggles. Her laugh don't sound nice to me, more like little hard slaps than anything else at all. "Sure I am." She smirks. "Can't you see my face?"

"You got a damn ugly face." I laugh and lean back. "Lucy Sam ain't got any ugly face."

"Shut up." She spits, standing up like she's going to run. "Shut up, you stupid boy, you. Just 'cause you ain't been home all this time don't mean nothin'. My children's growed now and that goddamn Ben done run off to live Outside. Now you get yourself over to that bed before I call them Norichinkas to take care of you themselves."

That old woman, she walks herself right up to me and grabs the back of my shirt. Next thing I know, I'm lying myself down on some hard mattress. All them lights still on bright and the room filled with peoples groaning themselves to sleep. Lucy Sam, she's suddenly all gone, and I shake my head, trying to remember how the hell I even end up here. Suddenly I hear this sound like a puppy dog, like one of our little sled puppy dogs, moaning and whimpering when its mama ain't there no more. Back Hooper Bay, we got ourselves ten dogs, and one of them follows me every day. That dog dies frozen out on the ice. I see its eyes looking back at me now.

So I sit up and look around. Them cots lined up solid,

mounds of bodies breathing up and down all around. I hear the moaning again and wish it away. But don't you know, it's coming from underneath my stinking bed.

I lean over. No one on that cot next to mine. Moaning once more. I look down.

That's when I see him. This guy lying flat on his face, crammed between two beds, right smack on the floor. He hardly fits there at all.

"Hey you." I poke at him with my foot. "You better get yourself up onto that bed." He don't move. He don't even moan.

Maybe he's dead, I think. Maybe that's what this is about. I poke him again with my heel and this time he shifts and groans again. Suddenly I feel something wet on my own foot and look down. My sock's covered red, my stupid sock's covered in blood. "Hey," I say again, "hey, what the hell?"

And then I look closer. This guy's neck is dark with blood that drips down the back of his shirt.

"What the hell?" I say. "What the hell's goin' on?"

I can't see his face but notice he's real tall and his long, thick hair is matted up with blood something bad. I reach out to poke him again but feel my head spin.

"Hey, what ya doin'," I hear myself say, but before I know what is what, I fall back into my own bed.

Just before that whole room turns black, I see the letters on the back of his collar, just under where his hair falls below. Them letters spell out something "River." Can't really read all of what they say. "Something River." And then I don't see nothing at all.

Next day I ask that new lady, "What happens to that guy passed out on the floor?"

"What guy?" This lady is gussak, and she's real thin and tall.

"The one on the floor next to me. Looks like he's hurt real bad."

"Oh, you mean the John Doe." She's counting papers on her desk.

"That his name? That guy who's hurt. His name's John Doe?"

She looks up and laughs then. Them teeth are yellow and her red lipstick looks all smeary to me. "That's not his real name. We call them that when we don't know."

"Don't know what?" I ask. My head's hurting and that stupid room's all warm.

"Don't know the real name. Isn't it time for you to go?"

"But how'd he get all hurt?" I ask. " Did someone fix him up real good?"

"Not that it's any concern to you," the lady says, not even looking at my stupid, brown Yup'ik face, "but he's picked up out by the jail, just lying in the mud. They think he's drunk and gets himself into a fight. But before the

220

medic even gets here, seems like he just ups and disappears."

"Disappears?"

"Yes, disappears. When we check on him this morning, his bed is empty and he's nowhere to be found. What's it to you, anyway? You need to concern yourself with your own problems right now."

"Sure," I say as she finally hands me back my boots. "I got me problems of my own."


Thelma Cooke is lying on the front room couch with her arm across her face. She don't look up when I walk by. "How come your little sister ain't hopping all around?" I ask her. "You getting some rest from that little silly kid?"

She moves her arm and I see her face all puffed up red. She tries to sit up but then lies back down again. I look around but ain't nobody but the two of us in the whole place—then I remember Wednesday mornings them kids go up by the old school yard to play.

"Well, see ya, I guess," I say, somehow wanting to get out of the room quick as I can, but just as I turn I hear her speak.

"Please." Thelma Cooke is making little whispery sounds. "I need some help. Don't feel so good at all." Well, I ain't really sure what she means by help so I don't say anything, just stand real quiet and don't say a word. "Please," she murmurs again, pulling herself up real slow and shaky,

221

"can you help me over there?"

I can see she's pointing toward the honeybucket room, and I'm wanting to get the heck out of here as soon as I can. But there's nothing left to do, seeing no one else is around. I can't exactly pretend Thelma Cooke's talking to anyone else at all, so I walk over and kinda set my hands under her shoulders and help lift her up. We stagger for a minute, then settle ourselves steady.

She leans against me, all soft and pillowy, smelling more like summer berries than anything else at all, and I can't help taking myself some quick sniffs as we rock there back and forth. But soon we's stumbling forward to the honeybucket room and by the time she closes the door, I'm not feeling like leaving at all. I just stand me by that door, hands jammed down in my pocket, listening to Thelma heave and ho.

When it's all over and she totters out slowly, leaning against the wall, I reach out for her all over again. And Thelma kinda falls forward, right into my dumb ole arms, and we walk, taking tinier and tinier steps, into the girls' dormitory room. She sits down on the edge of the bed, neither of us saying nothing, and I lift her feet until she's laying herself all the way down. Then I reach for her thin, frayed little blanket and pull it right up to her neck. She smiles just a little smile, murmurs out some air all feathery and sweet. She closes them pretty eyes and sighs until I know she goes right to sleep.

I tiptoe outa Thelma Cooke's room, feeling her soft sighing slip and slide right upside my battered, leathery heart.

This day the pool hall's empty, and I look around for an old butt or two. Someone's left a smudged glass with a little bit of something at the bottom and I drain it, licking my lips. Whiskey. A wisp of warmth flutters.

That Katie Santini's sleeping right there in the chair, her red blouse popped open so you can see a white bra. I walk by her hardly looking, somehow don't feel like looking at all, and hike myself up a notch so as I can see over at the bar. George's locked everything up, not a bottle or can around, and I feel myself shudder like I'm standing out in the cold. I hug myself; my hands is freezing, and my stomach feels all knotted solid and cold. Want a drink. Need some bootleg, but there ain't none around.

I look back at Katie Santini and see her wobble and then slide to the floor. Then I notice some bills falling outa her pocket, three ones and even a five, too. Don't take me a minute to bend over and snatch them bills right up off the ground. I run outa that pool hall toward the package store. I run all the way up there without stopping for nothing at all.

I open my eyes and she's standing over me. The receiving home walls are swaying back and forth, up and down;

the ceiling spins. She nods. She smiles, and I groan. My head's hurting like I never feel it before and I think the air right in front of me smacks every time I turn around. "Shhh," she murmurs, "don't try to move." My eyes close and I hear her humming. I inhale and smell summer berries, summer salmonberries all warm and sweet under that damn summer sun.

When you hold this whiskey bottle up toward the sky, it changes color. Clear to yellow to green. I sit outside the pool hall, a fifth in one hand, about a quarter of booze left inside. When I tip the bottle over, the gold slides to one side, then back down again. I take another gulp, holding the liquor in my mouth for a minute, then swallow. The hot explodes. My head nods, then drops forward. I don't hear no one even calling my name.

Crowded at the Sleep-Off tonight. Someone pushes me and I feel my arm sore. My mattress's wet with something, but I'm too tired to even turn around. I crawl myself up into this little trembling ball; I wind myself asleep, all tied up in somebody else's stiffened, stinking, cold-piss piece of sheet.

Thelma's braiding her sister's hair. "Tickles!" the little girl squeals. "Tickles!"
Thelma just laughs and puts down the white ribbon.

"Your hair's too short, Rosie." She smiles. "Maybe next month we can try again."

"But I want braids now." Rosie stamps her feet, then pulls on Thelma's hands. "Pick me up, Thelma; wanna piggyback ride now."

"Oh, Rosie, not now." Thelma sighs and shakes her head. "Ain't feeling so well right now. Maybe later."

"You always say that. You always say later. How 'bout you, mister?" She spins around, looks like on one tiny foot, and sets them itsy hands on her little skinny hips. "How 'bout you givin' me a piggyback ride up and down all over the house?"

"How 'bout no?" I almost snap, wishing she'd go off for her nap, but instead don't say nothing. I see Thelma bend her head to one side and then smile right at me. And before you know it, there I am, running back and forth and all around again, with one little Rosie girl clamped onto my back. She's laughing and hooting, yelling "Faster, faster, mister," until I just gotta stop. And then she slides right down to the ground and runs straight outa the room. "Hey, Mrs. Lady," I hear her yelling, "Hey, Mrs. Lady, I got me a piggyback!"

"Thanks, Edgar," Thelma says, and then stands up slowly. "That's a nice thing you do, I'm glad you do that for Rosie. She's asking for a long time now."

And then she leans herself backward just a little, both hands on her hips. She leans herself a little backward, and that's when I suddenly know. Her white shirt is long and loose, buttoned most the way all up the front, but the last few is missing, her belly roundish through the flap fluttering open wide. She stands up straight again and looks right at me, hair clipped up top of her head like some kinda black crown, her cheeks flushing all different kinds of pink. The air gathers, then streams out behind her, the shadow of something small on back of the wall.

"Thelma," I say, surprised at my voice, "Thelma, how much longer?"

But she just shakes her head and smiles at me. "Shhh," Thelma Cooke says, "shhh, don't tell, but now it ain't gonna be long."

# PART
# FOUR

*Deep sky is,*
*of all visual impressions,*
*the nearest akin*
*to a feeling.*

—Samuel Taylor Coleridge,
*Notebooks*

# LORRAINE HOBBS

*Bethel, Alaska*
*Summer 1969*

Rosie Cooke wiggles her four-year-old little ragged self into the receiving home kitchen, then right up into my face, her gray sweatshirt covered with brown stains (I don't even want to know what from). She's a dirty little thing, her black, uncombed hair all matted together and her thin face smudged with colorful markers or finger paints of every possible color in the whole wide world. Her wide pink mouth is like a haphazard slash across a dusty brown face.

"Whatyadoin'?" She sniffles, wiping her arm across her crusty, dripping nose. I keep washing dishes and don't look at her. "Whatyadoin'?" she asks again, this time pulling on my pure white polyester bell-bottoms with fuchsia trim.

I immediately picture an entire row of miniature, multicolored fingerprints at the bottoms of both knees.

"Hey," I say, kinda kicking her off with one foot, my Playtex rubber-gloved hands still in the dishwater. "Knock it off, will you? These pants are winter white, if you haven't noticed."

She's quiet for a minute and then shoots me a crooked smile. I notice two teeth missing smack in the front of her mouth, leaving a red, gummy gap.

"When do you lose your front teeth?" I ask, rinsing the final dish. "You sure do look like you're missing a few in there."

She shrugs.

"Evelyn Sugarbush tells me new ones ain't never gonna grow back. She tells me I'm gonna always have a big hole right here." Her face falls for a moment and then she demonstrates by sticking her tiny tongue through the exact spot where the teeth are missing. "Lost 'em when I fall down them receiving home steps one day."

I dry my hands on my apron and shake my head in disgust. If there's one thing I can't stand, it's someone lying to a little kid. Not that I really care or anything, but it still just ain't right to tell a kid something that's not so.

"Hey, Mrs. Lady," Rosie continues, watching me untie my cotton-candy-pink, freshly starched apron, "what-yadoin' now?"

"Come on, get outa here." I'm just about at the end of my rope with this kid—ain't as if I got extra time to waste on receiving home critters, what with meal planning 'n' all. Haven't even decided what to make up for dinner tonight. "I have a lot of important work to do. Maybe you better

230

get on back to your sister or Mrs. Hobbs. Ain't it nap time or nothing?"

She don't say a word.

I slowly tap one foot on the floor. I'm getting more than irritated that I can't lose the big-mouthed kid.

She sends this loopy grin across her face and don't take her eyes off me. It's one o'clock and I can usually slip in a free twenty minutes to read a new magazine or massage my fingernails with Crisco All-Vegetable Shortening while the kids are resting, although lately, I find myself a mite bored with all them beauty articles. Reading on dressing and looking like that grinning Mary Tyler Moore or sappy Dinah Shore—what *does* Burt Reynolds see in her, anyways?—just don't seem to fire me up in the way it does before. I guess I have more pressing concerns on my mind these days.

"Don't you have to take a nap or something?" I say to the annoying runt who is staying right by me like white on rice. "Where's your sister?"

Rosie's sister, Thelma Cooke, don't ever say much but usually keeps her eyes right on her little sister; don't let her out of her sight for nothing. Thelma's real pretty, with wide, pink cheeks, black eyes, and gleaming dark hair she sometimes wears loose all the way down to her waist. Every once in a while, I look at her out of the corner of my eye, kinda jealous of that thick, black hair and the graceful way she moves. Sometimes I'll secretly watch Thelma braid her

231

hair when she's talking to Rosie, her long, pale fingers flying in and out between the dark strands: bright waves rolling through black waters.

Funny how people can look so pretty mainly on account of how they move themselves, how they hold their heads up or keep their backs perfectly still. Thelma can be sitting there, doing nothing but watching Rosie, but you can see this special way about her. It's as if her beauty shoots right up through her skin, straight out from the most delicate of bones. And it seems like nothing ever bothers her neither; you ain't about to see Thelma Cooke get steamed up about nothing. She has this way of drawing into herself like no one else is around.

She inhales the plain old gritty air around her and blows it out sweet.

She don't talk much to no one. She don't say much of anything at all.

I look down at my scrawny, chatty, fidgety self and shake my head. I may be doggone smart and have many talents, but when it comes to grace and beauty, well, there ain't one ounce of that in my whole, entire body. And I don't think it'll be coming my way any time soon.

"Thelma gotta go the clinic." Rosie sits herself right down on a chair and starts to suck her thumb. "She's gonna get the checkup. Not me. I ain't gonna get no checkup never again."

"Hey, stop that," I say, reaching to take her arm. "Don't

be sucking on your thumb at your age—what you sucking your thumb for? Don't look very ladylike."

Her thumb disappears farther down her mouth and she looks down. I see her other hand grip the chair seat real tight like. Her tiny knuckles turn white. "You know, the other kids gonna tease you some if you keep sucking that there thumb like some little baby," I tell her, leaning over so that my face is close to her face.

She closes her eyes and turns her head away.

"Well, if that ain't the rudest thing I ever do see." I stand up, both hands on my hips. "I know that you're only four years old 'n' all, but that ain't no excuse for being impolite. How'd you feel if I close my eyes and turn my head from you in the middle of your talking?"

Rosie giggles, thumb still in her mouth.

I feel myself get angry.

"What's so funny?" I ask. "If you think it's so doggone funny, then you see if you like it when someone does the same thing in front of your rude face." I bend over again till our noses are almost touching, then shut my eyes and turn my head. I hear Rosie start to giggle again and feel wet fingers squeeze my nose. "Hey, knock it off!" I stand up and wipe off my nose quickly with a sheet of double-strength paper towel. "What do you do that for, anyway?"

She shrugs, her eyes wide. "Why don't it honk?" she asks, peering up into my face.

"Honk?"

"Make your nose honk. Thelma does it."

"Thelma makes her nose honk? Gimme a break. Hey, get outa here, kid, will you? I surely have more important things to do than listen to a silly little child. Come on, I got work to do. Make my nose honk!"

Rosie don't move. She crosses her little arms. I notice two fat tears trickle down one sunken cheek.

"Hey, quit that. Quit that crying, will you?"

Not that I give a hoot or anything, but nothing bugs me more than seeing a little kid cry. Something about a child about to bawl makes my stomach wind up real curly and tight. Rosie screws up her small face. Her skin starts to turn pink and she opens up her small mouth real wide. I think I can see all the way down her throat to her slimy, quivering little tonsils.

I know trouble is coming my way. Rosie starts to bawl.

And it ain't like she is crying nice and soft or anything, nothing like that, no; she lets out these crashing sobs like to bring the whole house down. I feel my insides start to jiggle and shake.

"Quit it, will you," I say again. "Look, stop your crying and I'll give you a slice of 1-2-3-4 Cake I make up with Post Grapenuts cereal and Hershey's Kisses. Here, I'll get out a piece for you right this very minute. Only stop that crying, will you?"

Rosie sniffles loudly and swings her little legs. Her red sneakers have a hole at the toe of one foot and the mismatched laces are frayed at the edges. I can see where someone has knotted one lace together where it breaks clear off.

"Want some 1-2-3-4 Cake?" I ask again, encouraged that the explosion of sobbing has stopped. "Make it up myself, just last night. Gonna serve it for dessert tonight, but I'll give you a piece early on if you promise not to bawl."

Her thumb edges to her mouth and then falls to her lap. She wiggles in the chair for a minute, as if her body's a-itching all over.

"Why's it called 1-2-3-4 Cake?" She sniffles.

"'Cause you can make the whole thing while counting up from one to four. It don't take any time at all. Come on, I'll get you a piece."

"I like cake," she says, suddenly still. "Thelma gives me cake whenever I want."

"Hmm." I look at her sideways while opening the refrigerator door. A small, lopsided grin creeps over her face, and I can't help but chuckle just a little myself. "Thelma gives you cake whenever you want? You sure is a lucky son of a gun. My mama don't give me any desserts 'cepting when I eat all of my dinner."

Rosie pats her cheeks with both hands and squeals.

"I jokes! I jokes!" She laughs gleefully. "Thelma don't really give me cake whenever I want. I trick you good, don't I, Mrs. Lady!"

"Yeah, yeah, whatever."

I slice off a small piece of cake and lick my fingers. If I do admit it myself, this cake is a work of art, what with the Hershey's Kisses lined up real neat around the edges and covered good with rainbow sprinkles. Four perfectly white marshmallows stick up in the center, held together by two toothpicks and surrounded by a yellow ring of Dole's canned pineapple (my own personal touch). There ain't nothing better than a good-looking piece of professionally made pastry confection, if you is to ask me.

Rosie digs her fork into her piece of cake, trying to break off a bit, but nothing seems to happen. She attacks the slice again, this time utilizing all of her skinny little arm. Still no luck. She tries one more time, hitting the edge of the cake with all of her might, and sends it popping like a Ping-Pong ball, straight on up to the ceiling.

*Splat.*

For a minute I think it's going to stick, but to my surprise and extreme horror, the cake drops down right in the center of my sprayed, recently teased bouffant french twist. I reach my hand up to touch and feel a wet, gooey mess.

"For pity's sake!" I screech (while also thinking on a few less refined words). "What in God's name are you doing? Lookee here what you do! This cake's gotten all over my hairdo and chocolate surely ain't recommended for no revitalizing treatments or nothing. I can tell you that!"

I take a slippery glob in my hand and throw it right at

Rosie's pinched little face. Understand, I know it ain't the grown-up and mature thing to do. I know it ain't a gesture befitting a person of my stature and responsibility, but it seems like I just can't rightly help myself. Some kinda urge tickles up in my belly and I let that piece of cake rip right into Rosie Cooke's surprised face. The cake lands on her chin, a pointed brown goatee.

For a minute she looks startled and I hold my breath, then her whole entire face breaks open wide. Rosie starts to laugh. I reach over and spread the chocolate up over her lip.

"Look!" I guffaw despite myself. "Look, Rosie, you is growing a real, sure as tootin' mustache and beard."

"I'm dessert," she announces proudly. "Now you and Mrs. Hobbs can give me to all the kids for dessert."

"Well, I don't know about that." I start to clean her face with a wet paper towel. "I'm not sure what Thelma would say about that. Just think, this morning she left a little sister behind and now she comes back to a piece of choco-late dessert. And all of them kids is expecting my famous, extra-special 1-2-3-4 Cake. Think they might be just a little down in the mouth if all's they end up with is a piece of your face."

She starts to laugh again and then all of the sudden, to my absolute and complete surprise, she swings her spindly arms around my neck and pulls me into a damp hug. Before I realize what's even happening, my very own arms squeeze her back tight, and I wonder what in the heck

I am doing with a dirty little orphan girl hanging on to me like I'm the only one left in this here whole, entire world.

So, don't you know it, Rosie and me, well, we kinda become a twosome of a sort. Not that I get any thrill outa a four-year-old following me around wherever I go, but this kid surely gets it into her skull that I'm her friend for life. And it's clear that there ain't nothing much I can do about it, even if I want to.

"Oooo, Miss Lorraine," Rosie calls to me right as I set my foot in the front door every afternoon. "Oooo, Miss Lorraine! Lookee see what I'm making for you!"

And every day I have to go straight over to Rosie's cot, before I do anything else at all, before I even put down my books or stop to give my mama a proper afternoon greeting, and right away I have to watch Rosie finish gluing together two splintery Popsicle sticks or scrawl a picture on a piece of torn, colored construction paper. You can be sure that Evelyn Sugarbush and Jimmy Pete are right there to make fun, cracking some joke or another about Mutt 'n' Jeff or Siamese twins. Don't you know that they sneak around spying and, as soon as I get close enough for touching, watch as Rosie throws her arms around my neck, jumping up and down until her cot starts to shake. I swing her away from those two's squinty eyes, I can tell you that, surely don't want someone little and innocent as Rosie victim to any shaman curses happen to be shooting across the room. Then Thelma, always sitting right there, will put a gentle hand on her sister's tiny back.

"Rosie, that'll be enough," she will say quietly. "Let's leave Lorraine alone for a minute so that she can get to her work."

"I don't wanna leave her alone," Rosie will scream happily, smudging my Perfectly Peach rouged cheeks with a million wet kisses. "Miss Lorraine's gonna stay with me today. Stay with me!"

"Now, Rosie," I'll say in my most grown-up manner. "Why don't you finish your artwork first? I'll be back to play with you in a little while." But every day, no matter what Thelma and I say, Rosie'll just hold on all the tighter. And every day, no matter what we do, I end up shrugging my shoulders and carrying her with me back into the kitchen, where I got to start preparing the afternoon snack and evening meal. Rosie will climb right up on the kitchen table, plain as can be, and grow a foolish grin right over that silly face. She'll sit there, real quiet and content, watching me rustle up a new recipe until it's time for her nap. Then, just as if I'm not standing right there in front of her, she'll slip down from the table and stagger, yawning, back to her cot. I can't help my smiling as I watch her go, the kitchen all filled up warm with her murmurings and drowsy little-girl breath.

239

Evenings, I barely crawl home, exhausted, what with working so hard all day, and the last thing I need is a conversation with anyone, especially Mr. Samuels. Each time I turn around, it seems he's right there at the kitchen table eating on one of Mama's home-cooked meals or dozing in that same chair. So I'm not pleased when I try to sneak past him one night on the way to bed and I hear him call my name. Mama's out visiting over at the Norichinkas—the older Norichinka girl is just back from a visit down Dillingham—and I surely don't feel much like entertaining this foolish old man.

"Lorraine Hobbs," he calls again as I tiptoe to my bed.

There just ain't no way for me to keep pretending I don't hear.

"Yes, Mr. Samuels." I sigh and turn around.

He wags his finger at the sink and smiles. "Bring an old man some water. Sure seems like my throat's real dry."

I sigh again. It just don't make any sense that a full-grown adult can't haul his own self up and get his own doggone water. But I bite my lip and pour him a cup.

"Hmm." He smiles again and don't you know, I see some water dribble down his chin.

"For God's sake, Mr. Samuels. Take a napkin or something."

I decide right then and there that I will absolutely have to kill myself before I turn disgustingly decrepit and old.

"Them folks come up here from Outside believe in God's sake." Mr. Samuels nods and motions me to sit down. I don't move a muscle. "Them missionary folk." He continues, slowly wiping his chin with a tattered denim sleeve. "Long time ago them missionaries tells us that God creates the world in six days."

I nod and tap my foot. He nods back and grins. For the first time I notice the color of his oval eyes, deep green, not the typical Yup'ik brown I would have expected. When he blinks, looks like those green eyes gleam larger and larger. Just like a cat, I think to myself, like a big old lazy tabby cat. His head rolls forward for a minute and then he jerks it up, smiling foolishly at me all over again.

"Back then, we believe different. We believe the world begins when Raven scratches out the earth with his claws. That shaman, he tells them missionary workers not to build the church on high ground."

"What church? What shaman?"

Is it possible the old man is really losing his mind? I hear tell of old folk who go looney all of a sudden one day and start talking crazy nonsense. I surely do wish Mama would walk through the door.

"The church. That church." He waves his arms and looks like he might suddenly leap out of the chair. "Our shaman, he tells them. He says, 'Peoples, don't build your mission on the high Kuskokwim River ground. Our river will eat out the earth from underneath.'" Mr. Samuels bows his head and then whispers, "You see what happens, Lorraine Hobbs. You see how far the hill falls and that mission church comes right down."

Neither of us speaks for a minute. I think of the crumbling riverbank at the edge of town where us kids used to play, and the old church skeleton, its boards rotted, its frame tilted, the foundation hidden and overgrown.

"You're telling me the shaman knew what would happen? That he knew that riverbank would fall?"

Mr. Samuels grins and nods, then points toward the door. I turn around and see my mama is standing there, smiling. Mr. Samuels winks at her; she laughs and winks right back.

Don't you know, sometimes I feel invisible, like no one even remembers me at all.


"Don't got no mom or dad," Rosie Cooke says to Mary Joseph cheerfully. They're both sitting on the receiving home floor, combing their battered dolls' hair. Evelyn and Jimmy Pete are quiet (for a change), playing Parcheesi in the corner.

I hold my breath and wait to hear more.

"You gotta have a mom and dad," Mary replies, giving her nude Barbie doll a good whack on the head with her pink plastic brush. "Don't want my dolly to have no stupid, dumb ponytail." Mary is six, two years older than Rosie and a full twenty pounds heavier. I watch her round face redden as she pulls at the offending hair.

"Do not. Do not gotta have 'em." Rosie firmly sets her baby doll on the floor. Two strands of yellow hair have been tied messily with a rubber band, and its pink, plastic face is covered with purple and yellow crayon marks. A large wad of Scotch tape covers one ear.

"Do too."

"Well, I don't."

"Don't what?"

"Gotta have a mom and dad."

"Sure you do, stupid." Mary gives Barbie's hair one good yank, and threads of white rayon float up in the air. Evelyn looks up and Jimmy Pete starts to laugh.

"I ain't stupid. You are." I see Rosie look to me for help and then cross her arms across her narrow chest.

"Well, then how do you get yourself born? If you don't have a mom and dad you can't get born!"

"Can too!"

"Cannot! Can't get yourself born any other way, ain't that right, Miss Lorraine?"

"Well," I mumble slowly, not really wanting to get in the middle of this conversation, "I guess you really can't."

"Told you so! Told you so!" Mary hugs Barbie to her chest and laughs gleefully. "I told you that you need a mom and dad."

Rosie looks at me accusingly. She bows down her fuzzy head, and I see her shoulders start to quiver. I feel

Evelyn's and Jimmy's eyes burn into my back.

"Rosie," I say, walking over to her, "there's nothing to cry about. Just 'cause you have to have a mom and dad to get born don't mean that—" But before I can even finish my sentences, she stands up and kicks her doll across the room. It goes whizzing right by my left ear, and she runs right out of the room. I stand there for a moment, not exactly knowing what to do.

"Now you've done it." Evelyn smacks Jimmy Pete on the shoulder for emphasis.

"Ain't my fault, Miss Lorraine," Mary whines, seeing my distressed expression. "Ain't my fault that Rosie Cooke's a crybaby."

"Oh, shut up your big mouth, Mary Joseph," I snap despite myself. And then I give that poor, mangled Barbie doll a kick hard enough to match Rosie's and march myself right out of the room.

Rosie's lying flat on her cot, facedown, her head dangling right over the edge. She's wearing a pair of blue jeans at least two sizes too big, and they bunch up at her hips, leaving white and red cowboy underwear exposed. I look closer and notice the cowboys each ride different colored horses and that they all raise tiny rifles in one hand.

"Hey, where didya get the cowboy panties, Rosie? That's pretty neat underwear." She doesn't say nothing, but quickly reaches backward and pulls the pants up to her waist.

I sit down next to her.

"Don't mean to hurt your feelings, Rosie," I say. "Sorry if I make you feel bad." I notice she is drawing a picture with a fat red crayon. Looks to me like she's drawing pictures of some animals, maybe birds.

"But you tell a lie to Mary Joseph," I hear a garbled voice say from the other side of the bed. "I don't have no mom or dad. They both die fishing down Bristol Bay. Long time ago. The water snatches them right up."

My heart wobbles a bit and then settles down.

"That sure ain't fair, is it? Don't seem fair to me at all." I put my hand on her back gently as I can. "I know how you feel, Rosie. I don't got no daddy and that kinda makes me feel real sad."

She puts her crayon down for a minute and raises her head to look at me. Her eyes are all puffy and her skin blotchy and wet.

"You don't got no daddy?"

"Nope."

"Oh." She's quiet for a minute and then suddenly sits herself up. "Well, then why you tell Mary Joseph all that stuff? You don't have a mom or dad neither."

"No, no," I say, trying not to smile. "Everyone has parents. Just that not everyone's parents is alive. Sometimes, things happen. I have a daddy once, long time ago, before I even remember. And you have a mom and dad long time ago too."

She wipes her nose on her sleeve and nods. "Don't

remember their faces, how they even look at all."

I nod and she reaches for my hand. Rosie holds my hand to her cheek for a minute and then kisses it quickly.

I feel my heart bounce loose around my chest until my lungs start to hurt.

"What are you drawing?" I quickly ask her, trying to hold back my own tears. Won't do this child no good to see a professional woman of my stature in tears.

"Oh, nothing." She sighs and then reaches for the paper. "Just a bunch of birds. Different kinda birds."

I look at the picture and smile. Rosie draws five birds in a row, her markings uneven and wobbly. "Do they have names?" I ask.

She nods and points. "Tommy, Sally, Cooke, Thelma, and Dove."

I gasp at the familiar name and look at the Dove bird closely. This bird is different from the others. It has the face of a boy and what looks like wings attached to human shoulders.

"Rosie," I ask slowly, "why does this bird look like a person?"

She shrugs and bounces on the bed. "I dunno," she answers. "I dunno. 'Cause Thelma likes a boy named Dove. She says he's real handsome and real brave. Ain't that a funny name, Lorraine, ain't it funny to have a name like a bird?"

"Rosie"—my heart is pounding faster and faster— "Rosie, are you sure Thelma knows a boy named Dove?" She nods happily and gives me a quick hug.

I hug her back.

And it's not long before I find Thelma reading a book on the receiving home couch. She doesn't look up when I sit down and puts her finger on her place on the paper when I start to talk. I can see she doesn't want to be disturbed. Edgar Kwagley is sitting on a chair next to her counting a mess of change from his wallet.

"Thelma," I say quickly, trying to ignore Edgar's heavy sigh. "I'm sorry to disturb you 'n' all but got a very important question to ask straightaway. I need your help with some information." She nods and I continue.

"I was just talking to Rosie and she says something about this boy you know. Dove. Rosie says you know this guy named Dove from school. Is that true, 'cause I'm trying to find out some stuff about someone with the same name, where he is 'n' all. Where do you meet him? Do you know where he is or where he's from?"

"Who's asking?" Edgar interrupts. "'Cause there ain't no way you're going to get anything bad out of us. Anything bad about him. Hear he's in enough trouble as it is. Do all your friends over at the jail set you up to this? Why don't you mind your own business and leave us alone?"

"You know him too?" I can't believe what I'm hearing and tap both feet on the floor so the rest of my body will keep still. Thelma nods.

"From down Edgecumbe," she says softly. "He's down Edgecumbe for a while last fall. He gets kicked out and I don't hear anything about him since."

"Wait a minute." I take a deep breath and try to avoid screaming out loud. "Do you mean to say that Dove Alexie's at Edgecumbe with the two of you? You mean all this time I could have found out about Dove from you?"

Edgar frowns and Thelma shrugs.

"What the hell," Edgar mutters. "Who cares what you want to know?"

"But we would tell you if you ask." Thelma puts a soft hand on my knee. "And I don't really know him that well at all. Just sat next to him in class and hear about what he does. How he is brave."

"I don't know about brave, but that goddamn kid's got a lot of nerve," Edgar continues. "All us kids down Edgecumbe can't believe what he does."

"What?" I ask quickly. "What does he do?" I see Thelma and Edgar exchange a glance.

"Got to check on Rosie," Thelma says, standing up. "I'll be in the back checking on Rosie."

"He beats up a goddamn asshole gussak teacher." Edgar smiles, leaning right into my face. "He don't take no crap from no one and beats up on this teacher till there ain't hardly nothing left. And then they kick him outa school and send him to jail or reform school. Hear he's in some special school for criminals or in jail somewhere. Who cares—it won't be long till that kid gets hisself free. He ain't about to be locked up anywhere. Not Dove. Not Dove Alexie."

Edgar reaches over and flicks an imaginary particle off his arm. "You don't want to mess with that guy at all, little Miss Receiving Home. And it ain't any of your business what a kid like that does, anyway. Ain't no gussak business of yours at all." He leans back in his chair slowly. "Don't even know Thelma knows about him, her being so quiet and all. Nobody talks about what happens, but we think about that crazy mixed-blood boy every once in a while. He stands up for all of us. Ain't nobody do what that Dove boy does."

So it turns out that Thelma and Edgar really don't know much, don't know much about Dove at all. But it hurts my heart to hear how Dove messes with a teacher, how he hurts someone real bad. Arnie tells me about it before, but I guess I really don't believe him. Always seems to me that there's more to the story than that. But Thelma don't want to talk about it, can't get anything out of her at all, and she ain't never going to really give me the time of day. And anyways, it turns out that neither of them actually know Dove, just run into him once or twice in person. But just as I'm mulling over my new tidbits of information about Dove being at Mt. Edgecumbe, something else happens that almost makes me want to stop searching for Dove or caring about anything else at all.

Rosie leaves. That's all I got to say about that. I really don't feel like saying nothing much more at all.

Turns out that Thelma gets pregnant and is sent back home to Sleetmute, and Rosie, well, Rosie goes to a stupid foster placement in Fairbanks.

Might as well be New York City. Might as well be China.

Who cares? She's just a silly little kid.

I lie on my cot at night, the light from that mean old moon slithering through the window and hitting me hard right between the eyes, my heart squeezed tight, my insides aching so bad that I can't even move, and I don't want to see that lonely, lonely world out there in front of me when I awake. Dove Alexie's all alone and hurting, waiting somewhere by himself, his body longing for some kind human touch, and Rosie Cooke's burying her tiny face in somebody else's arms. She don't even have her own sister to hold her no more.

I feel the entire universe bubble out of control, its moon and planets losing their place. Don't want to get up in the morning. Seems like the whole wide world slowly empties itself out, my very own heart draining right over the edge.

*

The day Thelma and Rosie have to go separate ways, I don't even like to think on that, looks like the whole receiving home crowd is about to break down and cry. Mama's standing at the door, arms crossed over her chest, her head dropped down, and all the other little kids are hanging around, trying not to tear up. The social services lady from Fairbanks is pulling my little Rosie right out of Thelma's shaking arms and I never to hear such a pitiful sound as Rosie's moaning. Like to make your whole heart crumple and break. She's sobbing and trying to hold on to her sister's shirt, making this high-pitched moan that sounds like an animal dying. Thelma's just standing there, frozen, her arms glued to her sides like she can't move, and her skin turns this yellowy white. She don't say nothing; it's as if she's dead.

We all stand around in this half circle, wanting to do something, wanting to hold each other's hands. But no one does nothing; no one says a single word. Even old Edgar Kwagley don't look so good, pacing up and down, hands jammed into pockets, head hanging real low.

"There, there," the social services lady keeps repeating, "there, there." But Rosie keeps wailing and to top everything off, Quimuckta begins to scratch at the door, matching Rosie's cries with his own harrowing howl. Both of them together make my skin crawl, and I do have to admit that my throat gets all choked up and my lower lip might tremble just a smidgen. In fact, after both girls are taken away, I lock myself in the laundry room and have a good cry.

Funny thing, I don't remember crying like that, real hard and long like that, since I was a little kid myself.

Funny thing, who would think that I'd ever find myself sobbing over two pitiful receiving home kids, even if one is the most special little girl ever does find her way to this here earth.

I try to pull myself together, I really do ("Meditate Your Way to Emotional Fitness," *Inner Essence*), but I can't seem to forget the sound of Rosie and Quimuckta wailing together. And I'll never forget the look on Thelma Cooke's frozen face. But there's nothing to be done about it now. Rosie's living up in Fairbanks with her new foster parents and Thelma's sent all the way back to Sleetmute. They say, come a few months, after she gets back her strength, she'll have to finish school at Mt. Edgecumbe again and leave the baby behind. It don't seem right the way things turn out. Don't seem right at all.

Two weeks since Rosie and Thelma leave. I'm sitting on the receiving home couch trying not to think about anything sad. I'm trying to keep my poor, tired old eyes open. My back is hurting and all of my petite fingers is sore from standing in that doggone receiving home kitchen and rolling up about ten thousand halibut fish cake balls for the prison and receiving home kids.

It's almost midnight and Mama's still nowhere to be

found. She usually works the Saturday-night shift so the regular overnight social services lady can get some time off. Mama ordinarily stays at the receiving home all Saturday night until seven the next morning, but tonight she's gotta do a whole mess of sewing and asks me to fill in.

Under ordinary circumstances I would absolutely never spend my precious Saturday night in this here stupid receiving home, but at this particular time, I'm needing a few extra dollars to order me a set of ten-karat gold star-shaped earrings with matching moon-glow necklace choker and anklet bracelet all for just twelve dollars. I saw it myself in the newest Sears catalogue summer insert and know the minute I spy the glossy photo advertisement that I just got to have the very same whole entire set. Mama says that I waste my money on trivial items but there's nothing wrong with trying to raise one's down-in-the-dumps spirits with replicated fine jewelry every once in a while. And I'm definitely in need of some cheering up these days.

Anyway, Mama promises she'll be back by eleven o'clock or midnight at the latest. She gets this big order from one of the teachers up at the school who's getting married and needs a wedding dress made from the new Butterick fall pattern. Mama shows me the picture and I just about roll over and die from jealously 'cause it's so beautiful. The dress is all shiny with puffed satin sleeves and a bodice covered with tiny silver-cased diamonds. The hem's got white netting along the trim, lined with satin and sequin bows. I get a stomachache from thinking hard on that dress and wanting it for my very own self. Or maybe from wanting somebody for myself. Somehow, I know that it ain't the dress making my innards all aquiver, but the idea of finding someone who is special to me, someone who cares and someone I can care for, no matter what.

Oh, well, it's not exactly as if I got any place to wear a fancy gown or any current beau to even get myself hitched up to, for goodness' sake. And believe it or not, I'm beginning to think that my ongoing attraction to the most ornate and beautiful of garments might be just a touch superficial. I even surprise myself, but I do think that it might not be a bad idea to start toning down my outfits a tad. I guess being faced with life's sadnesses starts to change a girl.

Good thing it's summer and still light outside or I might throw in the towel and lay my head right down on the arm of this here torn-up brown vinyl couch. Seems like all I feel like doing is sleeping these days; Mama says that's a sign of someone who's deeply and most certainly sad and depressed. I can feel her keeping a careful eye on me; I can feel her concern. But I just can't seem to do anything about it; I can't seem to shake it and cheer myself up.

I close my eyes at night and see Rosie Cooke's lopsided grin and wonder how she can just disappear. I see Dove Alexie's beat-up face and the loneliness in his eyes. Seems like everyone I learn to care about just ups and vanishes. Even though I try to comfort my own self with beauty treatments and gold trinkets of every kind, nothing really works; nothing's the same anymore. I walk around as if in a fog, of course always fulfilling my professional obligations in a most timely manner, but knowing that extra-special energized spring in my step is missing. If I didn't know better, I'd think that Evelyn Sugarbush puts some nasty, old-time shaman curse on my poor, pathetic, tired life.

I check my watch again. Midnight exactly. Guess Mama musta falled asleep and there's nothing left to do but make myself comfortable and wait on till morning. I must fess up to being just a bit annoyed. But, as much as I hate to bunk myself up for the night, I gotta admit that it's unusual for Mama not to fulfill her responsibilities and she is lookin' a bit peaked these days what with sewing for the wedding and pretty much taking over the receiving home. I make a note to give her one of my oatmeal and evaporated milk customized facials come Saturday.

I start to do a head check but the roster's not on the bulletin board behind the couch and I'm too weak tired to walk all the way around and count little bodies. Seems like everyone's here anyways, 'cepting Edgar Kwagley. He's probably out partying at the pool hall, like usual. I don't got no time for Edgar these days since he don't tell me who is the direct 'cause of Thelma Cooke being sent away. And I know he's sitting on some particularly vital information; I'm not sure how, but I'm absolutely certain he knows all about it. I can hardly believe that a levelheaded girl like Thelma finds herself in that particular kind of personal trouble. I don't even want to think on that.

The receiving home doors is all locked up good and tight so I just take a mighty long stretch and begin my evening calisthenics, starting with touching my toes ten times without bending my knees even a little, but give up after only three touches. No use in overexerting myself when I'm forced to sleep in a new environment and don't have the proper products for my evening cleansing and moisturizing ritual. I sigh and run my tongue across my teeth and wish I could have me just a touch of my favorite Pepsodent spearmint toothpaste. Just as I'm heading for the kitchen to look for an evening snack, I hear a crash at the front door.

"Goddamn it to hell!" someone is yelling from outside the home's front door. "Hey, open the damn door. You can't keep me outside!" The voice is quiet for a minute and then I hear something hit the door hard, maybe a hand or a foot. "Goddamn it to hell, Lorraine, let me in."

Edgar Kwagley. I recognize his voice.

I turn off the front room light so I can't be seen and walk quietly to the door. "Go away, Edgar Kwagley," I say softly, real calm like. "You're gonna wake up all the little kids if you keep yelling that way."

"Who cares if I wake up anybody. Nobody cares. Just open the door 'cause I wanna get some sleep."

I recognize the slur in his voice.

"Go away, Edgar," I say a little louder. "You've been drinking and I'm not going to let you in no matter what. Go away or I'll call the Sleep-Off."

"Don't wanna get picked up by the Sleep-Off. Don't wanna go back there. Come on, will you. Last time at the Sleep-Off, Lucy Sam gets holda my boots and won't even give them back. Lucy Sam, she says, 'My new old man's gonna look sexy in these damn good-looking cowboy boots.' She says, 'I'm gonna get me these here boots for my new old man.' And that Lucy, she won't hand over my god-damn boots. They take 'em right off your feet when you're passed out on one of the cots at the Sleep-Off. Right off your feet when you don't even know." He quiets down for a moment and then starts up again. "Come on, Lorraine, I know you're in there. Give old Edgar a break. I ain't gonna bother you none, just want to lay me down and get some shut-eye. Ain't even got me a bottle, ain't even got a bottle with me. Come on, let ole Edgar in to sleep."

I sigh and open the door a crack. He's leaning against the trailer, head dropped to one side. He looks up and smiles. His face looks greenish, the skin all droopy. For a minute he has the face of an old man.

"Wanna drink?" His breath is sharp and he takes a swig from an empty bottle.

"Thought you don't have nothing with you," I say.

He shrugs. "Got nothin' with me, Lorraine. Why don't you check me over, why don't you see for yourself.

Listen, you gonna let me sleep inside or what?"

I hesitate, then nod.

He smiles and stumbles on by, leaving a small breeze of beer and tobacco behind.

"Now, you make sure to be real quiet," I instruct, closing the door. "Don't you be going around waking up all the babies, or I'll be forced to call Sleep-Off, I absolutely surely will."

He turns around and smiles again. "What ya doing all alone by yourself, Miss Lorraine?" He laughs. "Ain't you got no boyfriend to keep you warm nights?"

I take a deep breath. I see Edgar Kwagley sloshed a few times, but usually in the late afternoon or when there's other folk around. Usually he just passes out on his cot and don't bother no one. But this time it's real late at night and ain't nobody else 'round here at all. I feel my stomach tighten.

"Shut up," I say, turning to face right up to him. "Shut up and go to bed."

"Hey, Lorraine," he says real low, almost a whisper, "why don't you come here for a minute. Now, don't be hurrying away from me none."

He reaches out and touches my elbow and then pulls me to him with both hands. I stiffen and don't say anything for a minute. He smells mixed-up sour and sweet— beer and chewing gum. I push him away.

"Don't you be laying your hands all over me. I ain't some girl over at that there pool hall." He laughs. I notice his eyes look half closed, the pupils wobbling.

"They're not coming back," Edgar Kwagley says suddenly. "My daddy, John Moran, my aunties, my sisters, Thelma Cooke, they all ain't coming back to me."

I hold my breath.

He looks at me, for a minute his eyes all still.

"I know, Edgar," I finally say softly. "I know about that."

"Hey, Lorraine." He smiles suddenly. "Come on over here, why don't you. Ain't you lonely with no man of your own? You can't tell me you ain't lonely with no man around."

I stand completely still. He moves his own self up to me and then pulls me close again. His shirt is rough against my face and I inhale his mixed-up smells and close my eyes. My head is drawn tight to his chest. I can almost hear his heart beat. I can feel his muscles flutter.

He pulls his head back and looks down at me, his arms still tight around my waist, our chests pressed together. I look right into his black eyes. Neither of us blinks. He sighs and bends down his head. His lips brush mine and then I feel his tongue push inside my mouth. Real cold and wet, it feels like some kinda wet, floppy fish gone all squirmy in my mouth. Edgar pushes his tongue hard in and out, even along my cheeks and chin, and I try to figure what the heck to do. No one ever gives me a tongue kiss before; in fact, no boy ever gives me any kind of real kiss at all and I'm not exactly favorably impressed. I feel the prickle of saliva drying all over my cheeks and chin.

My whole entire body starts to buzz and I feel my face burn.

"Come on," he whispers in my ear. "Come on back inside with me. I know how to make you feel real good. You'll see. Come with me back inside. Let me show you how to feel good."

And then it's as if I suddenly wake up and come back to life. I push him away and wipe off my mouth.

"Ah, Lorraine," he says weakly, stumbling backward. "Ain't you even gonna come back inside and lay with me just for a little while?"

I look down at my feet. I notice that my green velveteen slippers with tartan plaid lining are torn at the seams. I can hardly believe it, but I want to lay myself right down on that narrow little bed and put my head on Edgar Kwagley's square shoulder. I'm not so sure about the kissing part 'n' all, but it seems that the rest would be fine. Just laying and hugging sleepy in the quiet dark. Missing Thelma and Rosie together. But before I look up to say anything at all, he is already walking away, his head down and muttering to himself, almost as if he's walking in his sleep.

"They never does come back," I hear him mumble under his breath. "Them peoples, they leave for good. And they never gonna even come back to me at all."

I wipe my mouth again and hug my chest. The front door blows open slowly, but there ain't nothing there but a little bit of night full of big, empty shadow.

# ANNETTE WEINLAND

*Bethel, Alaska*
*Summer 1969*

The Anchorage Westbard Hotel is dark and I stand in the threshold for a long moment, my eyes stinging with heavy ribbons of smoke, my back aching from sitting crammed in between two brawny pipeline workers on a crowded Wein Air Alaska flight all the way from Bethel. I squint and notice that the room is long and narrow: a small, rectangular dance floor up front surrounded by microphones, a set of drums, and a curved mahogany bar at one end of the room, the other filled with small, round tables. It seems as if each and every table is full. There is barely any room to move; the noise, the chatter of voices are deafening, and I suddenly feel the urge to turn around and head right to the door. What am I doing here, anyway, a minister's daughter alone in a big city, far from home in a room full of music and smoke and liquor?

It's the first time I have ever defied my father.

But since my brothers are safe back in Bethel with the

neighbors, and Father has refused my phone calls to his office, I'm determined not to worry about anything and try to concentrate all of my attention on finding answers to some of my questions. I grip the wall, steadying myself, while surveying the faces in front of me. An enormous man with a protruding potbelly, blond beard, and dark eyebrows pushes by, his striped shirt hanging out of his pants and his red suspenders falling from both shoulders. I step away as a small Japanese woman in a white gauze blouse scurries after him, holding a bottle in front of her like a torch in the darkness, and I try to scan the faces at the bar.

My eyes move across the dance floor to the tables, looking at a blur of strangers, Native, Asian, Caucasian, young and old, some standing, some sitting, all drinking. A tall, dark woman waves one hand above her head and then falls suddenly into the arms of a soldier standing nearby. He is short and thin; he laughs and kisses her full on the mouth. I look away, embarrassed, and hear a woman behind me giggle. There's a loud crash. Someone has tipped over a whole table, and a small crowd of waitresses and busboys appears with mops and brooms. They huddle together like schoolchildren on a crowded playground.

And then suddenly I see him. In the shadows of hunched figures and smoke, a tall man slowly stands and motions to me. His wide marshal's hat is on the table and his badge flickers on his chest; it shines a path through the hazy smoke as I slowly wind my way along the maze of tables, tripping on someone's foot, knocking into the back of a chair, holding my arms across my chest as if in battle. He smiles and extends a hand to steady me.

"There, there, Miss Weinland." His voice is deep and guttural, coarse, just a little slurred. "Watch where you're going. Don't look like you're used to meeting up in a drinking hole like this. How old are you now, anyway? I guess I should have thought of that before inviting you to get together with me here, your being the minister's daughter and all. But your message sounded important, seemed like you need to see me straight off, tonight. Can hardly ignore the call of a lady in distress. So cheers to the lady and cheers to distress."

He chuckles to himself and pours a drink without sitting down. I watch, somehow fascinated, as the glass is drained, and look up, trying to study the imposing profile of a lawman.

The marshal is out of town more often than not, and I realize I have never really met him face-to-face before, but have only caught glimpses from afar. Every once in a while, I'll notice his lanky frame lumbering up to the Bethel jail, always a cigarette in hand, usually his large hat in the other. Sometimes we'll bump into each other shopping for groceries at Northern Commercial, but I don't believe that we've ever stopped to talk. I don't think we have ever acknowledged one another's presence, and I'm a little surprised that he recognizes me now.

Close up, he's much taller than expected, but lean and wiry as I remember, his torso long, his chest broad yet somewhat concave, his wide, thin shoulders hunched forward as if uncertain. And his face, a face I don't remember at all, barely having spent a moment talking to him in the past, startles me. It's thin and long, deeply tanned, almost burnished, his ears burned red and his skin pleated with lines, some light scratches and others creased long and deep. It's the sun-nicked face of a hunter, someone who spends long hours outside, probably in the far north. While Bethel remains overcast and rainy during the summer, they say that the Arctic interior simmers with brutal July and August heat. Every once in a while, town residents join expeditions to hunt bear or simply explore the miles of exposed wilderness, but I've heard that the marshal likes to camp way out in the wild, in the deep interior north of Mt. McKinley Park, and even do some mountain climbing. Folks around town talk of the dangers, of his foolishness. Why put oneself at risk? Some say he just went a little crazy once his young wife left him several years back, but I know from my personal experience it's not wise to listen to gossip; there's always someone willing to talk about someone else's troubles. It's one of the consequences of small-town life.

The marshal smiles at me again and the lines in his skin crack open, making his face look like it hurts: a long river at break-up slit open wide. He is older than I remember, maybe forty-five or even fifty.

"Miss Weinland?" He reaches behind me to pull out the chair and I see the back of his neck, burned red, where it meets the white untouched skin under his shirt. A familiar scent drifts toward me: smoke, singed kindling, burned embers from an outdoor fire. He sits down across from me, swinging his long legs over the chair, and pours another drink into the shot glass. His light-brown hair is thin and graying, but tousled, boyish. He pushes it off his damp forehead with a wide, unsteady hand.

"I'd offer you one, Miss," he says slowly, staring down at the glass and rubbing its rim with one finger, "but don't imagine you're the drinking kind."

I shake my head, somehow mesmerized by the gold glow of liquid in front of me, his broad, thickly grooved hand holding the delicate oval of glass.

"Thank you anyway." My voice sounds high, shaky, the voice of a little girl, and I clear my throat. "Listen, Marshal Nicholsen," I begin slowly. "I'm really sorry to impose on you like this, I know that it's very sudden and unusual. . . . I'm sorry to bother you in the middle of your conference and all, but as I said on the phone, it's very important that I talk to you immediately."

He laughs and lifts his glass to his lips. The gold disappears in one gulp, and he wipes his mouth with the back of his hand.

"I wouldn't worry about that, Miss." He smiles. "It ain't as if I'm busy with meetings this time of night. And you know"—he smiles again and leans forward just a bit—"there really ain't a whole bushel of work I've been doing lately, anyway. It ain't as if anything of any real meaning really ever gets done in these here conferences. Why, it's one meeting after another, mostly just a bunch of corrupt old men who are too big for their own britches, talking a lot of bull crap and needing an excuse to get away from home. And God only knows, I've been spending my whole summer listening to plenty of their shit."

I flinch, and he sighs.

"Hey, I'm sorry. I apologize, I really do. . . . That's just the way I've been raised to talk, kinda rough, and always hanging around these law-enforcement types, well, they're not the most refined of company." He laughs sarcastically. "But guess that cursing like a sailor ain't hardly the kind of language a young lady like yourself's been weaned on." He pulls out a toothpick from his front pocket and unwraps it slowly and then pops it suddenly into his mouth. "You and your family's from the big city, ain't that right? I remember your daddy saying something about that."

He leans back and stares at me, his arms spread out on the small table in front of him as if holding it in place. I realize that he's a more than a little tipsy. His reputation as a drunk comes back to me, and I shift in my chair.

"Marshal," I begin again, "I want to talk to you about

something important, something that you ought to know." I look down at my hands and see that they are shaking. "This isn't easy for me," I hear myself say, my voice drifting off into clatter around me. My flesh prickles cold, my skin along both arms gathers itself together, tightening. "And I'm not sure if I should even be here at all. But I've been meaning to get in touch with you for a long time now, only never could work up the courage. . . . I'm only sorry that it wasn't sooner."

I lose my breath and hear his chair scrape the floor and he is suddenly sitting next to me, his rough hand over my cold one.

"It's okay," he whispers.

Someone sets another glass on the table and grazes my back with a sharp elbow. I lower my head further and try to inhale slowly. My body bubbles with freezing water and I feel myself shake. I breathe carefully, but only tremble faster and faster until I bite my lip hard, anything to stop. If only I could disappear out of this room, right now— anything to disappear—and in horror see my own tears puddling on the back of his broad hand. For a moment I think of the flat tundra's back filling up with small ponds and lakes, and I picture Bethel. I am overcome with homesickness and nausea. This is a nightmare, a bad dream. Why am I not back in my small Bethel house with my four brothers? I yearn for the familiar—the babies, even my father. Home.

"Here, drink this." A glass appears in front of me and I shake my head. "Just a sip," he says. "You'll see. It'll make you feel better. Never failed me yet, I'm sorry to say."

I shake my head again but hold my hand unsteadily around his as we tip back the glass together. A small sip and then another. My mouth warms and my tongue thickens.

"Better?" he asks softly.

I nod.

"Good." He leans back and looks at me, his brow furrowed, his eyes silvery, kind. "Seems like you have something worrying you might bad, young lady. . . ."

I feel myself start to shake again.

"Hey, now, hey . . . don't be starting that again." His voice is hoarse. "Here," he continues, "let's just let things be for a second, maybe that'll make it easier. Give yourself some room to breathe. We got all evening, don't we, 'less you have some place you got to go."

I shake my head, too embarrassed to look up, and take another slow sip. The liquor slithers down my throat, giving me air and slowly clearing a path to breathe.

"Listen," I say quietly, keeping my eyes down, "I am so sorry, Marshal Nicholsen, I really am. I'm so sorry to bother you, but I really think this is a mistake, that I've made a big mistake coming here. This just isn't right. I'd like to forget about all of this, if it's all the same to you. Please. Can we just forget about all of this now?"

He doesn't say anything for a moment and I hear him

rustle in his pocket. Out of the corner of my eye I see a thin cigarette rolled between his thick fingers, the filmy edge of transparent paper licked. I notice his teeth are slightly crooked and chipped. He lights up and inhales slowly, a fleck of tobacco sticking to his lower lip. I start to stand but my knees are wobbly and I sit down again.

"So," I continue, "let's just forget about this, if that's all right with you. I really don't know what's come over me anyhow, just silliness, that's all it is. I do need to get back home to my brothers first thing in the morning, so I think I should make it an early night. And I do thank you for your time, Marshal, for taking this time and everything. But I should be going now. I need to go right now."

I stand up again and he stands up next to me, extending a hand. His long fingers are stained with nicotine, his skin chapped, leathery against mine.

"Anything you say, Miss." The handshake is warm and firm. "You're quite a young woman, Miss Weinland, to have come this far, and I know you'll make what's wrong right. But if there's anything I can do . . ."

The air swells around me, the liquor making me dizzy, and I look up into his face. His eyes deepen, darken. I hear the music begin again and someone begins to sing: *"Good morning, starshine, the earth says hello. . . ."* My eyes suddenly fill up with tears again and somehow, I find my way out of the warm, smoky, unfamiliar room.

✳

I wake up suddenly, startled, not sure of where I am. My head throbs with a piercing, unfamiliar pain. The room is pitch-black except for a red glow on the wall, and I hug myself. I blink and feel immediately claustrophobic, locked up in the dark, as if in one of the dank Bethel jail cells, but then the black turns bottomless and I reach out in the blank space as if attempting to find a reference point, something tangible. I grope around wildly, trying to make sense of the incomprehensible.

The immense void only deepens.

Terrified, I breathe slowly so as not to hyperventilate, and concentrate on the small red blaze floating in front of me. My eyes sting, as if irritated by smoke, and I blink again. The blaze sizzles, its form slowly reconfiguring, then sputters, shrinking into shape. I close my eyes and then open them again quickly. Four recognizable letters: E-X-I-T.

The hotel. Now I remember why I am here.

I reach to turn on the light and look at the time. Midnight. My headache worsens and I wonder if the hotel store would still be open and if they carry aspirin. Staggering, I reach for my sweater and knock over a small basket of toiletries on the bed stand. White bottles wrapped in plastic tip over and a small note flutters to the floor: "Your Maid Today: July 20, 1969—Astral Hughes. The Anchorage Westbard Hotel Housekeeping Staff Wishes

You a Pleasant Stay and a Memorable Journey." The bottles roll back and forth at my feet—shampoo, conditioner, moisturizing lotion—and a transparent shower cap crackles under my toes. A small globe of soap is wrapped in silver paper, pleated at the center and tied with a narrow golden ribbon. I turn as a miniature sewing kit slips to the floor. Tiny needles jingle, then divide: filaments of light scattered over the cold, dark floor.

I quickly pull the sweater over my head and feel it scratch against my skin; I imagine my chest suddenly discolored, tattooed with delicate, translucent scrapes and engravings.

My flesh tingles, a spreading firmament of illuminated scars.

No bra, no socks, no hose. What would Father think? All of his law, rules, and regulations about how to dress, how to act, what to say . . . I see him standing before me in the front room, his arms crossed, his mouth pursed, his words slow and even. "Annette," he would say, sighing, sucking in the air as if tasting something sour, "what is that you are wearing? What were you thinking of, that unbecoming sweater and your hair uncombed? Go fix yourself up and remember, you are still and always the minister's daughter."

I smile to myself and spin around twice, the cool air filling up the inside of my skirt so that I am moving forward with barely any effort at all.

✳

It's strange to stand in an empty elevator at midnight, not really even knowing where I'm going. The doors open quickly and a couple in evening dress smile at me from the dusky corridor, faces bright, eyes shining, their slender arms flung around each other's shoulders, as if preparing to suddenly leap forward. Both barely older than eighteen or nineteen, they suddenly embrace. The elevator closes without them and I see their vivid image become smaller and smaller until it is only a bright wedge of color between the drab metal doors. Another jolt and the chipped doors creak open once more, the glare from the lobby's fluorescent lights making my head ache all over again.

A whole new universe: a bustling, vital world at night.

Not exactly used to after-hours life, I am totally unfamiliar with the phenomenon of nighttime activity and feel suddenly uneasy. At this very moment, my own household back in Bethel is asleep, dead to the world by eight o'clock each evening, all of our doors locked, all of the lights out. One of the many fixed, unnegotiable rules of the home. Once again I am struck with how much of the world I have missed, fear robbing me blind.

I blink and rub my eyes, as if from a long sleep, suddenly waking to discover an unexplored continent, the underside of the planet earth. I drift into the lobby and am surprised by the crowd, everything lit up as if in daytime, people congregating by the registration desk and crowding by the one television set. I crane my neck but am unable to see the screen.

There are signs to the lobby store one level below and I follow them down the enclosed stairway. The clerk smiles at me, a middle-aged Yup'ik woman, chewing gum, wearing a red calico *kuspuck* and watching television behind the counter. A purple and gold scarf is tied loosely around her neck and long, silver, beaded earrings graze her shoulders. She wears a large gold button: "Give Peace a Chance."

"Need any help?" she asks, eyes glued to the television. "Aspirin?"

She points behind me without moving her eyes and I survey the wealth of merchandise in front of me, amazed. A rack of magazines and newspapers lines one wall with a display of colorful bumper stickers above: "Alaska, the last Frontier," "Alaska—Land of the Midnight Sun," "Barrow—Come to the Top of the World." And postcards: Anchorage, Juneau, Fairbanks, Sitka, Prudhoe Bay, the Alaska Marine Highway Ferry.

I turn around and see an amazing assortment of cellophane packages lining a long glass shelf: Souvenir of Alaska—Authentic Moose Cakes, soft dolls dressed in white rabbit fur, tan skin shoes in every size. To my right, five white mugs covered with gold and black maps of the state rattle as I pass, and black vinyl wallets embroidered with the Alaskan state flower, forget-me-not, fill an open cardboard box. My eyes move to a basket of brochures offering tours: Glacier Park, Skagway, Haines, Earthquake Park. I pick up the Earthquake Park pamphlet and finger it absently: "Make the time to visit the site of Anchorage's destruction, left exactly the way it was on that fateful day in 1964."

"Earthquake Park?" I turn to the clerk. "Can you tell me where it is?"

"Oh, yeah." She turns the television's volume up and unwraps a new stick of gum. "Just three blocks down the street from the hotel. Take a left at the side entrance, go down two blocks, and then a left by the new McDonald's. Can't miss it. Jeez," she says suddenly. "Will you look at that. Who woulda thought."

I cross the aisle to the counter and look at the television. The picture is grainy, but two figures covered in white float over what looks like an American flag. I grip the counter. I had forgotten. I missed the original broadcast hours before, so I am relieved to have a second chance.

"Houston." I hear a faint voice from afar. "Tranquility Base here. The Eagle has landed."

I hold my breath.

"Eagle, we copy you on the ground. You've got a bunch of guys about to turn blue. We're breathing again. Thanks a lot."

The clerk turns to me. I see her eyes fill with tears and her mascara slides down her rouged cheeks, two tiny black

274

avalanches. Her mouth opens and closes. I hold out my hand and she squeezes it hard.

When he opens the door, I can see that I have awakened him. One arm leans on the door frame, the other across his face, his eyes. He nods and opens the door wide.

His room is smaller than mine, the bed pushed against one wall and the bureau set at the end like a footboard. I notice a glass, a bottle of whiskey, and his badge, a small star, shimmering on the edge of a mirror-topped bed stand.

"Have a seat." He motions to a flowered chair.

I shake my head.

"I'm sorry to intrude, Marshal Nicholsen," I begin, "but it's time I talk to you about what's on my mind." He nods and motions me to sit again, but I don't move.

"It's Arnie," I continue, my voice quavering, my own breath tasting acrid and bitter. "He's kept a young boy behind bars, and he's hurt him. I know, I saw the whole thing."

The marshal doesn't say anything for a moment, then sighs heavily, rubbing his long, ropy arms. He is wearing a pair of gray sweatpants with a blue insignia—Alaska Department of Corrections—and a white T-shirt exposing skin burned dark past the elbows, then pale white.

"Miss Annette," he says slowly, rubbing both arms as if cold, "exactly what is it that you're talking about?

Something happen tonight? You all right?"

"No, no, I'm fine." I rub my temples, suddenly over-whelmed by the relentless pain. "Nothing has happened here, Marshal Nicholsen, nothing tonight. I'm talking about Bethel, about the Bethel jail and about Arnie Hanger, your assistant marshal."

"Arnie, ah . . ." He hesitates for a minute and then sits down at the edge of the bed. "Arnie from home? What's he done now? Still can't believe he ups and leaves town without proper notice."

"I think he's hurt someone, a young boy." The words slip out easily and I steady myself on the chair. "Please, I need you to help me with something. I need you to help find someone Arnie hurt before he left town. I know I should have come to you sooner, and it may just be too late now. But if there's anything at all I can do to help now, I want to know that I've done the right thing. It's important for me to do what's right. I need to help find this boy to put my own mind at rest."

Suddenly Lorraine Hobbs's bright, freckled face flashes in front of me and I feel a new urgency to find her young mysterious friend. "Some sixteen-year-old who Arnie locked up and hurt, someone who seems to have disappeared right off the face of the earth. One day he was up at the jail and the next he was gone."

"This don't have nothing to do with that Hobbs girl, does it? I seem to remember her name mentioned in some

276

letter from the council." He scratches his head and grins. "'Cause if it does, I wouldn't pay no nevermind. Why, that little child's full of all kinds of tall tales and stories and shenanigans.'"

"You don't believe her?"

He shrugs and reaches for a cigarette.

"It ain't that I don't believe her," he replies. "It's just that I'm gonna need a lot more solid information before using up the taxpayers' money to hunt down some imaginary lost boy. Seem to remember something about the town council advising her to stop writing them falsified correspondence. Now this young Lorraine Hobbs"—he sighs—"well, she's the perfect example of a child ready to dream up some story just to get a little attention for herself, just to get some kind of notice."

I take a deep breath. I feel myself getting angry.

"What makes you think little Lorraine has something real and concrete?" he continues. "What makes you think that there ever is such a sixteen-year-old boy in the first place?"

"I think I saw him myself. One Tuesday up at the jail. The very first day Arnie brought him in. Of course, I don't know for sure, but I think that I might have seen that same boy Lorraine has been talking about."

"Couldn't be. How do you know it's the very same child? What's his name anyway? Doug, Dove . . . I seem to remember his name from the letter."

"Alexie."

"Yeah, that's it. Dove Alexie. Thought that young Lorraine girl made up that crazy name all by herself." He almost chuckles.

"But the point is"—I hear my voice rising—"she didn't. She didn't make up the name and she didn't make up the boy. I think I saw the boy myself, and he looked as though he had been beaten up by someone pretty bad."

"Wait a minute—let me think a minute now." He stands up suddenly, hands to his forehead. "Christ, that's right. Of course, what an idiot. I don't know why I didn't think about this before."

"Think of what?" I lean toward him.

"Annette." He turns and sits down again. "Two weeks ago when I was back in town, old Sara Oscar bangs on the prison door and starts jabbering about a beating, about seeing a beating of some boy back some time ago in April. Said she couldn't report it before 'cause I was out of town and she didn't know where else to go. She's yelling about the jail and Arnie, talking real fast, and I gotta admit that I might have just been nursing a beer or two. So my memory's not great on the subject, but I think I took some notes. I know I took down some notes for a formal report even though I wasn't exactly sure what in the hell she was talking about."

"Do you think it's the same boy?"

"Could be. You never know." He's kneeling on the floor by a battered canvas knapsack and tossing piles of crushed papers into the air. A leather flask, two small decks of cards, and a rusted pocketknife all roll to the floor. He turns around and sighs. I hear him curse softly under his breath.

"Not there?"

He shakes his head and fingers the papers piled around him. "Don't that figure?" he says, almost to himself. "The one time I might could actually help." He stands and shakes his head again.

"Look," I say, bending to help gather the papers on the floor. "It's okay; don't worry. It's really not your fault. And the fact that you remember what Sara had to say, that you think it's the same boy, well, that makes a big difference. I can't wait to tell Lorraine and imagine she'll be pretty happy to know that somebody else saw something."

I try to neaten the papers in my hands and one yellow slip floats to the floor.

"Hey, wait a minute." He extends a long arm to catch it midair. "Hey, wait, this might be the very thing that I'm looking for, the notes from that afternoon. Thought I had them somewhere."

I feel my throat tighten.

"You're sure?"

"Wait." He sits down on the bed again, his hand raised

as if asking for silence. Suddenly his face breaks into a smile and he hands the paper to me. "Yes, I'm sure. It's all here."

I look down at the notes in my hand. They are written in black ink, his handwriting surprisingly small, surprisingly neat:

7/5/69
Bethel: 5:30 P.M.
Bethel resident Sara Elvira Oscar, 81, makes a report regarding a beating that allegedly took place on 4/30/69 at approximately 8:30 A.M.
Alleged victim was male, approximately fifteen to twenty years old, average to large.
Height: around 6'.
Race: unknown.
Build: average to large.
Source extremely agitated. Claims that "someone from the Bethel jail" was beating alleged victim with long iron pipe or some other blunt instrument.
Alleged perpetrator: male, approximately 30–35 years old.
Hair: light brown.
Build: average, muscular.
Height: around 5'10".
Race: Caucasian.

I hand the paper back. "Good." I smile and notice the pain in my head has suddenly disappeared. "This is just what I need. I mean, it's nothing definite, but at least we have a beginning, a real lead, finally something tangible. At least we know that there is a real boy somewhere and that he's been done some serious harm."

I inhale deeply, and all at once, I understand how important it is to right what is wrong, and notice how I am suddenly steady on my feet, my shoulders level, my head high. I will reveal what is hidden, what needs to be spoken, and instantly know I will never have to turn that tiny jail key and take what is not mine anymore. What I already own is of enough value; I need not sneak and steal ever again.

Marshal Nicholsen smiles back at me and reaches to shake my hand. The silver badge on the small table beside us suddenly flickers, its reflection tripled in the mirror below. For a minute, I think I see the star tremble, then slowly rotate full circle: an interrupted cycle now nearly complete.


Earthquake Park is larger than I imagined and I hold his sleeve to steady myself. He is wearing a light-blue wind-breaker and its nylon fabric is slick against my touch. When the wind around us lifts, I can hear a ghostly whistle, a faint hum.

"Five years ago." The marshal's voice is low but seems to echo in the pale haze. "Good Friday, 1964."

I nod.

"I remember. But it seems so much more recent than that."

We don't say anything then, but stand quietly at the edge of the huge crater, its center churned, the rocks and earth turned inside out, exposed. Everything has a pinkish ash, quivery in the mottled light. I feel myself drawn forward and his arm tightens around me.

"Hey there." He laughs. "Steady."

It must be close to three A.M. but the midnight sun is relentless, dropping its foggy breath, illuminating every hidden crevice, each crack, all fractures of the earth, and the flickering from the new McDonald's behind us casts an eerie neon glow.

"You know they walked on the moon yesterday," I tell him, imagining that distant surface, firm, brand-new. "Can you believe it? I saw it myself on TV."

He doesn't say anything then, but kneels down, taking a fistful of luminous dust in his hand.

"I read somewhere," he says, as if my own words were never heard, "that no one, no scientist, no one at all, has ever been able to account for the deep mysteries of space or the force of gravity, the shape of the world. Don't that make you wonder, don't that make you think about it all? Why, look at this here in front of us, the whole earth flipped all the way upside down and nothing to explain exactly why. Another inexplicable law of nature, that just when things seem settled, something happens to rip it all apart all over again. No one really knows exactly what causes an earthquake, do they, but some think it begins with slight tremors that turn violent, that most come from stresses built up way down deep inside, below."

"I thought earthquakes and floods are caused by comets." I try to remember my science books from long ago. "And that comets were formed at the same time as the sun and all the planets, but that most of them just float directionless, the uncontrollable, unpredictable 'exiled children of the solar system' that wander in the freezing outer regions of space. I heard that somewhere. Comets are supposed to hover somewhere in the most remote, desolate spots behind the planets, easy to forget. I remember now. That the earth's oceans were originally formed by their falling, the comets' crashing below. Not exactly according to the Bible."

He smiles.

I continue slowly, the text of my schoolbooks suddenly flashing before me like photographs. "Every once in a while, the gravity from passing stars pulls on an unsuspecting comet until it is finally sent flying out from its isolated place in space into orbit around the sun. Most stay in orbit, but every once in a while, one will escape and hurl itself toward us. Maybe that's the real cause of earthquakes. At least that's the way I think it works." Suddenly I feel somehow embarrassed. "But I'm not really sure. Think that's what I remember from my studies. Funny, what you remember and when it all comes back to you."

I close my eyes and feel myself suddenly jolted into space. My eyelids tremble, a single, diaphanous tail of light arches in the dark, behind the void between my pupils and their fluttering, incandescent lids. My eyes fly open. The earth rumbles and a turbulent expanse of deep-sky planets vibrates above, then below, quickly exchanging position.

I lose my breath. My heart beats faster as if I had been running.

A harmonic cluster of stars from beneath glows.

The marshal sighs and looks up.

The wind picks up, the dust blows white, then dark purple. The earth's mantle raises its broad shoulders around us, the crust settles; we await fortification of the core.

# PART
# FIVE

*"The human life in the North
is like that illumination the moon is casting.
The . . . tenderness of the relationships
[is] such a bright source of comfort
that the long winter does not seem
too cold to us, or too dark."*

—Sally Carrighar,
*Moonlight at Midday*

# LORRAINE HOBBS

*Bethel, Alaska*
*Fall 1969*

After Rosie and Thelma leave, seems like I begin noticing how many kids really do have it hard, have no special place to ever go, how they never do get to even stay anywhere very long at all. Can't really imagine what it feels like to be moved around like that, to have no place to call your own. Over the short time I work at the receiving home, lots of the children I get to know are sent away and a bunch of new ones appear before you can say boo. 'Course Rosie and Thelma's leaving's bad enough by itself, but it's really just the tip of the iceberg, to tell the honest truth. Mary Joseph goes to a foster family up Kotzebue, Amanda Edwards to some missionaries down by Dillingham, and Eleanor Paul to Sitka, where she'll be living with some teacher from the college. Lots of others too, seems like so many, I can't even remember them all, and that's pretty piti-ful when you take the time to consider them kids is people, just like you and me. Seems like no one ever remembers them, remembers who they is and where they're from.

Soon it's time for the high school kids to start packing up to go back to Mt. Edgecumbe, and I feel kinda sad when I see old Edgar putting his things in his ragged duffle bag. Edgar and me, we never do talk about that night he comes in all liquored up—it's almost as if nothing even ever happened. Strange, as I watch him getting his stuff together, strange to think just a few days ago, he's holding me close in his arms, he even lets me know how his heart hurts. Doesn't make much sense, but when Edgar starts with his packing up, I don't know, something makes my stomach feel funny even then. I try to catch his eye to ask if he needs any help getting his belongings together, kinda hang around him, trying to say good-bye, but he ain't got no use for the likes of me.

Mama says I'm starting to have feelings for these here orphans. She thinks I'm starting to grow up and think of others instead of always studying on myself. I don't know about that. I do know, though, that it sure is easier not to be bothered; it's easier when your heart ain't always about to turn over completely upside down.

But of course those snots, Jimmy Pete and Evelyn Sugarbush, don't get sent nowhere at all. Don't get sent to Mt. Edgecumbe until the spring; something about age and grade. Just my luck. Doesn't it figure that the very two brats give me the most trouble stay right where they are, ready to bug me any given moment.

"Where'd ya get the outfit?" Jimmy Pete'll say as I'm cooking up some Fancy Fruit Salad with crumbled Nabisco vanilla wafers for extra crunch. "You look like you come right out of a real-live circus."

"Yeah?" I'll be sure to snap right back. "And when's the last time a slob like you actually goes to the circus? I'll bet my new black and white paisley culottes that you never go to any real live circus at all."

"Oh yeah?" he'll say, looking down.

"Yeah," I'll answer.

And then we'll both stare evil into each other's eyes until one or the other gets tired and just moves on along.

Then that Evelyn girl, she's even worse. She may be smart and know a bunch about them stars and planets, but that ain't no excuse for a poor, snotty attitude. And always pretending to zap me with some magic curse, as if I believe any of that mumbo jumbo.

"Watch out," she hisses right into my poor ear. "You watch your step, Miss Fancy-Pants Lorraine Hobbs, or I'll work on a curse you'll never forget."

Those two nasty kids just hook up together real good and set their minds to torturing me every second of their stupid lives.

One afternoon, when I'm sticking new powder-blue shelving paper on the receiving home entry way floor to cover them old, ugly cracks, I hear Evelyn Sugarbush and

289

Jimmy Pete having a mighty peculiar conversation over a game of checkers. My ears perk up real good, but I pretend not to notice and keep trying to fit that doggone sticky paper over the chewed-up parts of the linoleum floor.

"Remember that guy reading dirty magazines the day we go up to visit the jail?"

"What guy?" I notice Jimmy's staring long and hard at the board. As far as I can tell, that boy never beats the likes of Evelyn yet, and they play that dang game morning and night.

"You know." Evelyn crowns a king without even skipping a beat. "That sleazy guy sitting at the desk reading magazines? The one who throws us out that day."

"Oh, him." Jimmy starts to move a black piece and then changes his mind.

"Hurry up, Jimmy." Evelyn sighs. "You're taking forever each time it's your turn."

"Am not." He slowly moves his black checker, only to be double jumped by Evelyn's red one.

"Well, I read in the paper that he gets himself killed up Prudhoe Bay. Just last week. Is in some kinda drunken brawl and ends up hitting his stupid gussak head real hard on the floor. Dead as a doorknob. The guy who decks him gets hauled off to jail."

Jimmy takes his eyes off the board and sits up straight.

"Killed?" he whispers, eyes wide. "You sure? How do you know something like that?"

290

"I just told you, dummy. Read it in the *Kuskokwim Kronicle* this morning. Here, look for yourself." Evelyn walks by me and snatches Mama's paper right off the couch. "Lookee here," Evelyn says to Jimmy, acting like I'm not even in the same room. "Here's the article. Even a photograph of that sorry excuse for a gussak."

I can't resist turning around. "Hey," I finally say, "hey, let me look at that."

Evelyn and Jimmy both stare at me.

"You don't need to look at nothing," Evelyn says, handing the paper over to Jimmy. "Why don't you mind your own business, anyway?"

"It's not even your paper." I start to burn up mad. I feel my heart start to beat real fast and my face go all hot and red. "That's Mama's *Kuskokwim Kronicle*, and you have no business looking at it without her personal permission."

"Well, that goes to show you, Miss Goody Two-Shoes. I do have permission. Mrs. Hobbs tells me I can read it any time I like. She says she admires a young girl like me being so interested in current events."

I look at Evelyn suspiciously. It does seem strange that a crazy Yup'ik like her would take the time to read the newspaper. Or even understand it, for that matter. Evelyn's the same age as me and I never look at anything but the *Kronicle*'s fashion column. And that amounts to a monthly article by Edna Frank on what refreshments the school board serves at the Christmas assembly. I must say that I'm kinda impressed that old Evelyn reads the newspaper every day, that she even wants to. Even so, I'm not sure I want to mess with the likes of her, shaman or no shaman curse.

"Just let me see it for a minute," I finally say. "I know that Arnie guy real well. You say he got hisself killed dead?"

"That's the only way to get killed these days," Evelyn sneers. "Never hear of anyone killed up alive."

"Shut up." I'm getting sick of this girl's nasty mouth. "I mean it. Let me see the article. It's important."

"Take it easy, why don't you." Evelyn throws the paper at my feet and I pick it up, my hands shaking. It's a picture of Arnie, all right, him wearing some old T-shirt says "White Lightenin'" and a familiar grin spread over his big ole face. Underneath, a short article reads:

# Late-Night Brawl Ends in Tragedy

By Steven Roberts
KUSKOKWIM KRONICLE EDITOR-IN-CHIEF AND STAFF WRITER

**SEPTEMBER 15**. Like many others living and working in the often lawless Prudoe Bay camp, Arnie Hanger, 31, Bethel's former second assistant to the U.S. marshal, lost his life Saturday night in an unprovoked brawl that took place in the camp recreation room. According to Sam Phillips, camp supervisor, Hanger had been drinking and accosted Martin Kurtz, 42, of

Kotzebue, Alaska. "Never witnessed anything quite like it," Mr. Phillips is quoted as saying. "One minute, everyone's standing around, playing a friendly game of pool, and all of a sudden, this crazy Hanger guy jumps Kurtz from behind. I've seen this kind of cabin fever time and again," Phillips continued. "Some folks can't handle being isolated way up here in the interior for so long, left face-to-face with themselves. Some just don't have the inner strength."

According to witnesses, Hanger grabbed Kurtz by the neck, initiating a fistfight that ended in approximately $5,000 worth of damage and with Hanger dead. Kurtz has been arrested on charges of involuntary manslaughter and is being held on $20,000 bond at the Prudhoe Bay Detention Center.

Funeral arrangements for Hanger are being made by next of kin in Carthage, South Dakota, birthplace of the deceased. Longtime Bethel residents are shocked by Hanger's death, remembering him as a diligent worker and responsible citizen. "Arnie Hanger was a committed law-enforcement officer," said Bethel Mayor Everette Plumb Sunday morning. "I have nothing but good to say about this exemplary young man."

"Exemplary, sure," I say to myself, handing the paper back to Evelyn. "Sure is true that you can't believe everything you read."

"You mean you really know that guy good?" Jimmy asks me, his last checker scooped up in Evelyn's skinny hand. "How do you get to be friends with such a jerk?"

"That question should answer itself." Evelyn laughs.

"I had a professional relationship with Arnie this summer," I reply smugly, choosing to ignore her rude and unnecessary comment, "seeing as I'm hired to provide meals—breakfast, lunch, and dinner—for the Bethel prisoners. And he was particularly fond of my Chipped Beef Marinated in Canned Cream of Celery Soup."

"Well," Evelyn says slowly, "then you find yourself working with pure evil."

"Wow," says Jimmy, impressed.

"Why pure evil?" I ask. "Don't you get your facts a little mixed up? Arnie's the one gets hisself knocked off. How do you figure him to be in the wrong?"

Evelyn shrugs. She looks away.

"Evelyn, don't you even hear what I say? How do you figure Arnie to be evil when he's the one gets killed?"

"I don't know," she says softly. "I don't know how I know but I just do. I can tell by looking at his picture, by just hearing his name."

"Give me a break. Surely you don't believe I'm buying that." I try to cough up a little sarcastic laugh, but somehow, my insides feel frozen up cold. Something about the way Evelyn's talking is giving me the authentic, full-blown, heebie-jeebies from head to toe.

"She knows what she's talking about," Jimmy blurts. "Believe me, Evelyn knows what she's saying. She can tell about somebody just from seeing a picture or holding a piece of clothing. No kidding. You know"—he lowers his voice to a whisper—"Evelyn's a shaman."

I don't say nothing but feel a shiver crawl up my spine. I don't believe Evelyn is really a shaman or anything at all, 'cepting for an annoying and obnoxious girl. On the other hand, she does have two different colored eyes and surely does have a creepy way about her.

I watch as she stands up, her hands squeezed together tightly. She don't say nothing but stares, as if deep in thought, out the receiving home window. I stand up behind her and try to see what's so god-awful interesting, but nothing's out there but that doggone, mangy Quimuckta dog whining and pawing at the receiving home door. My spine suddenly tingles again, and I move away from the window right quick, just as if a big bolt of lightning's about to strike its way on through.

"Mama," I say that night as I'm trying to wind my blond hair around extra-large Campbell's soup cans, "do you believe there's such a thing as a person finding out things just from looking? I mean, you know, seeing a picture or holding a piece of clothing. There's a name for it, you know. What's it called?"

"You mean ESP? Extrasensory perception?" Mama's cutting Mr. Samuels's hair with her sewing scissors, and he catches each clump of coarse black hair in his wide hands. I wonder why Mr. Samuels's hair never does turn white. Surely he's old enough.

"Yeah, that's it. Do you believe in such a thing? Seems to me that it's all a bunch of crazy talk. What do you think?"

Mama doesn't say nothing for a minute, concentrating on a particularly troublesome spot on the old man's head. He giggles as she tries to cut behind his ears.

"Well," she finally says, "I'm not so sure. There's a lot of things in this world can't be figured out the old-fashioned way, I can tell you that. Folks all through history been staring up at the beyond, trying to figure out the stars. Just when you think you've got the world all sized up, something happens to completely confuse the dickens outa you; something just can't be explained. There's still a lot of mystery in this here universe and we don't always understand how the world works or why people do what it is they do. But thank goodness for that. Thank goodness for a little mystery. Nobody rightly knows what makes the world go 'round, I can tell you that."

"Them gussaks think they know the world with science," Mr. Samuels suddenly says, startling me with his deep voice. Mr. Samuels usually don't join up with Mama's and my conversations, and I'm feeling a little peeved that he butts in.

"We're not talking about science," I say to him curtly.

"Mama and me's discussing a very complicated subject. Too hard to explain."

Sometimes I wish Mr. Samuels would just up and go home, I really do. I have more than enough of his hanging on to my mama and taking up more than his share of room at the kitchen table. The only trouble is, I can't seem to figure out a way to get rid of him ("Should I Have Stopped Her from Seeing Him? A Daughter's Tragic Regret," *Family Life*). But it sure seems like Mama still gets her heart stuck on keeping that old coot around, and I notice she's always doing all kinds of things for him too, spoiling him silly, if you is to ask me. She cooks for him, cleans for him; she even reads the *Kuskokwim Kronicle* to him, seeing as his old eyes is going bad. Why, every Friday evening, after a hard day of sewing and working over at the home, Mama hurries right up and makes Mr. Samuel his weekly wild rhubarb pie. I come in the front door come Friday evening and there she is, happy as a clam, covered with flour and rolling out a double crust on the kitchen table. Funny, but tired as she must be, Mama always looks happy when she's making Mr. Samuels his pie. It just makes me sick, it really does.

Guess it must be true that doing for someone else can make you feel good, no matter what, but I wouldn't know much about that. Got no one to fix up any pie for, got no one of my own at all.

Mama sighs heavily and Mr. Samuels laughs. "When

you can't explain, Lorraine Hobbs," Mr. Samuels says, smiling, "then you don't talk science. You talk of the spirit world, the world the Yup'ik know long time ago."

"Oh, please." I'm not feeling ready for another story of long ago.

"Lorraine." Mama sets down her scissors and gives me a mean ole look. "Don't you be sassing Mr. Samuels here. You'd be surprised to learn how much he knows, what a wise man he really is. You might learn a pinch from our friend right here if you is of a mind to. Don't always be so set in your ways, daughter, or you'll never learn nothing about this here universe. Know too many cranky folk 'round here, never learn to look at the world straight on. You better start opening your young eyes to the ways of others if you don't want to end up a sad, sorry, lonely, forgotten, old narrow-minded woman."

I look up at Mama, surprised. Her face is all flushed up red-purple and her hands is shaking at their sides. I don't remember seeing Mama that stirred up for a long time. Mr. Samuels shakes his head and takes her hand in his. They look at each other for a moment and I see Mama's face quiet down quick. Mr. Samuels smiles and stands up. All kinds of hair drift to the floor at his feet, and don't you know he ain't about to clean up that awful mess his own self.

"Lorraine Hobbs," he says slowly, as if I'm stupid or deaf, "you come with an old man tonight, and we gonna see them things can't get explained at all. Late at night, 'round ten o'clock. I gonna show you them things you never see before."

"Well, I'm sorry, Mr. Samuels, I surely am." I try to control my urge to yell and run right out the door at the thought of spending time alone with him tonight. Just what I need with a Fancy Peanut Fruit Canned Apricot Cobbler to be baked by morning. "I got plans to do some cooking tonight and don't think I'll be able to join you at all."

Mr. Samuels just shakes his head and laughs as if I've said something particularly funny. He shakes his head and says the same thing all over again. "Late at night, 'round ten o'clock. I gonna show you them things you never see before."

Mama smiles and pats him on the shoulder while I grit my teeth and try to keep myself from screaming right out loud.

And there's no getting around it. No matter what I do or what excuses I give, I still gonna have to meet up with Mr. Samuels and listen to what he has to say. No point spending time fretting—if there's one thing I learn this crazy summer, it's that it's better to bite the bullet than sit around worrying. If Mama is of a mind for me to spend time with that peculiar old man, well, so be it. Sometimes I do rightly impress myself with my very own grown-up maturity.

And so at exactly ten o'clock, I'm sitting at the kitchen

table, tapping my feet and wondering for gracious sake's alive where in the heck he is. Mama's at some social services meeting about moving the receiving home to a different trailer, and there's no sign of Mr. Samuels at all. Finally, just as I'm about to give up and moisturize my elbows and the heels of my feet with Pond's night cream for problem skin repair, there's a loud bang at the door and Mr. Samuels walks slowly in, carrying a small brown paper bag.

"Well, Mr. Samuels," I say, "here I am. What is it you're meditating on now, if you don't mind my asking? Working up some old Yup'ik spell or magic to send my way? I gotta warn you ahead of time, ain't much that fools Lorraine Hobbs, especially in the area of magical tricks and the like."

He looks at me suddenly, and then sighs. "Ah," he says, almost to himself, "ah, that's right."

"What's right?" I'm definitely losing my patience with all this gobbledygook. If Mr. Samuels thinks I'm going to be swayed by his hemming and hawing, he's got another thing coming.

"Almost forgot, Lorraine Hobbs." He smiles. "You're coming with me tonight. An old man's mind is sometimes thick as ice."

"You mean you forget about telling me about things I don't understand?" I feel my face flush up hot with anger. "I'm sitting here waiting for you to show up, and you don't even remember that we're to meet at all? And what's in that paper sack, anyways? Why'd you bring a bag of tricks if you ain't remembering meeting up with me tonight?"

"Ah," he says again, and I begin to wonder if he knows any other words. "Cheese balls, special at Northern Commercial tonight. Three jumbo bags of cheese balls for two ninety-nine."

"Mr. Samuels." I'm definitely riled up now. I'm pondering the mysteries of the universe, and he's chowing down on cheese snacks.

"Okay, okay," he says with a little chuckle. "You come with me to the water, and I'll tell you of things the Yup'ik knows."

"That's better," I say, relieved to get things straight. It's not exactly that I want to spend time with the old fool, but I do have some curiosity about the world beyond science. And it don't hurt a girl none to work on developing all sides of her life ("How to Be More Spiritual," *Quest*). But we're not even halfway out the door when Mr. Samuels stops dead in his tracks and looks back longingly over his shoulder at the bag on the kitchen table.

"They'll be there when we get back, Mr. Samuels," I say, my voice dripping with sarcasm. "Now don't you worry your head none, them cheese balls are sure as shootin' gonna be there when we get back."

Mr. Samuels don't say nothing then, but I hear him give a real deep sigh as I pass him at the door.

*

"So, Lorraine Hobbs," he says as we walk slowly down the dusty road, "what do you know of the shaman way of life?"

I hesitate for a moment, scanning the horizon to make sure nobody I know sees me with this hobbling old man.

"I dunno. Not much. But I do happen to make an acquaintance who says she's a shaman, not that I'm one to believe her. But there ain't any more shamans around here these days, are there? And anyways, what's so doggone important about shamans? Although truly, I could care less."

He doesn't say anything for a moment and then points toward the river ahead.

"The first missionary come down the Kuskokwim River many years ago, when the Yup'ik shamans got lotsa magic, lotsa power. That's changed now—today, the missionary got the power, but shaman still got lotsa magic."

"So?" I know that I'm being rude but can't seem to stop myself. Listening to him drone on and on about something I'm not the least interested in isn't my idea of a pleasant evening. I bite my cheek to stop from saying anything else.

"So," he says, ignoring my tone of voice, "so, them days long ago the shaman visits the moon and the land of the dead. Them days, the shaman makes the weather, sees the future, makes the sick well, and helps the animals agree to get captured. Respects nature. Makes all the animals happy to know that they will be shared."

"Visits the moon and the land of the dead?" Give me a break. This old man must think I'm some kinda idiot to buy this drivel.

"Some things can't be explained, Lorraine Hobbs. Just part of the way things is, how nature is. Mysterious. We can't always figure on the way things happen just out of our reach. The shaman knows this, visits the moon in search of what will be, and the moonman keeps all the souls of both men and animal. The shaman is the first to see spirits in dreams, first to see the dead."

I stop walking for a minute and think about Evelyn Sugarbush.

"Mr. Samuels," I say slowly, "do you think that there could be any shamans left today? What if somebody says she's a shaman? Let's say I am to believe in this hocus-pocus, how'd I know if a shaman is real?"

He doesn't say anything for a minute.

"If a Yup'ik says she is shaman, then it is so. She sees with her heart, not with her head." The old man avoids my eyes and looks longingly at the river's edge.

"What are you looking at, Mr. Samuels?" Maybe it's his tone of voice, but somehow I find myself kinda interested in what he's saying. Somehow, I begin to believe that Evelyn Sugarbush just might be what she says she is. He doesn't answer.

"Mr. Samuels?"

"Oh, nothing, Lorraine Hobbs." He rubs his hands

together gleefully and grins. "I'm just thinking that the Tundra Shack over there might got a new shipment of ice creams in last night. I'm hungry for that double-stick Fudgsicle pop."

I can hardly believe my ears. "What?"

"Never mind. Got me plenty Reese's Peanut Butter Cups in my pocket. You hungry? Want a Reese's Peanut Butter Cup?"

For a minute I'm speechless, then hear my own stomach growl up a storm.

"Well, okay," I finally say. "Maybe just one." He grunts with approval and hands over the candy, smashed flat in its wrapper. "Can't eat them Snickers or Milky Way bars," he says sadly. "Them candies pop my dentures right outa my mouth. Same thing with them Chocolate-Vanilla Bubble-Gum Pops. Maybe good thing that the Tundra Shack always closed down these days. Keeps an old man outa trouble."

"I'm awfully sorry to hear that you're having troubles with your teeth, Mr. Samuels, I truly am."

My mind is reeling; trying to stay with this old coot is not an easy job. First we're talking about shamans and the moon, then suddenly we're having a conversation about the nature of teeth and candy. Just as I'm recovering from this peculiar change in topic, he pops two peanut butter cups into his mouth, stretches his arms out at his sides, and starts singing some strange tune.

"Mr. Samuels," I say quietly, not wanting to interrupt

any important ancient ritual, "I think we're talking about shamans."

"Ah." His arms drop to his side and he kneels at the river's edge. "Too many new peoples now, too many people from too far away, bringing different kinds of rules. Telling us how to live and how to be. Even the air around us changes. All them people eating up the summer's air. And that Kuskokwim River water's all poison now. No one respects its laws today, but long time ago, the river keeps us alive. We drink from it. We travel on it. Everyone healthy. Now the water's black with garbage, filled with the empty dreams of disappointed peoples. And one day soon"—he sighs deeply—"them big barges gonna spill poison oil into the water's veins and into the water's heart. Then all the animals, all the fish and birds, we ain't gonna see them no more. Then the world will be a different place all over again. But that day's still to come, when the water's world deep below's gonna change. Long time ago"—he looks up and suddenly smiles—"them days the people, they trust the land, the water, nature. Everyone happy them days. Don't even know we're poor. Don't even know what we don't got. Them missionaries say that our people are savage but gets better, learns the law of their church, and grows a better soul. Not me, not this old man, I think them church laws no good for nothing. Man gets weaker, not stronger. Gotta fight to keep our old soul. Long time ago man has the brave shoulders of nature, before the missionaries poison the river with their words and when the Yup'ik dance away their boats and dogs."

By now I'm ready to give up entirely, finding it impossible to follow any clear train of thought. I sit myself on the river's edge next to him and don't say nothing. I'm just waiting to hear the next thing coming my way.

"Long time ago," he continues, "the Yup'ik passes cold winter months dancing and feasting. Them dances honor souls of the animals we need for food and clothing. Also honor dead friends and family. Them missionaries"— he pauses and makes a scrunched-up face to demonstrate his disgust—"they think the Yup'ik is filled with demon and work to make change, to end what we believe, to stop the shamans, to stop the dancing. Work to stop Yup'ik Messenger Feast. All gone now. No more dancing things away."

"Yup'ik Messenger Feast? What's that, anyway? And what the heck does it mean to 'dance things away'?"

"Don't hurry an old man, Lorraine Hobbs," he says, reaching in his pocket for yet another treat. To my extreme disgust, he pulls out a can of snuff and stuffs a wad up into his gum. "Hmm," he says happily, "hmm." I start to ask again, but keep my mouth shut this time. I watch him sigh contentedly and stretch his legs out one by one.

"The Messenger Feast," he finally continues, "is the time all villages invite each other to dance away food and cloth and boots and houses. Them old men, they get most

306

of the good stuff, first the old men get things, last the young ones. The Messenger Feast lets us show how much we respect each other, nature, and all of the animals, because we share everything we catch. Since we share with all of our friends, everything is used and nothing is wasted. This way, we know the spirits of animals will return as partners the next winter. And so on and so on. In this way, we know our people will always have food for our children and their children. We stay close to nature and with each other, as one."

"Do you mean to tell me," I ask slowly, scratching the dusty ground with the tip of my finger, "do you mean to say that you give away all of your things to your friends? Without asking for any money or nothing?"

He nods. "Other things more important than money. Helping and caring for each other more important. Respecting, trusting in nature. We dance and make up songs which ask for new things and which show respect. If we need a new sled and the other village has sleds, then we ask for that. If we need warmer weather, we ask for that. Dancers and singers wait outside the *qasgig*, then go inside when singers call for them. Everything set up just right them days, which villages go to dances, which dance group sings to each other, which songs is sung. Village gives away most things honored the most—great honor to be the one gives things away to others. The people, they care for each other then, know how to help when others are needing and know how to see that need in their dreams. You know, the shamans sees us in their dreams and knows how to make things better, what to do to make things right. Now dances just for fun, not for asking or giving things away.

"Missionaries stop all the dancing because they think we dance away what we own and are being wasteful, uncivilized. Think we will be lazy, learn not to work at all. But you should see them days back then. All the old folks sit on benches around the outside of the *qasgig* room, real happy—boats, traps, gingham cloth, rifles, we dance all things away back them days. That *quasig* gets filled up with soot from the seal oil lamps, but we don't mind. We get hot and tired. Still don't mind. Still dance. Sometimes we dance two nights. Sometimes we don't want to ever stop. Happy times, them days. Messenger Feast, shamans, spirit dreams . . . the world much bigger then. . . . Now the world such a small place. People nowadays, they don't remember what came before, they only believe in now, what they see now and what they're told, don't try to see anything else. Lotsa magic out there"—he stops and waves his wrinkled hands at the sky—"and lotsa magic here"—he pats his chest lightly. "But nobody wants to use it no more. Nobody got no use for what they can't always understand. Funny, to me, men is more savage today than long time ago. What the missionaries see before was the gentle heart. Today, men's hearts is savage. Today, men's hearts is cruel."

His voice trails away and neither of us says nothing for a minute.

I notice the inky sheen of water before me and suddenly realize that the flow of river and sky must look as they looked generations before, that I am seeing the same tug of blue-black currents reflecting the same far-flung heavens the elders once saw, and that I am in the same place where they must have once stood.

I shiver. Sitting here, just Mr. Samuels and me, I feel myself suddenly shrink, minuscule under the smoky halo of planets, the sweep of space. The night wind hums, and time, the years between us, seem to just spin silently away.

We are the elders, warming ourselves around a fire, our eyes on the stars above. Maybe things do change, folks gonna leave each other, hurt each other, disappear, maybe nothing ever stays the same at all, but in a way those blurry objects above remain constant, shimmering and gyrating in all kinds of crazy and mysterious ways, but still always there, year after year, decade after decade, offering us clues to our beginnings as well as to what's ahead. As we sit here together, Mr. Samuels and me, just the two of us, one young and one old, everything else seems easily forgotten: Mama, Rosie, Thelma, even Dove Alexie and all of my troubles, hurts, and woes.

Days are shorter now, fall here so soon, and it's kinda sad to see the gilded summer nights fade away. I realize that there's not much time left and I need to learn what it is I have to know.

"Who gets to be shaman, Mr. Samuels?" I finally ask quietly. "How do you get to have shaman powers in the first place?"

"Funny thing, Lorraine Hobbs." He spits some tobacco juice right on the ground in front of him. I try to ignore the brown stain covering a corner of his mouth. "The shamans must visit them spirits in their dreams. They gotta visit them spirits and bring all of them back into the day. Not so easy for everyone. Funny thing, them little children got no friends or family, them who grow up wild and all alone, all those little childrens feeling real lonely and sad, them the ones like to spend time in their own dreams. Them lonely little ones happy to leave this world behind and dream in the stars above. Them lonely little ones like to go at night by themselves and bring spirits back with them into the day. The small child, something different in him than others, something in him wild and can't be tamed just like the world of nature, maybe got no mom, got no dad, maybe got some mark on his skin, maybe looks different in some way. That child, you know, the one the village don't like and the one some say is bad, the one living way off on his own . . . them little childrens love to make friends with the spirits in their dreams and them little children grow up to be shamans that way. They keep their hearts open to the spirit world that most folks scared to see. Lots out there that most people never even see.

"Nowadays all the young peoples think that things difficult to understand, that people who are different and alone is real bad, but us old folks, we see it as some kind of good mystery and magic, something precious to save." He smiles and pats my shoulder with a gentle hand. "If Lorraine Hobbs got no mama, if Lorraine Hobbs got no one else, who knows?" He laughs to himself and pats me again. "If you is Yup'ik, who knows, maybe you is shaman too."

I try to smile back but a sudden chill walks right up my arms. I think of Evelyn Sugarbush. I think of where she is from, I think of her dead parents, and I think of the two different colors of her shaman eyes.

"Lorraine Hobbs," Mr. Samuels says quietly, pulling something from his pocket. Funny how I never notice before what a tall man he really is and what a large shadow he casts; the ground by my feet quivers with his broad, imposing profile. "My auntie got a friend who's shaman once. Long time ago up by Unalakleet. She says this necklace only for them little childrens. She gives me this necklace when I'm just a small boy and tells me to give it to another child when I grow up. Guess I grow up by now." He chuckles and drapes a piece of string over his hands; I see a small carving shaped like a crescent moon swing back and forth, all glittery in the foggy night. He closes his hand suddenly and reaches for mine. Mr. Samuels puts the moon necklace right in my own hand.

"Never get no child of my own." He smiles. "Too busy chasing all them pretty women to settle down to just one wife. You take this charm from me, Lorraine Hobbs, something tells me you gonna see things real soon wearing the moon day and night."

I take a deep breath and look. The carving is white, looks like ivory. I wonder how many other children have worn it before. I wonder where those children are right now. "Thank you," I whisper, a little embarrassed by the tears come sudden to my eyes, "never see anything as pretty as this before."

Mr. Samuels nods his head.

"It's the moon, it's half a baby's heart, it's anything you want. Every time you look, you see something new. See with your eyes, Lorraine Hobbs, see with your heart. To know the universe, you gotta understand everything small. An old man is tired," he continues quietly, "and passes his eyes to a young child. Who knows"—he smiles again— "who knows what you gonna see and what changes this gonna bring."

I lift the string over my head and feel the carving knock softly against my chest. I close my eyes. I think I hear a distant beat from deep inside.

I think I hear a reply.


Evelyn and Jimmy are playing checkers again when I arrive at the receiving home the next day. Neither of them even bothers to look up when I come in or offers to help with my bags of groceries. Two packages of Oscar Mayer frankfurters slip out onto the floor with a giant jar of pimentos tumbling after it.

"You're cheating!" Evelyn says to Jimmy as if I'm not even around, and suddenly wipes all the checkers off the board with the back of her spindly arm.

"No fair," Jimmy squeals. "It's my turn."

"Is not."

"Is."

"Hey, Evelyn," I say, trying to raise my voice over the ruckus. "Hey, forget the checkers. I have something important to discuss with you."

"Yeah." She chuckles under her breath, folding the checkerboard in half. "Who cares?"

"Evelyn." I try as hard as can be to keep my patience. "I mean it. Can I talk to you alone? It's important, really." She eyes me suspiciously.

"How come alone?"

"Yeah," Jimmy whines, "how come alone?"

"Well, if you must know, it's of a personal nature."

I finger my sweatshirt's zipper nervously and feel the tiny ivory charm press into my neck. Lately, working at the receiving home, I've established a more practical wardrobe, and while it isn't particularly distinguished, at least I don't get my other clothes all ruined. At first I'm a mite worried about my personal reputation around town and what folks is going to think about Lorraine Hobbs not getting all gussied up no more, but when Mama notices, she don't make a big deal or nothing. All she does is look over her reading glasses and say, "Now that you're dressing more like me, daughter, folks gonna say you and me look just alike. Enough so that it looks like I done spit you right outa my mouth."

Of course, I don't say nothing then, choosing to ignore her teasing, but somehow it kinda makes me feel good that I could favor my mama even a little. She's no looker or nothing, but folks around here surely do admire her—wouldn't mind even a little if anyone starts looking up to me with newfangled admiration. I may only be fourteen, but I surely do think that I'm due some respect.

And I have to admit that it's a lot more comfortable to work in a sweatshirt and jeans than a dress and correspon-ding accessories. In fact, when you really think about it, there might be a lot more important ways to spend one's creative energies than on the maintenance of a complex wardrobe. Mama can hardly believe it, but I'm getting to appreciate the benefits of pure comfort.

"Look, Little Miss Hobbs, princess of the Kusko-kwim, I don't jump every time you snap your little gussak fingers. What do you want, anyway?" Evelyn stands up, stretches, and looks me dead in the eye. "You want my help, don't you?" she finally says. "Now that you need me, you're willing to speak with the likes of a crazy Yup'ik from Emmonak."

"I do. You're right and I kinda do need your personal assistance. At least I think I do, that's assuming you have those magical shaman powers you keep talking about."

"Not exactly magical powers," she says dreamily. "Not exactly magic."

"Then what do you call it? Not that I actually believe all of this mumbo jumbo or nothing."

Beryl Wiggins, a little five-year-old from Aniak, wearing a long, white sweatshirt and no shoes, runs across the room and trips on the checker box. I catch her in my arms before she falls down.

"Hey, watch it," Evelyn yells, as checkers spill out all over the floor. "I just clean this up. Stupid kid."

Beryl starts to cry and runs outa the room.

"You don't have to make her cry." I feel my face getting hot. If there's one thing I can't stand, it's the sight of a little kid crying.

"Stupid kid," Jimmy mutters under his breath and kneels to help throw the pieces back into the box. "We just finish cleaning this up."

"Me, not you, Jimmy. You don't do nothing much 'cept stand around." Evelyn glares at him and then turns to look down at her hands. She bends and straightens her crooked fingers and then looks me right in the face. "Tell me what you want," she finally says. "Tell me why you're here."

So I sit down on the receiving home couch, Evelyn and Jimmy on either side, and tell them all about Dove Alexie and the jail. I tell them about how he looks when I see him and I tell them about Annette Weinland, about Thelma Cooke and Edgar Kwagley, about Arnie and about Mama and me tryin' to get answers to one simple question: What happens to Dove Alexie? I tell them about my letters and about all the answers I get back, saying nothing at all. I tell them about Annette meeting up with the marshal in Anchorage and exactly what she finds out. Most especially, I tell them about the "can you help me get out of here" note that I still keep in my bedroom dresser.

"But why do you care about this guy, anyways?" Jimmy asks, seems like kinda nervously, holding onto a Raggedy Andy doll real tight, its soft chest embroidered with a divided red heart. "If you don't really know this Dove Alexie guy, then why do you even care at all?"

I'm quiet for a moment, not really knowing what to say ("Love Happens: Your Past Holds the Key," *Quest*).

"She meets him," Evelyn says suddenly, standing up and walking over to the window. "He asks her to help him and that makes them brother and sister."

"Well, I don't know if I'd go so far as to say that." I'm not so sure if brother and sister is what I have in mind. Evelyn nods and pushes up the window. She whistles and then says something in Yup'ik that I can't even understand.

316

The only word I recognize is Quimuckta, and soon I hear his familiar bark outside the door.

"Evelyn," I say to her from across the room, "are you going to help me or not? Because if you're not, then I'll find some other way. I know I can find some other way, no matter what."

"Shut up, Lorraine," she says, her back still facing me. "Shut up or I'm gonna call the whole thing off."

I don't say a thing. I realize she never calls me by my first name before.

The next Saturday we all sit around the kitchen table in my house, Evelyn, Jimmy, Mr. Samuels, and me. Mama's still over at the receiving home, helping get all the children to bed, but she's left a plate of pilot bread and salmonberry jam in the center of the table. Of course Mr. Samuels is chewing and grunting, eating more than his share, but I try to be more tolerant, seeing as he is helping me with the difficult problem of finding Dove Alexie.

At first Evelyn and Jimmy don't say nothing—they both look kinda nervous and all of a sudden I realize how young they both are. I suddenly realize that they're just children, just lonely children far away from home. Funny, how all of a sudden things can change right in front of your very own eyes.

"Have some pilot bread and jam," I offer Evelyn, hoping her energy'll get boosted so she can provide some real

317

assistance. "Mama and me, we put up the jam all by ourselves."

Right now don't look much like she can do much of anything, sitting there all hunched over the table, the "can you help me get out of here" note spread out in front of her, her eyes lowered way down. Mr. Samuels says something to her in Yup'ik and she nods. Quimuckta, lying under the table at her feet, is chewing on a bone or some other large object. I hear him slurping and grunting with delight.

"Hey," I say, "who let in the dog? Mama don't let no animals inside."

"Oh, please shut up." Evelyn suddenly looks up and both me and Quimuckta pipe down real quiet. "I'm trying to concentrate."

Mr. Samuels chuckles, his mouth full of bread, and Jimmy looks scared enough to run right outside the front door. I never do see anyone's eyes pop out so big and wide before.

"Look," Jimmy says to Evelyn, his eyes real big and round. "I don't say nothing about some evil, cold-blooded criminal, do I? Or some dead guy. No one says nothing to me about evil and death. I mean, I know the other day . . . but I think you is kidding. I think you jokes." He looks at me for a second and then nervously at Evelyn again. "You don't even need me, Evelyn," he continues. "I'm no shaman or nothing like you. I'm just some boy from up Russian Village."

318

Evelyn sighs and rolls her eyes. "Will you please shut up. Everyone. I can't think with all of you jabbering so."

"Well, excuse me." I stand up and pour myself a cup of Tang. "You know, Evelyn Sugarbush, just because you might be a shaman and everything surely don't mean you can say whatever the heck you want. No plain out 'n' out rudeness is ever really acceptable in any social circle, you might want to know."

Mr. Samuels clears his throat and Evelyn drops both hands on the table in disgust.

"Shhh," she continues, her thin, parched lips all knotted up together. "Shhh. I can almost see something now. It's dark and lonely and he's hurting real bad. He's all alone out here; I think I can see him walking out on the tundra all by himself."

"Well, can you see him or not?" Somehow I'm getting madder and madder. What's all this talk about "I think" and "almost"? Does the girl know what she's doing or am I just wasting time? She don't say anything for a minute. I hear Quimuckta startin' that chewing again and I look under the table.

"Hey," I yell out real loud, "hey, that dang dog's chewing up my best velvet and simulated pearl headband. Mama orders it all the way from Seattle." I crawl under the table and try to wrestle the headband outa Quimuckta's slimy mouth. "Give it here!" I scream. "Give it here, you godforsaken old mutt."

The dog pulls away from me real hard, then suddenly relaxes his jaws. I fall backward against Mr. Samuels's legs, the wet headband foamy with dog spittle. Of course, I hear Jimmy laughing and I struggle as Mr. Samuels helps me to my feet. He is shaking his head sadly, as if I'm the one do wrong.

"What you lookin' at, anyway?" I stamp my feet like a little kid. "Get your hands off me! Lookee here at my new party headband. It's all ruined. Just ruined."

I throw it down on the floor and run right out the front door like I just step smack into the middle of a hornet's nest. I know that I'm acting like a stupid little kid. I know it but somehow can't even stop. All of a sudden, thinking about Rosie and how sad she probably is this very moment, all of a sudden remembering Dove, thinking about his poor swollen face, and now that something awful really might could happen to him, all of a sudden I can't stop crying.

I sit down on my cracked wooden front steps and drop my face into my own stupid lap. The cold Bethel rain drizzles down my back and I shiver. Sometimes I feel so doggone lonely, I can't even stand it. Rosie whisked away right in front of my face, no one to talk to, no real friends at all. Mama too busy with Mr. Samuels and them orphan kids to pay much attention to me anymore. And Dove Alexie, the only person in this whole, entire world who needs my help. Dove Alexie's in real trouble and there ain't nothing at all I can do.

I pull out the tiny ivory moon from under my shirt and rub it between two fingers. It looks the same as it does yesterday and the day before that. I wonder who's kidding who and what the heck I'm doing wearing some old Eskimo charm made from a dirty animal tusk. Is this the way I'm gonna end up, after all my wishing and hoping for an exciting future . . . a lonely girl counting on a stupid charm and three crazy Yup'iks to help her see the light? I might as well wake up and smell the coffee; nothing's gonna ever change in this pathetic life of mine. I'm gonna always be plain old Lorraine Hobbs, a dumb old gussak girl who can't do anything that's gonna make any difference in this here universe. No way. Ain't gonna make any difference at all.

"Don't cry, Lorraine." I hear Evelyn's voice behind me and wipe my eyes with the edge of my flannel shirt. She sits down next to me on the steps.

"I'm not crying," I sniff. "I ain't about to blubber over the likes of you or Jimmy or anybody else."

"Oh."

Neither of us says nothing for a minute.

"Guess you want me and Jimmy to go on back to the home," she says quietly. "Guess you don't want my help no more."

I shake my head.

The evening air is full of fish and sand and mud. Everything looks flat and brown; everything looks like it's dying or already dead, them poor little houses strung out in front of me like some kinda stupid kid's broken necklace, sad gaps where beads once been. I can't remember the last time I really look at Oscarville, really see it for what it is, just the part of town where nobody wants to go. Who am I kidding, planning to be a fancy chef or Avon beauty consultant or anything important at all? My home is no more than a lonely, run-down shantytown, filled with lopsided, caved-in shacks made of tar paper, plywood, and tin. Old refrigerators sit out rusting on front steps, and abandoned cardboard cartons scatter in the dusty road. Everywhere you look, nothing but tundra—empty, flat, colorless space.

Funny, how folks call Alaska "the last frontier" and outer space "the final frontier." Seems to me the only thing that the two have in common is never-ending nothingness, far-off places where man hasn't even made a dent or left a permanent mark. Guess some see open space as possibility, while I feel the ache of its loneliness and the sting of its invisible edge.

A torn yellow box marked Pillsbury Moist Supreme Cake Mix blows across the road, the only bit of color for miles.

Suddenly I realize that my home looks like some kinda bombed-out war zone, some place abandoned and totally forgotten. And if I look deep inside my own self right this very minute, I'd probably see the same forsaken landscape reflected within. I'd hear the same gusts blow.

I gasp; a sharp pain shoots sudden across my chest like a shooting star. I hear a somber echo, and see each empty chamber, each dune of my lonely heart.

"Is he all right?" I hear myself ask Evelyn, the hollow sound of my own words scaring me. "Just tell me if he's gonna be okay."

She puts a scratchy hand on my hand.

"He's hurt," she says quietly, almost a whisper. "Dove Alexie's hurting real bad, but if you want, we can find him. I really want to help you find him soon as I can."

"Find him?" I turn my head toward her and feel her warm breath on my face. "How we gonna find him? How we gonna find him, anyway? Don't even have any idea of where he's at."

She studies the backs of her hands. She don't say nothing.

"Evelyn," I say straight out loud to her and everyone else who cares to listen, to the poisoned Kuskokwim River winding by, to all of the tired-looking Oscarville houses in front of me, to the kids in school whispering and calling each other names, to all the rotten people who would hurt a scared young boy, "is he gonna be okay, is he gonna make it alive? I mean, if he's all alone out there, if he's hurt and by himself . . ."

She slips her hand into my hand, she really does. Evelyn Sugarbush slips her little bent hand into mine and looks me right in the eye.

"He's hurt bad," she says in a faraway voice, "and I don't know what's gonna happen next. But we're going to find him as fast as anybody can."

Her stiff fingers feel fragile, breakable, and I hold them loosely, scared that if I squeeze too tight, something might break, something else might break and shatter into bits before my very own eyes.

And it don't take her long to get started. She wants to start looking for Dove right off, the very next day, and so for the entire week, I tell Evelyn everything I know about Dove Alexie, Arnie Hanger, Annette Weinland, Edgar Kwagley, and Thelma Cooke. I kinda wish I would bump into Miss Weinland, but hear that she's busy working long hours at the jail, now that no one takes Arnie's place. The last time I see her is right after the moon walk in July, when she tells me what she learns from the marshal up in Anchorage. I really appreciate her help 'n' all, and it makes me feel real good to know that even the marshal believes something is awry, but still don't got no real proof or evidence about what really happens to Dove or where he might be. Still nobody knows which way to look or how to help.

"What's she like?" Evelyn asks me one evening as I'm

stirring up a pot of lime Jell-O for my Tutti-Frutti Vegetable Medley.

"Who? The minister's daughter?"

"Yeah, her. What's she like, anyways?" Evelyn sticks a finger into the Jell-O mixture and then screeches and dunks her hand in the sink.

"I tell you not to taste. I tell you the Jell-O is hot." I hand her a paper towel and she makes a face to let me know how much her finger hurts. "She's real nice," I continue, "real nice but kinda quiet, you know, shy. And she always seems sad, seems sad and tired."

"She's scared," Evelyn says, sucking on the finger again.

"Scared? Scared of what, might I ask?" I'm getting a tad annoyed with Evelyn knowing everything before getting all the facts. All of a sudden, before you know what's what, right in the middle of your telling her an important piece of information, she'll just blurt out with something that makes no sense at all.

She shrugs. "I don't know what she's scared of, but don't really matter. What matters is they work together, Arnie and Miss . . . what's her name?"

"Weinland," I reply curtly. "Weinland. How come you can tell that she's scared but can't even figure out her name?" Evelyn shrugs but looks mighty pleased with herself. Again, I feel myself getting irritated. "And tell me again, how do you figure Dove ends up hurt so bad? I mean, I know he's beat about the face, I can see that when I first meet him, but he don't look like he's about to roll over and die. How do you really know how bad he's hurting for sure?"

She shrugs again and looks away.

"And don't be calling for that mangy Quimuckta mutt." Seems like every time Evelyn talks about Dove Alexie, she's looking for Quimuckta. I can't even bring myself to ask her about that—don't even want to know what that business is about.

"Lookee here," she suddenly says, hopping up on the small piece of kitchen counter. Under ordinary circumstances, I'd be yelling at her to get down, seeing as sitting on that particular stretch of counter is against receiving home rules. But since these is extenuating circumstances, I overlook the rule. "Look, sometimes I don't really understand how I know what I know. And does it really matter, anyway, as long as it's true? Sometimes I have these dreams, you know, all kinda dreams, especially when I'm a little kid. I don't always remember what happens in the dreams, but when I wake up the next day then there's something else that I know. Something'll just slip itself into my mind without me even understanding. If a person is dead, then maybe I visit the land of the dead in my dreams. That's what the shaman does, you know, sometimes it's stuff even I don't remember, even I don't understand."

I look up at her, a skinny little girl with a tight pointed face and two different colored eyes. If it wasn't for the eyes, you wouldn't even think she was different at all. She just looks like any other ordinary Native kid, anyone at all.

"Can I have a bowl of Jell-O now?" she asks, innocently, a little child pleading for a treat. "I don't care if it's all hot and runny." I pour her some in a cereal bowl and watch her gulp it up real fast, like someone's about to snatch it away. She wipes her green mouth with the back of her hand. She smiles. "Dove Alexie's lying somewhere out there in the tundra," she finally says, rubbing her stomach and giving one small burp. "As soon as you're ready, we can go find him."

"What do you mean 'somewhere out in the tundra'?" I grab the empty bowl away from her and toss it into the sink with all the other dirty dishes. "Aren't you covering a lot of territory? How we gonna find him somewhere out in the godforsaken tundra, for Christ's sake?"

"Well, she says slowly, "I guess I'm not sure. All I know is that he's out there and needs a friend."

"Try to remember," Evelyn is saying to me the very next day. Turns out, the more information I tell her about Dove, the more likely she's able to find him. It don't make a lot of sense to me, seeing as I'm bothering with her in the first place so she can tell me what I don't already know. But I do try to remember everything Edgar Kwagley and Thelma Cooke tell me. I try to tell her everything Annette Weinland finds out and what Marshal Nicholsen knows.

Evelyn is sitting on the receiving home laundry room

stool, smack in front of the sink, and I'm standing behind her, trying to set her short hair in clips. I try not to let on that I can't actually remember the setting instructions for this particular style, being as I don't get much of a chance to read my magazines these days, what with working at the receiving home and all. I try not to panic when the clips dangle right down from her puny scalp.

"Can't you just sit still one minute," I beg, putting down my genuine boar's hair brush in exasperation. "I ain't gonna be able to curl your hair at all if you keep shifting 'round."

The laundry room is real small, and it's hard to change position, even a little. When Evelyn wiggles, I find myself jumping all around, trying not to get squished up against the wall. An old metal ironing board is hanging there, its screws digging into my back.

"Just forget it." Evelyn grabs the towel off from around her neck and stands up. The stool gets shoved right into my stomach.

"Watch it!" I complain. "What are you doing anyway, for land's sake? You're likely to damage one of my vital organs if you keep on like that. And anyway, I thought you say I can fix your hair if I try and remember real hard."

"Well, you're not really trying." She gives the stool an extra push for emphasis. "I don't need my hair fixed anyway."

"Who says?" I look at Evelyn standing in front of me, hands on her hips. Her short black hair is uneven, the bangs lopsided and the rest of it standing up straight, all spiky, like she just sticks her finger into an electrical socket. One side of her head is plastered with shiny silver clips. I start to laugh.

"What are you laughing at?" She touches the top of her head gingerly, as if feeling to make sure there's still some hair left. She looks at me suspiciously and then throws the towel on the floor.

"Real mature, Evelyn," I say with disgust. "Pick up that there towel or I'll call Mama. You're acting like a big baby."

"Am not."

"Are too."

Nobody says nothing for a minute and we both try to stare the other one down.

"Just tell me," I finally say, wearily. "Can you help me or not? It's a few days now since we start all of this and we don't seem any farther along."

She starts pulling out the hair clips and shaking out her head like some kind of wild animal. I step back so as not to get sprayed with Dippity-Do styling gel.

"You don't even know what you're talking about," she says, handing the clips back to me one by one. "If you have some more accurate information, some real facts, or maybe a piece of his clothing or something belonging to that Hanger guy, well, that's a different story. That stupid old note you get isn't enough. It's a help but it just isn't enough for me to do my very best work."

"But I don't got nothing else, that's the whole point.

329

Can't you just look at the moon and stars or something and figure it out for yourself? Seems kinda greedy to me to tell you more and more before you can figure out anything helpful at all. Might as well try to find Dove Alexie all by myself." I can tell you, I'm feeling sick of the whole thing, sick of it and frustrated too. Sometimes I wonder why in the heck I'm bothering with all of this. Dove Alexie ain't no family of mine, don't even rightly really know him, and seems like I'm making a big deal outa nothing. Maybe nothing bad happens to him after all, maybe Evelyn don't know what in the world she's talking about, maybe she's even just pulling my leg. Why can't I just go back to the old Lorraine, content with my magazines and the refinements of my personal appearance? But somehow, I'm not satisfied with those things anymore. Somehow I get to be needing something else, something more. I sigh heavily. Just wish I knew what in heaven's name that something is.

Evelyn and I both stand there for a moment, not saying nothing, not doing nothing at all. The steam from the clothes dryer rises up high to the ceiling, then drifts and winds itself around Evelyn's skinny shoulders. She takes a deep breath and the haze thickens. For a minute it looks like Evelyn Sugarbush is going to vanish into thin air.

But she don't. She don't disappear and she don't come up with any other visions of Dove Alexie or Arnie Hanger or nothing. She and Jimmy still come over to the house some nights, still sit around the kitchen table with me and Mr. Samuels, eating graham crackers and pilot bread and drinking Tang or Mama's Russian tea. Sometimes we try to figure out what happens to Dove, sometimes we argue and everyone leaves mad, sometimes we just whip out a pack of playing cards and have a good time laughing.

Funny, soon it's hard to even remember that Evelyn and Jimmy are receiving home kids, just seems as if they're like anyone else at all, and sometimes, in the middle of a card game or while just making conversation, I stop and look around the table at my assorted companions. Strange to say, but if I really sit back and think about it, I realize that I've made three pretty good friends. Mr. Samuels still drives me batty with his slowness and confusing chatter; Evelyn often makes me furious, her snotty nose-in-the-air attitude enough to drive anyone to distraction; and Jimmy can also push me over the edge, imitating everything Evelyn does and never standing on his own. All in all, we might seem like a strange bunch to be hanging around together, an old man, two Yup'ik kids, and a gussak girl. Who can figure how this group even gets together? But it does, and I got to admit, even if it is just to my very own self, sometimes I sure like having all of them around, arguing, playing, laughing, whatever—it almost don't even matter at all.

Since school starts, things pretty much the same, them popular girls hanging out together and generally ignoring the likes of me and half the Bethel population. My teachers are okay, but I'm usually bored out of my mind and I find myself looking at the time all day, waiting for three o'clock when I can leave the stuffy classrooms behind and head out to my job at the home. I usually run all the way, the cool air feeling good on my cheeks, my book bag over one shoulder, my jacket flapping open wide. Sometimes Mama just starts to laugh when she sees me come in, my hair blown every whichaway, one sneaker left untied, my jeans rolled up at the cuff where I've tripped in the muddy road. "Land sakes, child," she'll say, grinning and reaching to help me with my things, "you look like you done get shot straight out of a volcano!" And she'll give me a quick pat and a list of things to do around the home.

Sometimes I'll have to start dinner, or set the table. Sometimes I'll have to fix the little kids some Kool-Aid and peanut butter–marshmallow cookies, and we'll all sit down together as I read them a story and they gnaw away at their snack. Every so often, I'll bring in my special fashion design markers from home and we'll draw detailed pictures of outfits we'd all most like to wear. The kids'll usually crowd around me, each one trying to get closer than the rest, although I do get a little irritated when they're rude or drive me crazy with endless chatter. But every now and then, I got to admit, I really get a kick outa them, their little faces smudged with paint and dirt, their scuffed-up shoes wobbling off the wrong tiny feet, the way they can't pronounce my name right and call me all kinda funny things, the way they fight to sit on my lap, even the way they take their naps, rosy cheeks smeared with crumbs and cinnamon sugar. They look at me, eyes lowered, a loopy half smile covering those screwed-up little faces, and burrow into my lap, wiggly and warm.

I hear old Mr. Samuels's voice: "To know the universe, you gotta understand everything small."

What I can't understand is that these doggone children always smell so good, no matter how disgustingly dirty they are, no matter if they even never change their sad, scruffy little clothes. And I can tell you, them kids definitely stay filthy no matter how often Mama and me change their clothes, full of mud and sand, wearing the most pitiful torn shirts and frayed little pants. If you see them walking down some Bethel street, they just look like ordinary poor little Native children; they look like everyone else. But somehow when they get here to the receiving home and you begin to know them and see them up close, well, something happens. They look different all of a sudden—their clothes and all that dirt don't even matter. Where they're from, why they end up here, none of that seems important to me anymore. All that matters is that goofy look on their faces and the way they keep on smelling so darn good.

I sometimes walk right by accidentally on purpose at night, particularly when I'm hurting from missing Rosie, and when them kids are lined up sleeping in their little cots. I take a good long whiff, that sweet damp smell, kinda like cooking vanilla, sinking slowly through my whole entire body and making me feel like I don't even want to go home. Seems like when I see them there whistling and snoring in their sleep, I just want to stay at the old receiving home forever, trying to listen to them silly kids' dreams and be right at their sides in the morning when they wake.

I feel like I'm learning about a whole new universe, like one of them moon astronauts, calling out, stunned, from outer space, viewing the whole world in an entirely different way.

The planets are spinning, the stars quiver, and on some radiant corner of the moon, we explorers are walking, steady and firm, on a newly discovered Tranquility Base.

✳  ✳  ✳

*Quimuckta stops ahead, his nose to the ground, then looks back as if to call us forward. Evelyn runs out in front, but me, Mr. Samuels, and Jimmy, we still hang back some. Jimmy looks at me and his face turns quiet, as if he's trying to remember what to say.*

*"Hey," he calls to me finally, "hey, you doing okay?" and I nod.*

*I feel the wind pick up and blow me back; I keep getting pushed backward every time I try to take a step forward and I look up ahead where Evelyn is standing. She seems far away, her clothes also blown back from her skin as if someone's holding her as she struggles ahead. I can hardly see her face, so pinched by the wind; her eyes look closed, as if she is crying.*

*Mr. Samuels takes my hand and I look at him, surprised. Each* step we take together is difficult, the force of the wind almost knocking all three of us down.

We stop several feet back from Evelyn and watch her drop to her knees. She is humming a mournful melody and its moan covers the tundra and fills up its hollow sky. Mr. Samuels holds on to my hand real tight and Jimmy moves closer to my side.

"Don't go," Mr. Samuels whispers, "don't go any farther," and I feel the muscle that is my heart tighten, ache, grow stronger, and then tighten again.

And then I see the body stretched out on its long back, arms extended as if trying to reach for the whole wide world with both hands. The moon slinks out from behind its clouds and shimmers defiantly so that I have to turn my head away, a white beam outlining the figure of a young boy lying cold on the tundra's warm back. I close my eyes. I don't see his face.

Quimuckta lies down flat by the body, and for a minute I can't tell the animal from the earth, the glittering fur on his wide shoulders blowing back and forth: silver tundra grass under a dark, sprawling sky.

✳ ✳ ✳

I bolt upright in bed and look around. I can hear Mama's heavy breathing and Mr. Samuels snoring just like always, and I look closely at the room around me to make sure that I'm really at home. I'm shivering and sweating at the same time and pull the thin blanket up to my chin. Just a dream, I say to myself, just a dream. But even as I lay back down in bed, even as I try to fall asleep again, I know that it's more than just a dream. I pull my knees up to my chin and start to cry.

The next morning, I don't feel like going to the receiving home after school. Maybe I'm coming down with a cold or the flu. I stop at the home to tell Mama that I'm feeling poorly. She has a bunch of little kids on her lap, Jesse Michaelsen from Napaskiak, Cecilia Bailey from Chevak, and Chrissie Sam from Kwethluk. Adoph Johns from Eek is hanging on to Mama's knees, and a new little baby whose name I don't even know is lying in a woven basket, wearing nothing but a diaper and a tiny T-shirt. I notice the blue and yellow flowered shirt is on inside out.

"Sakes alive, Lorraine," Mama says when she sees me, "I sure as shootin' is happy to see the likes of you. These here children are giving me a run for my money today and I'm mighty happy to have an extra set of hands." The baby gurgles and sways back and forth. I pick him up and feel his warm body sink into my arms; his diaper is damp. He gurgles again and I feel my heart lurch.

"This one's wet, Mama," I say. "I'm gonna change his little diaper and then think I'll go on home, if it's okay with you. Hate to leave you in a pinch, but don't feel right today. Coming down with some kinda bug or another." I lay the baby on the rug and pull out a diaper from where they're stacked at the bottom of the bookshelf. "Who's this one, anyways? Ain't ever seen the likes of him before."

"Her." Mama smiles. "Violet Rose, from Sleetmute." The baby coos at me as I lift her legs, and Mama shoos the children from her lap. She walks over to where I'm working on getting them diaper pins to close together real good and tight.

"Let me feel your head, Lorraine—it ain't like you at all to be sickly. Well, now, you feel cool enough to your mama's hand, but if you're not up to snuff today, might as well get some rest at home. Don't worry yourself none, I'll be fine with this boatload of little monsters. And this little one here, when you're feeling better, I think this little baby's gonna be your very special charge."

I hand Violet Rose back to Mama and stand up slowly. The baby's cheeks are flushed up pink and her black eyes stare at me, as if she's seen me before.

"See you later, then," I say, not looking into Mama's face. "I think I'm just gonna go straight on home." I reach over to give the baby a final pat and feel my mama's eyes right on me as I head out the door.

I pour myself a glass of water when I get home and sit down at the kitchen table. Mama's been making up a batch of *agutuck* and she leaves the mixing bowl smack in the middle of the table without cleaning it out. I stick my finger into the batter and give it a lick, but don't got much of an appetite at all. *Agutuk*'s a real treat to those of us used to it, but most gussaks will turn up their noses, seeing that it's made with whipped seal lard, sugar, and berries. I lay down my head in my arms. Folks gonna think what they gonna think, no matter what you say or do. You can get pretty down in the mouth, worrying on how everyone's just scared to death of each other. How they're scared of anything at all they ain't used to. Guess I gotta include myself, though it's difficult to admit; it sure takes me a long time to open up my mind to another way of thinking, to another way of life. But we're all in the same doggone universe, ain't we, after all? With the same sun and moon and planets and stars? Sometimes it's hard to remember that; sometimes it don't feel that way at all.

And if it ain't for ole Mr. Samuels and Evelyn Sugarbush, well, where would I be right now? Probably going along my merry way, not noticing nothing at all, only seeing the world from one little bitty viewpoint, through the narrow tunnels of my own two little beady eyes.

Not that things is so great, considering what I see in my dream and how it makes me feel. And yet, all this time, I'm not really believing Evelyn, but mostly thinking that she really don't see nothing at all. That she's just an ordinary girl. Sitting here now, I understand how much she does know and how she shares so much with me; seems like something breaks open way down inside, freeing up my heart so that I can see into the lives of others. It's kinda scary but it makes me feel all growed up, makes me feel proud.

I lean back and close my eyes. I try to see Dove's body

the way I see it in my dream, but I can't. All I see inside my eyelids is blackness and a few distant, flickering lights: faraway stars in a winter night sky.

There's a sudden knock at the door and Evelyn pops her head inside the house.

"Go away," I say. "I don't feel much like visiting right now."

Of course, she ignores my request and shilly-shallies herself right in the door. She just stands there, staring at me, but she don't say a word.

"Don't you hear me, Evelyn Sugarbush?" I almost yell, maybe a little louder than I should. "I'm feeling poorly and is just about to lay me down for a nap. You can stop by later, that is, if I am feeling better."

She don't say nothing and don't budge at all. Her head is down and that crazy mop of knotty black hair is sticking out all over the place, just like always.

"Lorraine," she finally says quietly, still not looking up, "I gotta talk to you. I gotta get it out and tell you the truth. I can't wait no longer." Something in her quaking voice surprises me. Something makes me keep my mouth shut up quiet. I stare at my hands.

"I ain't really shaman anymore," she continues, her voice all shaky as if she's getting ready to break down and cry. "I lie to you. I'm just like everybody else. I don't got no idea where Dove Alexie is right now. . . . Haven't seen him since that last time at the jail when I think I can help him,

339

I really do, but he ends up all alone and lost just the same."

"Wait," I say, confused. "What do you mean 'that last time at the jail'? When do you see him at all? Don't think you ever meet Dove at all. You learn everything about him from me."

"I don't exactly meet him," she responds softly, "and I know that I never tell you any of this before. I'm sorry, Lorraine, I really am. I get so scared, so scared all of the time. 'Cause it's really me who hurts Dove Alexie. It's me, Lorraine"—her voice is quavering again—"it's me who hurts Dove. Don't mean to, but it's me who lets him out and makes him end up all lost and alone."

I take a deep breath and step backward. Evelyn is talking faster and faster now and it's difficult to understand each word.

"I see Dove that first time I come to Bethel," she continues, "when they leave me there, when they stick me at the jail first, just for one night since there ain't no room at the home. And I see Dove then, I see how Arnie pushes him around and beats up on his face just for fun. Arnie tells me that I'll get the same if I ever open my mouth, and that he could cut up any dirty Native he wants and nobody'll even care. He's evil, that Arnie, I could see pure evil, and he beats on poor Dove just because he's from Stony River, because he's a mixed-blood and don't got no people of his own. And Arnie can't stand the fact that Dove stands up to a white man, that a mixed breed refuses to get pushed around. That

340

makes Arnie crazy. Any excuse, and he's all over Dove. Something would go wrong with Arnie's day, he'd drop his coffee or lose his keys, and he'd take it out on Dove. Some folks are like that, Lorraine, they really are."

Evelyn's shaking all over now, but she keeps talking real fast.

"Folks like Arnie think that people who are different, people with a darker color skin or who come from somewhere they don't understand, well, they think we ain't even human. That even our blood is some other color and our hearts some other shape. That we don't belong nowhere. But I can tell that Dove's special, different from the rest, that he's got a little bit of blood from all of us, gussak, Yup'ik, and Indian, too. Never know anyone like him before. They say he's bad, but I know different right away. Just think of it, a person with so many of us inside. Anyway, oh, I'm sorry I don't tell you this before but I'm so scared. I'm scared all the time now and can't face telling you. Anyway, one day after I'm living at the receiving home, this is before I get to know you at all, something makes me go back to the jail. Somehow, I have to see him, need to see if he's all right. I make it in the back door, down by the honey-bucket room where nobody goes, and see Dove sitting on the cell floor, his head in his arms, blood on the floor. He's all beat up even worse than before. And I don't know how I do it, can't figure how I work up the nerve, but something makes me have to help him, and I sneak the keys from the wall. I make sure Arnie's busy with Miss Weinland out front and I slip the keys right off the wall. Dove, I don't even know his name then, he just looks up at me, his face twisted up sad, and doesn't say nothing, doesn't budge an inch. I stick the key into the lock and twist as hard as I can, but nothing clicks. And I can tell you, Lorraine, I've never been so scared before, my whole body's wound up in a quiver. I'm shaking from head to toe. Finally I swing the door open and drop that key to the floor. Never run so fast in my life. Run straight out that back door. Don't even see if Dove gets out. And later," she continues, "a few days later I go back. Remember when Jimmy and me see you at the jail, the time you fall right on your face in the mud?"

"Humpf." I still don't favor thinking on that particular moment in time.

"Well, I'm going back to check on Dove then. To try and find out if he gets away."

"But why don't you tell me?" I interrupt, once I find my voice. "Why don't you tell me all of this before?" She shrugs and looks down.

"I'm just so scared," she whispers in a tiny voice. "Scared I might get in trouble with the marshal for messing in official law business and scared that you would hate me for not telling the truth sooner. Mostly, I'm scared I'd end up in jail."

"But you could have told me," I continue. "All this changes everything. So that's why Arnie pretends Dove's sent somewhere else by the Department of Corrections. That's why Arnie don't want to talk at all. Bet he wants to cover up, don't want nobody to learn he loses a prisoner, that someone gets away from his jail. He musta erased all the intake information in the hopes nobody would remember Dove's being there at all."

Evelyn nods.

"And then I'm at the receiving home," she says softly, "keeping all of this inside, worrying about Dove and where he is and all, when you start your talking about my helping you. I can't believe it. And at first it works, it really does. I do help and I see Dove all by hisself out there in the tundra, hungry and sick, his wounds bigger and bigger, but I see him alive. And then what I see changes, he's weaker and weaker, losing more and more blood, until one day he's lying out on the ground. But then nothing. I don't see nothing anymore. Got no dreams, got nothing. It's just all empty inside. Everything gone. I know you're waiting. I know you want to know. But there ain't no sense in your hanging around me anymore when I can't really even help find your friend at all." Her voice trembles and she presses her hands together in front of her, as if begging for forgiveness.

I look out the kitchen window. The wind's blowing up real good and a few empty tin garbage cans go rolling down the river path until I can't see them anymore. Way down the road a bit, I watch Quimuckta trotting toward my house, his ears pointed up as if he's listening for clues.

"So it's you, you're the 'her' in his letter. You're the 'her' I can't figure out at all. Dove knows you see him and must know you would want to help if you can. Guess he writes that note just before you let him go free. Guess we must first run into him pretty near the same time."

Evelyn nods and I walk over to where she's standing; I put my arms around her, the same way Mama puts her arms around me. Evelyn's body is thin—feels almost like a skeleton to me—and it seems as if her sharp bones prick right through my skin. I close my eyes and imagine my heart etched with Evelyn Sugarbush's bony imprint and permanently marked by tiny slivers of her dreams. She pushes away from me. I can see that she is embarrassed by my touch, but she still grips onto the corner of my sleeve with a shaky hand.

I inhale and feel a secret constellation of stars blink under my bones, and my whole insides grow a new, larger heart. It swings back and forth within like a huge clock, its ticking keeping time with the moon and all the world's lost, careening planets. I can almost see the universe snap back into place, and my own particular, unsteady spot rooting right into it.

I squeeze Evelyn's arm and walk over to the window. My picture imagination flashes a sudden scene of the receiving home, all the small children lining up for bed. Their scrubbed faces are upturned, their hands clasped as if praying; they wait silently, single file, for someone to remember their names and tuck them in safely for the long night ahead. Thelma Cooke's new baby wiggles in her small crib, her tiny fists opening and closing just like two perfectly shaped pink buds.

The front door blows open suddenly. Evelyn and me, we both stand up together and stop for a moment to exchange sighs. The small moon around my neck pulls me forward; an inner tide beckons.

Quimuckta sits outside the house, just as we know he will, waiting for us to come out so he can lead us directly to where we need to be.


It don't surprise me at all to see a crowd of people up at the jail and Steven Roberts standing by with a camera and tape recorder.

"Hey, Lorraine," he calls when he sees me and Evelyn. "Hey, maybe you're right about Alexie all the time. Turns out he might be up here at the jail before after all. And then gets himself loose. They think maybe they find his body way out on the tundra, that he was trying to find his way back home, or maybe it's just the corpse of someone else, a hunter, some other lost soul. Hey, how about an interview, since you know so much about all of this? How about seeing yourself in print? I may even have a real job for you up at the paper. Give you a chance to do a little investigative work, if your information pans out right."

I shake my head and try to elbow our way through the crowd. I see old Sara Oscar hobble down the jail steps, pushing through the maze of people surrounding us, looks like she's trying to make her way on home. She shakes her old wooden walking cane at Arthur Swanson, who sideswipes her on his rusty bike.

"Hey, you kid!" she calls, waving her free hand in the air. "Hey, you, you almost knock down an old lady. Better watch it, you stupid kid."

Someone steps on Quimuckta's paw and he whines.

"Knock it off," I yell, "nobody be touching my dog or you'll have to mess with the likes of Lorraine Hobbs."

"Shhh." Evelyn whispers in my ear. "Don't yell so loud in front of all these people." She's hanging on to my arm and keeping her head tucked real low. I know she ain't used to dealing with so many folks all together at once, and I try to smile at her reassuringly, but she keeps pinching my elbow till my whole arm throbs.

"Quit it," I snap at her, trying to keep my patience good as I can, "else you're gonna end up getting a good whack 'cross your pointed head." We push our way through to the door and I see Marshal Nicholsen standing by Arnie's old desk, talking with two gussak men dressed like trappers. The marshal's just standing there with his arms crossed over his chest, and the two trappers are talking up a storm in real hushed tones.

"Lorraine," he calls out when he sees me, "I've been

trying to run you down. Need to talk to you about that fellow, Alexie, the kid you were making such a stink about."

Me and Evelyn slowly edge our way up front, and I feel everyone's eyes lookin' straight at me. "I'm sorry to tell you," the marshal says, clearing his throat. "I'm sorry to tell you that a boy's been found, a body that we figure could be Alexie, but we still don't know for sure. Kind of confusing—some old-time label stamped on the collar of his shirt says Stony River which is way up north, but the body was found on the tundra right up at the base of the Pilgrim River Valley."

"Where's that?" I ask, my voice shaky.

"Not far," he answers, "just a little bit north by Big River. Now it still might mean nothing at all, could be coincidence, so don't get yourself all in a dither just yet. We still don't have any positive ID, not for the victim of the beating or for this here body we just find." The marshal scratches his head as if confused. "These two fellas here practically bump right into the corpse when they're setting up traps. And a good thing, too, with the body starting to decompose and all. Of course, this still could be some hunting accident. Ain't necessarily foul play at all."

I feel sick to my stomach. I lean against Evelyn and hear her shallow breathing. Nobody says nothing for a minute.

"But why don't anyone help him? Couldn't he find someone to help? Someone who would have stopped to take care? Why couldn't he find his way, why does anyone have to end out there all alone?" I hear my own voice sounding out of breath, just like I've been running.

"Can't honestly answer that one. Whoever it is, if it's the boy at all, or if it's some poor hunter." The marshal sighs. "But the strange thing here, the odd thing about this fellow, is that he don't have anything on him. Traveling without any gear, no gun, no knives, no backpack, nothing." He coughs as our eyes widen. "Now you remember, young ladies, we ain't even sure the body's gonna check out to be the very same boy."

I take a deep breath and picture Dove Alexie's Stony River home, a small wooden cabin, its dark corners filmy with spiderwebs, its windows locked shut, its floor made of leaves and earth. Deep in a hidden forest, he only hears the rinse of rushing river and only sees the thick fence made of stone.

The marshal pauses for a moment, then continues slowly. "Of course, we're planning a complete and full investigation into this here matter. I'll be going up the Kuskokwim over to Stony River myself. And, as I say, there's still a lot of questions need answering." I look over at Evelyn. Her eyes are closed. "If I know that a sixteen-year-old boy is holed up in the jail, you can be sure that all kind of hell would break loose, and I still can't figure how things get so out of control." His face softens for a minute. He almost looks nice.

I don't say nothing. Me and Evelyn, we just turn right

around and head out the door for home.

Quimuckta is waiting for us outside, wagging his tail, and he leaps off the steps as we leave. The crowd around the jail starts to scatter and Front Street looks like it does any other usual Bethel day. The dust kicks up gritty, the rocky sand gets in your shoes, the Roadhouse is clattering with the sound of plates breaking and voices arguing. A tangle of gulls chatter above us and thick circles of black mosquitoes buzz around each and every muddy puddle.

Evelyn and me, we just keep on walking ahead, faster and faster, not looking at each other, not saying nothing at all. When we cross that old shaky bridge over to Oscarville, we both break into a run. We see the receiving home in the distance, its crumpled tin roof catching the last of the evening sun and shining silver green in the spotty mist.

The front door swings open wide, and I hear a whisper of voices hum my name. Most of the lights are left on inside, and I know it's time to help all the tired little children get ready for bed ("How to Spot the Miracles in Your Life," *Community Circle*).

# EPILOGUE
## *Fall 1969*

*"Most frontiers have been
the hideout of scoundrels but,
happily for Alaska,
few scoundrels are winter types."*

—Sally Carrighar,
Moonlight at Midday

*"In our town,
we like to know the facts
about everybody."*

—Thorton Wilder,
Our Town

# Bethel Town Council Appoints Interim Prison Warden

By STEVEN ROBERTS

KUSKOKWIM KRONICLE EDITOR-IN-CHIEF AND STAFF WRITER

**NOVEMBER 4.** The Bethel Town Council has voted unanimously to appoint Miss Annette Weinland to the interim position of Bethel Prison Warden upon Marshal Cooker Nicholsen's retirement next month. Miss Weinland has been a Bethel resident for over seven years and has worked as a part-time administrator for the Bethel jail over the past five years. She is a native of Cincinnati, Ohio, and the daughter of Gerald Weinland, Bethel's local minister and Bible study director.

Bethel Mayor Everette Plumb has formally cited Miss Weinland's efforts in the ongoing investigation of a lost juvenile from the Stony River region. At yesterday's town meeting, he applauded her work at the jail in the sudden absence of U.S. Assistant Deputy Arnie Hanger and during Marshal Nicholsen's participation in the State Department of Corrections conferences held across the country this past summer. Marshal Nicholsen has also commended Miss Weinland for "doing the work of three people during a particularly demanding period in July and August."

When asked about future plans for the prison, Miss Weinland was quick to respond with her ideas for a work-release program in which nonviolent prisoners would participate in community service projects. Some of those projects will include working on the Bethel Honeybucket Squad, providing intake at the Sleep-Off Center, and assisting with the prison food service.

On the subject of the local prison food, an anonymous *Kronicle* source has recently learned of formal grievances initiated on behalf of the jail population. "It's absolutely fabricated truths and hogwash," an agitated Miss Lorraine Hobbs (Bethel prison chef) responded to these allegations in an unscheduled interview at the Bethel Tundra Shack yesterday evening, "that them folks at the jail would rather starve than eat from the likes of my recipe fixings."

Both Mayor Plumb and Interim Marshal Weinland were unavailable for comment.

# GLOSSARY

| | |
|---|---|
| *agutuk* | Otherwise known as Eskimo ice cream; made from whipped seal lard, sugar, and berries |
| **Aleut** | Natives populating the Alaskan Aleutian chain of islands stretching from Alaska to Russia |
| **break-up** | Time of year when weather becomes warm enough for frozen sea to begin to melt or break up, and transportation and fishing by boat are possible |
| **freeze-up** | Time of year when the Bering Sea on the coast becomes frozen solid and transportation to other villages is possible on the ice by dogsled or snowmobile |

| | |
|---|---|
| **gussak** | Caucasian, from the Russian word 'Kass'ag' (*Cossack*), the first white people in Alaska |
| **honeybucket** | Metal or plastic can used indoors as a toilet |
| **Lower 48** | All American states other than Alaska and Hawaii |
| *kuspuck* | Cloth jacket with hood, usually made out of calico material |
| **muktuk** | Whale meat |
| **Outside** | Anywhere outside of Alaska, usually in the United States |
| **pilot bread** | Hard crackers kept by bush pilots as emergency reserves |
| *qasgig* | Social and religious house used by men and boys |
| **Tlingit** | Natives of Southeast Alaska, originally from the interior of Canada |

**Tsimshian**     A Native American people indigenous to northern British Columbia and southeastern Alaska

**Yup'ik**     "Authentic people" (from *yuk*, "person"); natives of Alaska originating from Siberia and known for sea hunting culture

# ACKNOWLEDGMENTS

With the deepest love and appreciation to my extraordinary sister, Kathy Gosliner, who listened and listened; my agent, Anne Edelstein, and my insightful editor, Katherine Tegen, whose support and enthusiasm fortified me throughout; my friend and colleague Leah Johnson, who found me when I was hiding; writers Alice McDermott and Barbara Esstman, who read early drafts; American University Librarian Mary Mintz, who was so generous with her time; Julie Hittman, Alison Donalty, Andrea Vandergrift, and Janet Frick at HarperCollins, who tended to my manuscript with such care; my remarkable friend of thirty-five years, the indomitable Twig C. George, who led this book home; and to *the children of the Bethel receiving home, then and now.*